THE DARK OF THE WOODS

THE DARK
OF THE
WOODS

FAIRY TALES FOR MODERN TIMES

✦ EDITED BY ✦
ELLEN DATLOW AND TERRI WINDLING

ALADDIN PAPERBACKS
New York ✦ London ✦ Toronto ✦ Sydney

ALADDIN PAPERBACKS
An imprint of Simon & Schuster Children's Publishing Division
1230 Avenue of the Americas, New York, NY 10020

Paper-over-board edition May 2006
Introduction copyright © 2006 by Ellen Datlow and Terri Windling

Pages 1–166:
"The Months of Manhattan" copyright © 2000 by Delia Sherman · "Cinder Elephant" copyright © 2000 by Jane Yolen · "Instructions" copyright © 2000 by Neil Gaiman · "Mrs. Big" copyright © 2000 by Michael Cadnum · "Falada" copyright © 2000 by Nancy Farmer · "A Wolf at the Door" copyright © 2000 by Tanith Lee · "Ali Baba and the Forty Aliens" copyright © 2000 by Janeen Webb · "Swans" copyright © 2000 by Kelly Link · "The Kingdom of Melting Glances" copyright © 2000 by Katherine Vaz · "Hansel's Eyes" copyright © 2000 by Garth Nix · "Becoming Charise" copyright © 2000 by Kathe Koja · "The Seven Stage a Comeback" copyright © 2000 by Gregory Maguire · "The Twelve Dancing Princesses" copyright © 2000 by Patricia A. McKillip

Also available in a Simon & Schuster Books for Young Readers hardcover edition.
Designed by Steve Scott
The text of this book was set in Adobe Caslon.
Manufactured in the United States of America
First Aladdin Paperbacks edition November 2001
The Library of Congress has cataloged the hardcover edition as follows:
A wolf at the door : and other retold fairy tales / edited by Ellen Datlow and Terri Windling.
p. cm.
Contents: The Months of Manhattan / Delia Sherman—Cinder elephant / Jane Yolen—Instructions / Neil Gaiman—Mrs. Big / Michael Cadnum—Falada / Nancy Farmer—A Wolf at the door / Tanith Lee—Ali Baba and the forty aliens / Janeen Webb—Swans / Kelly Link—The Kingdom of Melting Glances / Katherine Vaz—Hansel's eyes / Garth Nix—Becoming Charise / Kathe Koja—The Seven stage a comeback / Gregory Maguire—The twelve dancing princesses / Patricia A. McKillip.
ISBN 0-689-82138-7 (hc.)
1. Fairy tales. [1. Fairy tales.]
I. Datlow, Ellen. II. Windling, Terri.
PZ8.W813   2000
[Fic]—dc21   99-38616
CIP

Pages 167–331:

Copyright © 2003 by Ellen Datlow and Terri Windling

"Greenkid" copyright © 2003 by Jane Yolen · "Golden Fur" copyright © 2003 by Midori Snyder · "Chambers of the Heart" copyright © 2003 by Nina Kiriki Hoffman · "Little Red and the Big Bad" copyright © 2003 by Will Shetterly · "The Fish's Story" copyright © 2003 by Pat York · "The Children of Tilford Fortune" copyright © 2003 by Christopher Rowe · "The Girl in the Attic" copyright © 2003 by Lois Metzger · "The Harp That Sang" copyright © 2003 by Gregory Frost · "A Life in Miniature" copyright © 2003 by Bruce Coville · "Lupe" copyright © 2003 by Kathe Koja · "Awake" copyright © 2003 by Tanith Lee · "Inventing Aladdin" copyright © 2003 by Neil Gaiman · "My Swan Sister" copyright © 2003 by Katherine Vaz

Also available in a Simon & Schuster Books for Young Readers hardcover edition.
Designed by Ann Sullivan
The text of this book was set in Hoefler Text.
Manufactured in the United States of America
First Aladdin Paperbacks edition April 2005
The Library of Congress has catalogued the hardcover edition as follows:
Swan Sister: fairy tales retold / edited by Ellen Datlow and Terri Windling.—1st ed.
p.cm.
Contents: Greenkid / Jane Yolen—Golden fur / Midori Snyder—Chambers of the heart / Nina Kiriki Hoffman—Little Red and the Big Bad / Will Shetterly—The Fish's story / Pat York—The Children of Tilford Fortune / Christopher Rowe—The Girl in the attic / Lois Metzger—The Harp that sang / Gregory Frost—A life in miniature / Bruce Coville—Lupe / Kathe Koja—Awake / Tanith Lee—Inventing Aladdin / Neil Gaiman—My swan sister / Katherine Vaz.
ISBN 0-689-84613-4 (hc.)
I. Fairy tales. [I. Fairy Tales.] I. Datlow, Ellen. II. Windling, Terri.
PZ8.M9867 2003
[Fic]—dc21 2002030409

10 9 8 7 6 5 4 3 2 1
ISBN-13: 978-1-4169-2480-7
ISBN-10: 1-4169-2480-9

CONTENTS

INTRODUCTION

by Terri Windling and Ellen Datlow

The stories in this book are based on classic fairy tales—but probably not the way you've ever heard fairy tales before. Most people think that fairy tales are stories meant for very young children, but hundreds of years ago tales of magic were loved by folks of all ages. The fairy tales we know today—like "Cinderella," "Hansel and Gretel," "Snow White," and all the rest—used to be darker, stranger, and more complex, up until the nineteenth and twentieth centuries. Then they were turned into children's tales, banished to the nursery (as J.R.R. Tolkien, the author of *The Lord of the Rings*, once pointed out) like furniture the adults have grown tired of and no longer want. Fairy tales were changed and simplified when they were rewritten for very young readers. And it's these sweet and simple versions that most of us know today.

But if you go back to the older versions, you'll see why people both young and old liked to gather before the hearth fire and listen to these marvelous stories on long, cold winter evenings. Fairy tales were scarier then, and the heroes and heroines were more interesting. Cinderella, for instance, was a smart, feisty, angry girl in the oldest versions of the story (dating back all the way to ninth-century China), not the helpless dreamer who has to be rescued by a prince, as we know her today. Little Red Riding Hood didn't wait for a passing woodsman, she outwitted the wolf herself—who was, in fact, a werewolf in older versions of the story. Happy endings were never guaranteed—particularly in the well-loved fairy tales of Hans Christian Andersen (where the Little Match Girl dies in the snow, the loyal Tin Soldier is consumed by fire, and the Little Mermaid loses her life when her fickle prince weds another). The old fairy tales, like all the best stories, were filled with all the dark and bright, all the failures and triumphs, that life has to offer. No wonder our ancestors have loved them for hundreds and hundreds of years.

All of the writers in this book loved fairy tales when they were young, and they didn't stop loving and reading them even when they grew to adulthood. Each writer has taken a favorite tale and made a brand-new story from it—stories full of strangeness, humor, dark magic, and wonder.

These are tales to lead you into the Dark Woods, where witches live and animals talk and magic appears when you least expect it. And here are a few standard words of advice when you enter that enchanted forest: Be kind to old women on the path (they may be fairies in disguise). Use magic wishes carefully (you'll get exactly what you wish for). Don't eat the food the fairies offer (it will trap you in their realm forever). And be sure to leave a trail of stones to find your way home again. . . .

This book is dedicated to . . .

Jane Yolen, who has been a good friend
to the old fairy tales . . . and to us.

Heidi Anne Heiner—
librarian, fairy tale lover, and creator of the
SurLaLune Fairy Tale Pages website.

And to all the librarians
who keep young readers supplied with magic.

FURTHER READING

Gary D. Schmidt *Straw Into Gold*
Ellen Schreiber *Teenage Mermaid*
Ellen Steiber *Shadow of the Fox*
Ursula Synge *Swan's Wing*
Debbie Viguié *Scarlet Moon*
Suzanne Weyn *The Night Dance*
Patricia C. Wrede *Snow White and Rose Red*
Laurence Yep *Angelfish*
Jane Yolen *Briar Rose*

SHORT STORY COLLECTIONS BASED ON FAIRY TALES
Robin McKinley *The Door in the Hedge*
Vivian Vande Velde
Tales from the Brothers Grimm and the Sisters Weird
Jane Yolen *Tales of Wonder*

RECOMMENDED FAIRY TALE COLLECTIONS
Angela Carter (editor)
Strange Things Sometimes Still Happen
Alan Garner *Alan Garner's Book of British Fairy Tales*
Maria Tatar (editor) *The Classic Fairy Tales*
Jane Yolen (editor)
Favorite Folktales from Around the World
Jane Yolen (editor)
Mightier Than the Sword: World Folktales for Strong Boys

Jane Yolen (editor)
Not One Damsel in Distress: World Folktales for Strong Girls
Jack Zipes (editor) *Spells of Enchantment*

ON THE HISTORY OF FAIRY TALES
Jane Yolen *Touch Magic: Fantasy,
Faerie and Folklore in the Literature of Childhood*

ON THE WEB
Heidi Anne Heiner (editor)
The SurLaLune Fairy Tale Pages:
www.surlalunefairytales.com
Terri Windling and Midori Snyder (editors)
The Endicott Studio Journal of Mythic Arts:
www.endicott-studio.com

THE DARK
OF THE
WOODS

The Months of Manhattan

by Delia Sherman

Liz Wallach was a pretty good kid. She mostly did her homework on time and pretty much got along with her father and was usually polite to her girlfriends. She wasn't perfect, by any means. She had been known to lie about brushing her teeth and she couldn't for the life of her tell her left from her right. But for a ten-year-old, she wasn't bad.

Liz lived with her father in a big apartment on the Upper West Side of New York City. Sometimes she went to stay with her mother in San Francisco or her grandmother on Cape Cod. She liked school. Things were good.

Then Beth Dodson came into her life.

Beth Dodson was the daughter of one of Dad's girlfriends. When the girlfriend became Liz's stepmother, Liz and Beth became stepsisters. Liz was ready to be happy about this. She'd always wanted a sister, and she kind of liked it that their real names were the same: Elizabeth.

But Beth had been perfectly happy being an only child, and she didn't like it at all that they had the same name. That was only one of the things she didn't like. She didn't like school and she didn't like Chinese food and she didn't like New York. It was big and noisy and dirty, and there were too many people living in it.

"Maybe she's shy," said Liz's father hopefully. "Maybe she'll get over it."

But Beth had no intention of getting over hating New York, or anything else. She whined constantly: about having to walk three blocks to the bus stop, about having ballet lessons at Mme. Demipointe's École de Danse.

She fought with her mother, and wouldn't speak to Liz or her stepfather except to say that she wished she were still living in New Rochelle with her daddy and playing soccer on Wednesday afternoons.

Things weren't so good anymore.

It was November, just before Thanksgiving vacation, when Liz got a special history assignment. She had to go to the American Wing at the Metropolitan Museum of Art and look at the furniture and write a paper about it.

Liz's stepmother said, "I can take you while Bethy's in ballet class. You'll have to be quick, though. Mme. Demipointe hates to be kept waiting."

Delia Sherman

By the time Liz and her stepmother dropped Beth off at Mme. Demipointe's and got to the museum, it was about 3:00 P.M. Liz's stepmother paid for two admissions, went to the restaurant, sat down at a little round table, and took a magazine out of her bag.

"Aren't you coming with me?" Liz asked.

"It's your assignment," said her stepmother. "It's better if you do it yourself. And remember, we have to be at Madame's by four-thirty."

"But I don't know where—"

"I don't either," said her stepmother. "Ask."

By the time Liz found a guard who wasn't busy with someone else, ten minutes of her hour were gone. Then she turned left instead of right in the Medieval Treasury and got lost, and asked another guard and got lost again. Precious minutes ticked away as she walked through rooms of paintings and statues.

Finally, at 3:45, she walked up a flight of stairs and through a glass door, and found herself in a small, dark room with nothing in it but a big, bright picture.

Wherever she was, it wasn't the American Wing.

Liz wasn't much of a crier as a general rule, but this was too much. Even if she started back now and didn't get lost once, she'd be late, and her stepmother would be madder than a taxi driver in a traffic jam and her assignment still wouldn't be done. "I must be just about the unluckiest person in the world," she wailed.

"Whatsa matter, kid?"

The voice was friendly, with a heavy Bronx accent. Liz wiped her face on her sleeve and looked around for a guard, but she was alone.

The painting caught her eye.

It showed the statue of Atlas at Rockefeller Center with twelve people standing and sitting around it. They were all ages, from a very little girl in a snowsuit with cat ears to an old man in a wheelchair, and all the races Liz had ever heard of, except maybe Native American. They were wearing all kinds of different clothes, too, from a little Hispanic boy in snow boots and a ski jacket to a young, white guy in Bermuda shorts. A pretty African-American woman in a sundress opened her painted lips and said, "What is it, honey? Maybe we can help."

Liz's heart started to beat very fast. She was startled, but not frightened. She'd read lots of books in which things like this happened. "I'm lost," she said.

"We also," said a Pakistani boy in baggy jeans and a hooded sweatshirt. "But you have found us."

Liz thought about this. "Would you like me to tell the guard you're here?"

The old man in the wheelchair laughed. He was pale and thin as a china cup, but his laugh was warm and strong. "No. Thank you. We prefer to be found by chance."

"Oh," Liz said, and glanced at her watch: 3:40. She'd thought it was later.

"What time of year is it?" The question came from

an Asian girl about Liz's age, dressed in a red slicker and boots and flowered mittens.

"November," said Liz.

"I hate November," the girl said, and stuck out her tongue at an old African-American woman leaning on a cane.

"It's not so bad," said Liz. "There's Thanksgiving and hot apple cider, and we get to go to Grandma's. And then it's almost December, and that means Christmas and I can go sledding in Central Park with Dad." She remembered Beth and sighed. "If he still wants to."

"January, though," remarked a middle-aged Latino man in an embroidered short-sleeved shirt. "January is very terrible."

"And February, and March," added a skinny, unshaven man dressed in layers and layers of brown jackets.

"I kind of like February and March," Liz said. "I like getting cold and wet and then coming in and getting warm and looking at the lights out the window. It's easier to go to school in winter, too. You don't want to be outdoors so much, unless it's snowing, of course."

"Of course," said a woman with a prayer shawl around her shoulders. "But April, you know what they say about April, no? April is the cruelest month, that's what they say."

"April showers bring May flowers," said Liz. "Besides, I like mud and the way it smells."

"Even in Central Park?" asked an old Hispanic woman with a cane.

"Especially in Central Park."

"And the summer?" asked a teenage girl with her hair in a million little braids and flowers painted on her nails.

"Oh, summer is neat," said Liz. "May and June can be hard because I want to be outside all the time and there's still school, but it smells so good and the days are getting longer and there's summer vacation coming and we go to Cape Cod, and that's the best."

"So you must hate the fall," said a little African-American boy in a very big parka.

"Not really," said Liz. "I miss my friends over the summer, and there's my birthday in October, and I love the leaves turning all red and gold and—" she stopped suddenly. "Listen. This is way cool, but I'm really late, and my stepmother is going to kill me. I really have to go."

"I think we can take care of that for you," said the young guy in shorts. "Can't we, September?"

The woman smoothed her prayer shawl. "I think we should, June. And the history assignment as well." She caught sight of Liz's face and laughed kindly. "We can't do it for you—that wouldn't be kosher. But we can give you the time to do it in. And directions to the American Wing."

"Bye-bye," said the little girl in the snowsuit. "Good luck."

And they were gone.

Oh, there was still a painting on the wall, but it was just a big canvas with bright blobs on it that only looked like people if you stood back and squinted hard. The plaque on the wall beside it read: THE TWELVE MONTHS OF MANHATTAN. PETER MINUIT. UNDATED.

Liz looked at her watch. It was 3:05 P.M. She had fifty-five minutes before her stepmother would be looking for her. She ran straight to the American Wing without taking one wrong turn, and looked at the furniture and took notes for her paper until her watch said 3:50, when she walked back to the restaurant without even having to ask for directions. It was magical.

As Liz came up to her stepmother's table, she looked at her watch. "Four o'clock exactly," she said, surprised. "Lucky for you you made it."

Outside, it was raining, a cold, thick November rain. There wasn't a taxi to be seen, and lots of people were waiting.

"We're going to be hours late picking Beth up," Liz's stepmother moaned.

Just then, a taxi pulled up right in front of Liz. The door opened, the passenger got out, and Liz's stepmother nipped right in, with Liz on her heels. Liz's stepmother told the taxi where they were going, and sat back as the traffic miraculously cleared to let them through. "What a piece of luck!" she exclaimed.

Liz hung on to her notebook and grinned.

From that moment on, things got much, much better.

Not only did taxis stop whenever Liz needed one, she always made it to the bus stop just when the bus was pulling up to it. Her dad gave her a sled for Christmas, and her stepmother liked the scarf Liz knitted for her. And she never, ever lost a card game. Old Maid, Go Fish, War—anything where luck counted, Liz just couldn't lose.

"Not again!" her stepmother groaned as Liz stripped her of her hoarded sixes and triumphantly laid down all her own cards.

"Look at the bright side, dear," said her father. "If we need money, we can just send her to buy a lottery ticket."

"I'm only ten," Liz objected. "They wouldn't sell me one."

Beth's mother glanced at Beth, who was looking as gloomy as the East River in the rain. "I'm tired of cards," she said.

"Monopoly!" Beth's stepfather said cheerfully, and got out the board. "I'll take the top hat. I never lose a game when I have the top hat."

He lost this game, though. Liz won it, mostly because she landed on Boardwalk, Park Place, and all the Railroads her first time around the board.

"Lucky stiff," her father said.

"Too lucky," Beth muttered, and went off to think about it. Ever since that trip to the museum in

Delia Sherman

November, Liz had been luckier than any human being had a right to be. Something had to have happened, something magic. It wasn't fair. Nice things were always happening to Liz, and only bad things happened to her.

Later, Beth challenged Liz to a game of Paper, Scissors, Stone. Unable to think of a reason not to, Liz agreed. Seven times, the stepsisters chanted, "One, Two Three, Go." Seven times, Liz won.

"That's not luck, that's magic," Beth said accusingly. "You have to tell me what happened. I want to be lucky, too."

Liz thought about lying, but it just didn't seem right. Beth wouldn't find the Months of Manhattan unless they wanted her to. And if she did find them, Liz was sure they'd be able to handle one eleven-year-old girl, even one as whiny and annoying as Beth.

So she told her stepsister all about getting really lost, and stumbling into a room with a magic picture in it. She would have told her all about the Seasons, but Beth didn't want to hear about it.

"I'm not a total idiot," she said. "If you tell me everything, it'll ruin the magic, right? I hate you, Liz Wallach."

Next day, Beth announced at dinner that her history teacher had given her the now-famous American Wing furniture assigment. It was due Monday.

"But the museum's a madhouse on weekends," her mother objected.

"We can make a family outing of it," said her step-father. "It'll be fun."

Beth pouted. "I want to do it by myself."

Her stepfather said, "Good for you, Bethy. We'll turn you into a New Yorker yet. I tell you what. We'll all go to the museum, and you can go to the American Wing and the rest of us will look at armor or something and we'll all meet in the restaurant for lunch."

And that was what they did. Liz, her dad, and Beth's mother went off one way, and Beth went off in another. She'd never liked going to the museum, so it wasn't very long before she was as lost and frightened as the most demanding magic would wish. The museum was, as her mother had predicted, a madhouse. Everywhere she turned, people bumped into her and glared at her. Thinking of nothing but finding somewhere quiet, she ran up a back stairway and through a glass door and found herself in a small, dark room with nothing in it but a large, bright picture.

In her fear, Beth had almost forgotten what had brought her to the museum. Almost, but not quite. She stared at the picture to see if it looked magic. It didn't. What could be magic about a bunch of street people sitting around a stupid statue?

"It was a dumb idea, anyway," she said aloud. "Everyone knows there's no such thing as magic."

"Who says?"

Beth jumped. One of the people in the painting, a

Delia Sherman

dark brown boy about her age in huge, baggy jeans, was scowling at her.

Beth said, "Remember my stepsister, Liz? She was here in November. You made her lucky."

Next to a guy in bermuda shorts was an African-American girl with long nails and lots of braids. "November," she said. "I know November. Is it still winter, out there in the world?"

Beth shook her head scornfully. "You guys are supposed to be magic, right? And you don't even know what month it is? It's December, for your information, and it's cold and wet, and I hate it."

"What about Christmas, and the snow?" asked the young guy in shorts.

"It doesn't snow in New York, not a real snow like at home. It just turns into slush and puddles that get into your boots. And Christmas isn't the same without Daddy. I hate winter here, every bit of it."

"And spring?" asked an old bum wearing about a million raggedy jackets.

"It never gets warm until June, and then it gets hot and muggy, and you can smell the garbage and you never feel clean. And then it gets cold again, just like that, and starts raining again, and there aren't even any pretty leaves to look at, like there are at home. I hate it. I hate it all."

The Months exchanged silent looks.

"Well," said the woman in the prayer shawl. "We

certainly know where you stand." Her voice was angry, in a cool sort of way.

Beth scowled. "You *asked*," she whined. "That's how I feel. I can't help it if you don't like it. Now you'll probably do something awful to me. It's not fair."

"Don't you worry, honey," said an African-American woman in a sundress. "We're going to give you exactly what you need. And I don't want to hear any of your sass, April."

The baggy-jeans boy shrugged and grinned.

The old man in the wheelchair lifted a hand like a white claw and said, "The luck you have asked for is yours. Now go."

Beth felt a giant hand shove her out of the little room. It kept on shoving her, right and left through the Saturday crowds, until she was, if possible, even more lost than she had been before. And then it left her, in the farthest corner of European Decorative Arts, in a room full of cloudy glass cups.

By the time Beth had found her way back to the restaurant, she was nearly an hour late. Her mother and stepfather, who had been wondering if she'd been kidnapped, were pretty mad when she showed up safe and sound. When they found out that she didn't have any notes on American furniture, they were even madder. And when she unluckily let slip that she didn't really have a paper due Monday, they were mad enough to fight all the lions in the Bronx Zoo and win.

Delia Sherman

The only person who wasn't mad at Beth was Liz. At first, it was because she thought that having major bad luck served Beth right. But before long, she started to feel sorry for her. Anyone would.

Beth couldn't walk down the street without stepping in chewing gum or doggy doo. Streetlights turned red when she came to the corner, and buses pulled away just as she got to the stop. When it rained, her umbrella inevitably blew inside out, and taxis going too fast splashed her with dirty water. She caught every cold that was going around, and in April, she sprained her ankle in ballet class. In June, she came down with the measles.

At first, all the bad luck made Beth meaner than ever. She was especially mean to Liz, who she blamed for ruining her life.

"It's pretty awful," Liz agreed. "But I bet there's a way to break the curse—there usually is, in fairy tales. Maybe if you apologized to the Months. Or at least made it up to them somehow."

"Apologize?" growled Beth. "Why should I apologize? They're the ones who should apologize, for doing this to me. You're a creep." She made a grab at Liz's braid, missed, and fell out of bed onto Barbie's Dream House, scraping her arm painfully.

"Oh, poor Beth," said Liz. "But it wouldn't have happened if you hadn't tried to pull my hair. Think about it."

Beth was too miserable to answer her. But later, when the measles were itching like crazy and even her mother didn't want to keep her company, she thought about what Liz had said. What were the old man's words? "The luck you have asked for is yours." Maybe she had hurt the Months' feelings. Maybe there was something nice about June in New York she just hadn't noticed.

She looked out the window. The sky was clear, a deep turquoise blue that made the buildings across the street look bright and sharp. A pigeon landed on her windowsill with a flutter of gray wings and cooed at her.

Okay. Maybe June in New York wasn't so bad after all.

Once Beth had noticed the pigeon and the sky, she began to notice other things. She noticed that her mother kept bringing her food and books even when Beth threw them on the floor. She noticed that the rocks Liz brought her from Central Park had chips of mica in them that sparkled like tiny diamonds. She noticed that her stepfather always came into her room as soon as he got home from work and told her how they'd all go to Cape Cod in July and build sand castles together. She noticed that she kind of liked it when he did that.

By the time she was over her measles and everyone went to Cape Cod, she didn't hate New York City nearly as much as she had. What's more, she could find both her shoes when she needed them, and the tunnels

Delia Sherman

under her sand castles didn't cave in, and the sand fleas bit everyone in the family, not just her.

It was like magic. By the time school started in the fall, Beth was down to little things that could happen to anyone, like losing pencils and leaving her gloves in taxis. She pretty much got along with Liz and was usually nice to her stepfather and mostly did her homework on time. She tried Chinese food and discovered that she liked it. In fact, Beth Dodson had become a pretty good kid.

That Thanksgiving, Beth and Liz decided to go back to the Metropolitan Museum to find the Twelve Months of Manhattan and thank them. But although the sisters did their best to get lost, they never found the back stairs that led to a small, dark room with nothing in it but a big, bright picture.

Delia Sherman's all-time favorite books are *The Merrie Adventures of Robin Hood* and *Fairy Tales from Many Lands*, which is where she first learned about the "Twelve Months" and the importance of being polite to people you don't know.

She is the author of two historical fantasy novels, *Through a Brazen Mirror* and *The Porcelain Dove*, and the forthcoming young adult time-travel novel *The Freedom Maze*. She is also coeditor of *The Essential Bordertown*, an "urban fantasy" anthology for teenage readers, and of *The Horns of Elfland*, a collection of stories about music and magic. She was born in Japan, grew up in New York City, and now lives in New York and Boston.

Cinder Elephant

by Jane Yolen

There was once a lovely big girl who lived with her father in a large house near the king's park.

Her mother had been called *Pleasingly Plump*. Her grandmother had been called *Round and Rosie*. Her great-grandmother had been called *Sunny and Solid*. And her great-great-grandmother had been called *Fat!*

But though she was bigger than most, the girl had a sweet face, a loving heart, a kind disposition, and big feet.

Her name was Eleanor.

Her father called her Elly.

Now Elly and her father did everything together. They rambled and scrambled over the rolling hills. They bird-watched and dish-washed and trout-fished and star-wished together.

In fact, they were happy for a long long time.

But one day Elly's father grew lonely for someone his own age; someone who laughed at the same jokes;

someone who knew the words to the same songs; someone who knew the steps to dances like the turkey trot and the mashed potato and didn't think those were just food groups.

So he married again, a woman so thin, it took her three tries to throw a shadow. She had two skinny daughters. One was as skinny as a straw. One was as skinny as a reed. They had thin smiles, too. And thin names: Reen and Rhee. And hearts so thin, you could read a magazine through them.

Reen and Rhee smiled their thin smiles all through the wedding and the very next morning they made Elly their maid.

They made her do the dishes. They made her make the beds. They even made her sit in the fireplace, where she got covered with soot and cinders.

To make matters worse, they called her names:

> *"Elly, Elly,*
> *big fat belly,*
> *Cinder Elephant."*

So Elly cried.

But crying only made things worse. It made the soot into mud pies and the cinders into bogs. So Elly stopped crying.

Elly may have been big, but she wasn't stupid. She did the sisters' work without complaining, and she did it very well. And in her spare time—which meant long after her stepmother and the skinnies were asleep—she read books. Books about football and baseball, books about tennis and golf. It was how she preferred to get her exercise.

One day as Elly worked in the kitchen, two little bluebirds peeked in the window.

Elly guessed they were hungry, so she gave them each a crumb of bread.

Just then in came the skinnies, Reen and Rhee, one thin as a reed, one thin as a straw. "Mama, Mama," they screamed in their thin little voices. "Look what Cinder Elephant has done!"

Their skinny mother came quickly in her best running shoes, size five and a half, narrow. (Very narrow.)

She took the bread crumbs away, saying, "Cinder Elephant, this is all you will get for *your* dinner. Dieting will do you a world of good, and you will thank me for it later."

Then she turned to her skinny daughters. "I have great news. Prince Junior is home from school."

"The PRINCE!" Reen and Rhee squealed, for of course they had heard of him. He wore great clothes. He had straight teeth, which in the days before dentists took a lot of doing. And he was sure to inherit the kingdom.

The sisters smiled their thin smiles and ran to their

bedrooms to pick out their prettiest dresses to wear just in case they should bump into him.

Elly stayed on in the kitchen pretending to cry. But as soon as the skinnies were gone, she gave her bread crumb dinner to the bluebirds, anyway.

They ate it in one gulp each, singing:

> *"The bigger the heart,*
> *The greater the prize.*
> *You will be perfect*
> *In somebody's eyes."*

Fairy-tale birds always sing like this. It's annoying to everyone except the heroine.

Meanwhile in the palace, Prince Junior had just had a serious talk with his father, the king.

"Time to get married," said the king. "Time to grow up. Time to run the kingdom." The king always spoke that way to his son: short and to the point. Pointed remarks were his specialty.

"I am not in love," said Prince Junior.

"Doesn't matter," said the king.

"I am not even in like," said Prince Junior.

"Doesn't matter," said the king.

"I don't even know any girls," said Prince Junior.

"*That* matters," said the king. "Time to think about it." So, the king began to think.

Jane Yolen

It took hours.

It took days.

It took help!

At last the king came up with a plan. "Time for a ball," said the king.

Prince Junior was pleased. "Oh, good," he said. "I like balls." He meant he liked footballs and baseballs and tennis balls. (Though he wasn't terribly fond of moth-balls. They stank something fierce.)

"Your father means a fancy-dress, drinking-champagne-from-slippers ball," said his mother, the queen.

Prince Junior groaned. He really preferred watching birds to that kind of ball.

"Invite everyone in the kingdom," said the king, "as long as they are girls. Send them to every shop girl, cop girl, mop girl, prop girl, and champagne-in-the-slipper girl in the kingdom."

"And," added the queen, "no invitation—no admittance."

So invitations went out on creamy invitation paper, and every girl in the kingdom was invited except for Elly beecause her skinny stepsisters tore up her invitation. Then they made Elly pick up the creamy pieces.

On the night of the royal ball the skinny stepsisters swept out of the house, in yellow gowns, skinny as straws and looking like brooms. They rode to the castle, and their skinny mother went with them. And to the castle as well went every shop girl, cop girl, mop girl, prop girl, and champagne-in-the-slipper girl in the kingdom.

But Elly stayed at home staring into the cinders. She had no invitation to the ball. Even worse—she had nothing to wear.

At ten o'clock there came a noise at the kitchen window. It was the bluebirds.

> *"You gave us something*
> *Yummy to eat.*
> *Now we are back*
> *With a marvelous treat."*

Elly threw open the window.

In flew the bluebirds with all their bird friends carrying a large gown made of feathers. Blue feathers from the bluebirds, gold feathers from the goldfinches, green feathers from the greenfinches, and brown feathers from the owls.

They slipped the gown over Elly's head before she could say a word.

> *"You look beautiful," sang the bluebirds.*
> *"As trees in the fall*
> *And now you can set off*
> *For Prince Junior's ball."*

Jane Yolen

Actually, with all those feathers, Elly looked more like a big fat hen.

And as much as she wanted to go to the royal dance, Elly knew a thing or two about balls herself. She knew she could not get in without a proper invitation. But she did not want to hurt the birds' feelings.

So instead she said, "I have no dancing slippers. Size nine and a half, wide." (Very wide.)

The birds flew away all atwitter and did not return until eleven o'clock when they pecked excitedly at the kitchen window.

"Let us in, let us in,
We've come with a treat:
A pair of new shoes
To put on your feet."

(Please remember that the expression "birdbrain" was invented by someone who knew quite a bit about birds.)

Elly opened the window, and in flew the bluebirds with all their bird friends, carrying two big slippers made of twigs and grass, which they slipped on to Elly's feet.

"How do I look?" Elly asked.

Actually she looked like a big fat hen sitting on a nest. But the birds all thought she looked beautiful and said so.

Elly did not want to hurt their feelings. But she still had no invitation. So instead she said, "I have no carriage to ride in. And if I walk to the palace, I will be too late for the ball."

> *"Here we are*
> *Birds of a feather*
> *And so we all*
> *Must flock together,"*

the birds sang.

And before Elly could ask them what they meant, they had lifted her up and up and up.

The wind blew under the arms of the feather gown. And away Elly flew with the flock of birds to Prince Junior's fancy-dress ball.

By now, of course, it was nearly midnight.

Prince Junior was tired of talking about things he did not enjoy, like the weather and the price of fancy dresses. He was slightly sick from all that shoe champagne. So he went outside to the terrace for a breath of fresh air and to do a little bird watching.

He had just put his field glasses up to his eyes, when what should drop from the skies but a giant hen on a nest.

Prince Junior was amazed. He stared at the hen's lovely round face through his glasses. He checked his field guide.

There was no such hen among the chickens.

It was Elly, of course, come to the royal ball even though she had no invitation.

"Sorry to make an end run around the guards at the door," said Elly.

"You know football!" said the prince.

"And baseball," said Elly.

"What about tennis?" asked the prince.

"Adore it," she admitted. "Golf, too."

Prince Junior was not so sure about golf. So he asked slyly: "And mothballs?"

"Stink something fierce," said Elly.

"I think I love you," said the prince, smiling at Elly with his perfect teeth.

Just then a big wind blew across the terrace, lifting Elly in her feather dress back into the air.

One of her slippers fell off, landing in the undergrowth.

Then she was gone, blown back home before answering Prince Junior's declaration of love.

By the time she was dropped onto her own front porch, the feather gown was a ruin. She put the remaining slipper on the windowsill over the kitchen sink and filled it with ferns.

Poor Elly.

Poor prince.

The skinny sisters came home in a twit. That is not a kind of carriage. It is a kind of temper tantrum. They were so mad, they could barely talk. So they yelled.

"PRINCE JUNIOR IS A LOON," yelled Reen.

"WHICH IS A KIND OF BIRD," yelled Rhee.

"HE IS IN LOVE WITH A FAT HEN," they yelled together.

Elly just smiled into the cinders. It was a happy smile and a sad smile, too. But she didn't tell them anything. Would you?

Prince Junior found the slipper the very next day, when he was out bird watching, which some people do to ease an aching heart. He thought the slipper was a nest and he went to put it back in the tree.

But then he took a second look. "I know what this is!" he said. (He was pretty smart for a prince.) And he picked up the slipper and ran inside.

"I want to marry the hen who fits this grass slipper," he told his parents.

"Glass slippers are more usual," said his mother.

"Princes marry swans—not hens," added his father.

Then they sighed.

But Prince Junior was adamant.

So he searched high. (Very high.)

He searched low. (Very low.)

In fact, he searched the entire kingdom. But all the girls had small feet, tiny feet, five-to-seven, narrow feet. (Very narrow.) The grass slipper fell off every one.

Jane Yolen

At last Prince Junior arrived at Elly's house, the very last house on the very last block, where Elly sat amongst the cinders.

The skinny sisters tried on the grass shoe. They wadded paper in at the toes and cotton at the heel. They put Super Glue on their insteps and duct tape on their ankles.

But, still, the shoe fell off. (It was, after all, a slipper, which is to say, it was slippery.)

And then it fell apart all over the kitchen floor. (It was, after all, only made of grass and twigs.)

"Oh, no!" cried Prince Junior. "Now how will I find my own true love?"

The skinny sisters were furious. "Elly! Come clean up this mess," they demanded.

Then they swept out of the room with Prince Junior while Elly swept up the room by herself.

When she was done, Elly got the other slipper, from the windowsill. She was about to put it on her big foot to show Prince Junior who she really was, when she noticed that the bluebirds had used the slipper as a nest. There were three little eggs hidden in the ferns. So she put the slipper back on the sill, and sat down again in the cinders.

Poor Elly.

Poor Prince.

And that would have been the end of that, except the bluebirds came back to the nest and began to squawk and talk in bluebird.

Prince Junior heard their cries. He ran into the kitchen with his field glasses. "Bluebirds!" he cried.

"*Sialia sialis*," said Elly, which is the scientific name that only bird watchers seem to know or to care about.

Prince Junior turned his glasses from the nest to Elly. Close up, he recognized her face. "My dear hen!" he cried.

"My dear prince!" she answered.

Then they kissed, and all that nonsense about slippers—glass, grass, or good sturdy leather—was forgotten.

Elly and Prince Junior were married, of course. They named their children Blue, Green, Goldie, and Owl.

As for Reen and Rhee, and their skinny mother, they were often invited to the palace because Elly held no grudges. But they never came. Their lips were too thin to ask forgiveness, and their minds too mean to understand love.

Moral: If you love a waist, you waste a love.

Jane Yolen

Jane Yolen, who has more than two hundred books to her credit, including the Caldecott-winning *Owl Moon*, has always loved fairy tales. In fact, growing up, she read all of the Andrew Lang Color Fairy Books, which included folktales from around the world. She says: "'Cinder Elephant' has more to do with the fact that I wear a size nine and a half shoe and went from rompers to a size twelve dress with no intervening steps than any deep love for Cinderella. I hated the Disney *Cinderella* with a passion. All those mice. All those birds. The birds in 'Cinder Elephant' are a satire on those twittery bluebirds."

Instructions

Neil Gaiman

Touch the wooden gate in the wall you never
    saw before.
Say "please" before you open the latch,
go through,
walk down the path.
A red metal imp hangs from the green-painted
    front door,
as a knocker,
do not touch it; it will bite your fingers.
Walk through the house. Take nothing. Eat
    nothing.
However,
if any creature tells you that it hungers,
feed it.
If it tells you that it is dirty,
clean it.

If it cries to you that it hurts,
if you can,
ease its pain.

From the back garden you will be able to see the
    wild wood.
The deep well you walk past leads to Winter's
    realm;
there is another land at the bottom of it.
If you turn around here,
you can walk back, safely;
you will lose no face. I will think no less of you.

Once through the garden you will be in the
    wood.
The trees are old. Eyes peer from the under-
    growth.
Beneath a twisted oak sits an old woman. She
    may ask for something;
give it to her. She
will point the way to the castle.
Inside it are three princesses.
Do not trust the youngest. Walk on.
In the clearing beyond the castle the twelve
    months sit about a fire,
warming their feet, exchanging tales.
They may do favors for you, if you are polite.
You may pick strawberries in December's frost.

Trust the wolves, but do not tell them where
    you are going.
The river can be crossed by the ferry. The ferry-
    man will take you.
(The answer to his question is this:
If he hands the oar to his passenger, he will be free to
    leave the boat.
Only tell him this from a safe distance.)

If an eagle gives you a feather, keep it safe.
Remember: that giants sleep too soundly; that
witches are often betrayed by their appetites;
dragons have one soft spot, somewhere, always;
hearts can be well-hidden,
and you betray them with your tongue.

Do not be jealous of your sister.
Know that diamonds and roses
are as uncomfortable when they tumble from
    one's lips as toads and frogs:
colder, too, and sharper, and they cut.

Remember your name.
Do not lose hope—what you seek will be found.
Trust ghosts. Trust those that you have helped
    to help you in their turn.
Trust dreams.
Trust your heart, and trust your story.

                      Neil Gaiman

When you come back, return the way you came.
Favors will be returned, debts be repaid.
Do not forget your manners.
Do not look back.
Ride the wise eagle (you shall not fall)
Ride the silver fish (you will not drown)
Ride the gray wolf (hold tightly to his fur).

There is a worm at the heart of the tower; that is
     why it will not stand.

When you reach the little house, the place your
     journey started,
you will recognize it, although it will seem
     much smaller than you remember.
Walk up the path, and through the garden gate
     you never saw before but once.
And then go home. Or make a home.

Or rest.

Neil Gaiman says: "When I was a small boy, my favorite fairy tale was probably 'Snow White.' I would stare, fascinated, at apples that were red on one side and green on the other, and wonder how you poisoned just half an apple, and whether the red half really did taste better than the green half. And it left me with a fondness for wicked and magnificent witch-queens that, it only occurs to me now, is probably why I put one in *Stardust*, my latest book, which is a fairy tale for adults.

"'Instructions' is, quite literally, that: It's a tale of what to do when you find yourself in a fairy tale. It's always best to be prepared for these things, after all."

Gaiman is also the author of the Sandman series of graphic novels and of the novel *Neverwhere*. He lives in Wisconsin.

Mrs. Big:
"Jack and the Beanstalk" Retold

by Michael Cadnum

Sometimes I complained too much, but there was a lot to complain about.

We couldn't live in the village among the joiners and the potters. We shook the ground when we tiptoed, and every time we napped in the town square we rolled over and crushed the Charter Oak or the Stone of Justice, or some other ancient monument beloved by man and boy. Our burps shattered windows in the chapel, and my stifled sneezes slopped duck ponds dry.

I started telling him it was all the fault of the pee-wee Englishmen, so tiny, their yells were squeaks. I flattened an ox by mistake one morn, out shaking dust off a doily. The ox-drovers cried out in terror, bovine mush all over my instep. "The Englishmen are too small," I said. "And not only that, the Englishmen are thieves!" This was the truth, as all giants know. Our kind always have some few tons of gold dust or silver nuggets tucked away. And we were always brushing away a couple of carter's boys or tanner's apprentices—trying to steal our nodes of ore.

One evening out watching the full moon come up, I trod on a milkmaid, and I knew then we had to make changes. It was bad enough having to scrub girl-juice off my best wooden shoe. It was the way my husband took it so hard that really troubled me. He brooded for days on why people-folk are so minuscule and easy to squish. And as tough as I like to sound, I don't like squashing maidens any more than you would.

Little by little his usual complacent, happy nature started to go sour. Before, he had been glad to wave at a passing farmhand. Now he frowned, and stuck out his lip, and started the beginnings of his famous poem. "I smell an Englishman," he would say, a picnic of villagers scrambling out of his shadow. "I smell the blood of an Englishman," he would say, shaking his fist, which was the size of a cow barn.

I encouraged him. "You smell the blood of a mite, is what you smell," I said. "A bunch we'd be well rid of." They had a strong scent: charred beef and tobacco, green ale and cheddar. You could nose a gentleman farmer and his lady half a league away.

I had hoped my beloved would be one of the Raving Giants, terrors of the earth, and devour the citizens of the countryside, like my great uncle, scourge of Europe. I'd hoped he'd be a Bard of the Big, like a few of my forebears. But, instead, he was a garden-giant, planting oaks and patting the earth around their roots. He had fine gold in bags of whale skin stitched together, and silver in schooner sails, but otherwise he was more peaceful planter than monster.

One day he hurried home with a gleeful expression, poplars shivering at his tread. He announced, in a voice loud enough to give a flock of passing geese a collective heart attack, "I've found a home!"

He'd bought it from a traveling peddler for a pocketful of pumpkins, he explained. It was acreage with a view, a mansion, plenty of garden space, but one drawback from the point of view access: It was in the clouds.

What sort of peddler? I thought to ask, but could not get the words out in my wonderment.

We had to stack carriages, oxcarts, sheds, and steeples one on top of each other, a teetering column, just so we could clamber up and take possession of the place. Once there, the pile tumbled back to earth with a dusty crash, and we were homeowners.

What sort of peddler indeed! I had cause to think in days and weeks to come. If I walked beyond where the wash was hanging, blue and yellow in the sun, I'd stumble and there it would be, the land way down there, cloud spinning off right under my feet. We feasted on gourds, squash, marrow, courgettes, that race of veggies that grows big. When the cloud-land parted, some of the yams tumbled down, all the way to the countryside below.

My husband would patch the cloud-field with some more of the stuff we walked around on, and rake it neat.

The view from the mansion was all thunderhead and sun, and sometimes a bird would make it all the way up to where we lived. He would alight on one of the melon plants that grew like weeds and peep around at things, bright and chirpy. I was learning to be a wiser giantess, and learned not to complain so much, even when my husband made up more of his poem, the verses of which could get on even a stone saint's nerves.

"I smell the blood of an Englishman," he would say, and then try out the words, "Peas, cows, drakes, drums, I smell the . . ." Or other random word assortments, until I wanted to scream. My father was the Giant Poet of the East, renowned among the deepest valleys for his alliterative verse. He's the wit who made up such famous phrases as *shilly-shally, hale and hearty, vim and vigor,* and other such word-pairs.

I explained the importance of form over meaning, of nonsense over simple declaration, and my husband, the poor dear, took it so to heart, he sulked. This pained me, because the truth is I was growing very fond of my huge hubby, isolated in the sky though we were.

His earnest humming in the cuke patch, his merry "Blood of an Englishman" yodel, all worked him ever deeper into my heart. I came to regret that I'd ever been critical in the first place. So when he burst in on me as I darned his breeches, and blurted out, "I smell the blood of an Englishman! Fee, Fie, Foe, Fum!" I clapped with appreciation, and patted his pink cheek.

I should have kept my mouth shut. "But wouldn't it be better back to front?" I began. And when he beamed, uncomprehending, I continued, "With the 'Fee, Fie' part first in the poem, the 'blood' part second?"

Such a sulk I have never observed in man or giant, a sulk of such deep duration, I was afraid he would never speak again.

Long days and somber nights he tugged the weeds, watered the crookneck and the summer squash with squeezed cloud, wrung out like sponges on the leafy vines. He met my eyes with sorrow, bearing up, brave-hearted, but thinking he had failed me, knowing how my family prized a turn of phrase. So there we were, solemn and quiet, when the terrible thing happened.

One day I was wringing the suds from my husband's knickers, and the next a human flea was squeezing through a hole in the cloudy field. Not one of the usual wear-and-wind holes, either, but a puncture made by a bean vine with leaves as big as me. I couldn't scream, I couldn't take a breath.

The lad was quick, and like a weevil he crept along the garden path, but by then my husband straightened in the garden, sniffing. Sniffing the bright air, he said softly, "Fee, Fie, Foe, Fum. I smell the blood of an Englishman." Gentle, like it was a love poem, an offering from his heart. Then he frowned. "I do!" he exclaimed. "I smell—"

He gathered himself, put one foot forward, and sang out, for all under the sky to hear, "Fee! Fie!" And continued on to declaim his entire, famous poem, the one they heard from Iceland to Crete that very instant.

We couldn't find the boy. The human pup got lost in the hall, and lost in the pantry, and lost in the parlor, too. All over the mansion we sniffed him out, but not a glimpse could we see.

Human as he was, I should have known. A giant's footstool, a god-sized spoon, a magnificent pair of breeches drying over a chair the size of a county were nothing to an English lad. He sought gold. He squirted through the chest-chamber, leaped up the side of a cask of gold, and bounded high, onto a sack the side of a guild house. He was a leaping-lad, digging and cutting with a cunning little knife, gold dust like summer wheat pouring out upon the floor.

He stuffed his breeches pockets with as much gold as he could cram, and leaped more slowly, jumped and scrambled. And then he stumbled, weighed down with twenty-four-carat powder, and rolled under my feet. In my fear that I might flatten him dead on the spot, I lifted one foot. I shifted another. I swayed.

I swung my arms, and fell with a crash that shook the cloud-land and shivered the billowing cumulus from north to south. My husband caught my look of pain, his eyes filled with shock at my distress, and ran after the human speck, bellowing the poem.

Michael Cadnum

The thief was clumsy, fat with gold, escaping the grasp of my angry spouse by a feather's span. I hurried after the two, gasping that I was not hurt, but now, when I wished my words had weight, they had no effect on large or small. The thief heaved himself to the stalk and shimmied down, leaf to leaf, falling, catching himself, until he was out of sight.

My husband hesitated—no giant can scramble, or bound, or spring to save his life. He took a deep breath and clambered down behind him, swaying the mighty beanstalk, leaves thrashing, covering the sound of my cry that I was all right, that my loved one need not avenge me. The thief had scampered all the way down to the landscape before my husband had mastered his grip on the leaves, and the thief began to work with a tiny ax, far below.

Who has not heard the story? How my husband fell, crashing through the green into the flat and distant earth? How Jack—for even robbers have names— hugged his mum and bragged of gold, and three beans exchanged with a peddler for a cow. While my husband lay like a hill, a mountain shaped like a man, stretched out with his last glance bright with love for me.

Fear not, Jack and Jack's mother, I wanted to say. Stay calm, villagers and geese. I sought no vengeance on a foolish lad, or harm to roof or heath. And be not afraid of my story's end, or believe it tells the demise of my beloved.

Even then I spied the creature I wanted, stealing down the hedgerows, the single cause of all my grief. I hurried after him, my shadow flowing ahead of my stride.

Sorcery that can ennoble the clouds with an estate, and sprout a beanstalk to heaven from three beans, can cure a giant poet of a fall. I sought the scurrying peddler with his magic wares.

He ran across a cow pasture, fled across a barnyard, staggered through daisies.

And I followed easily, bending, reaching. He was far too slow.

Michael Cadnum

Michael Cadnum has always been interested in stories about giants, and he thinks "Jack and the Beanstalk" is one of his favorites. Not only did the story have a very impressive giant, but it had a secret landscape in the clouds, which is another fascinating subject. He thinks we have all seen mountains and valleys in the clouds from time to time. What a wonderful kingdom for a giant the sky would be. . . .

Michael Cadnum's novel about Robin Hood, *In a Dark Wood*, was chosen by the Smithsonian as one of 1998's best books for young people. His most recent novels are *Heat* and *Rundown*.

Falada:

The Goose Girl's Horse

by Nancy Farmer

My troubles began when the queen of Elfland put Conrad on my back. As a fairy horse I was used to strange riders. The queen often asked me to carry royal guests. *Asked* me, you understand. I was no bumbling farm horse. The queen would say, "*Dear* Falada. Would you mind taking this dwarf (or gnome or goblin) for a tour of the royal gardens!"

And I would say, "Of course!" unless it was a goblin. Some of them like to chew on ears.

I was a beautiful mare. I had silvery-white hair and a long, silver mane. My golden horseshoes were fastened with diamond nails, and when I galloped, sparks flew up from my feet. Right in the middle of my forehead was a gray circle. It was exactly where a horn would have grown, if I'd been a unicorn. My great-grandfather on my mother's side *was* a unicorn.

So you see I was no ordinary horse. And when the

queen put Conrad on my back—without asking!—I was insulted. First, I should explain about Conrad. He was a human child. Every now and then the elves carry off a baby they find interesting. They call it *borrowing*, but I call it *stealing*. They keep this child until they get bored with it. Then they return it to the poor mother.

By that time the child has learned bad habits. The elves spoil it rotten. They feed it candy instead of fruit, never send it to bed on time, and give in to it every time it throws a temper tantrum. And believe me, those brats know how to throw tantrums.

Conrad was eight years old and no longer cute. The queen was tired of his screaming fits, so she put him on my back and said, "Take him around the garden. Don't throw him off, either. I know your tricks."

She was annoyed at me because I had dumped a pair of gnomes into a rosebush the week before. I couldn't see what the fuss was about. Everyone knows gnomes bounce. I trotted off with Conrad clinging to my mane. His fingers were sticky with chocolate.

"Don't hang on to me," I said.

"Make me stop," jeered Conrad.

"Good riders hold on with their knees," I explained patiently.

Conrad gave a vicious tug to my mane. "I could pull this out," he said. "I could stuff a pillow with it."

"You already have a pillow," I told the little monster.

"Maybe I want another one." He yanked so hard, I

saw stars. I actually felt a clump of my beautiful, silver mane being torn out! I stopped short, kicked up my heels, and tossed Conrad into the thorniest rosebush in the garden.

You could hear him scream all the way to the goblin king's palace in the mountains. He was only bleeding in a dozen or so places, but the queen was furious. "I'm sick of all the noise around here," she cried. "You, Falada, will be given a task among humans. If you do it well, I *might* let you return. And you, Conrad, are going straight back to your mother."

I felt sick. I was being banished from Elfland. Every now and then a fairy animal is given a task in the real world. That's where all those magic foxes, firebirds, and talking fish come from. The task is always unpleasant.

An Elf lord put a rope around my neck and took me along the misty road that leads to the real world. The first thing I noticed was the dirt crunching beneath my feet. Then I felt my first horsefly bite. The sun was too hot, the grass too dry, the water too muddy.

I saw myself in a stream. My golden horseshoes were gone. My silver hair had turned gray. Oh, woe, woe, woe! I was no better than a mangy plow horse on a turnip farm.

My task was to carry the princess Belinda to her future husband in the next kingdom. "Watch over her," whispered Belinda's mother, who knew I was a fairy horse. "She's a sweet girl, but rather foolish." The

Nancy Farmer

old queen sighed. "I suppose I babied her too much."

My heart sank when I saw Belinda. She was a soft, pretty child. She cried when a bird flew into the courtyard and snapped up a grasshopper. "Do something," she wept, wringing her hands.

"There, there," said the old queen. "The bird is only taking food home to her babies."

We started out. I walked carefully with the princess Belinda on my back. Behind me came a handsome black horse with Belinda's serving maid, Dagmar. Belinda clapped her hands when she saw anything new. Everything was a delight to her. She liked the trees and the squirrels that chattered at us from the branches. Every flower filled her with joy.

Dagmar, on the other hand, hated everything. She thought squirrels were only good for squirrel pie, and that trees should be chopped up for firewood. "This forest is probably full of bears," she sniffed.

"How I'd love to see a cuddly, wuddly little bear! Do they really drink honey?" cried Belinda.

"They eat people and drink blood," said Dagmar.

That shut Belinda up for a while, but soon she was warbling again. Everything was new to her, you see. She was a kind, happy girl.

When we got to the first stream, Princess Belinda said, "Dear Dagmar, could you bring me a cup of water?"

"Get it yourself. You aren't lame," said Dagmar.

"Don't let her get away with that," I told Belinda.

"You're going to be a queen someday. You must learn to give orders." But the girl was too afraid. She climbed down from the saddle and fetched her own water.

Later in the day we came to another stream. "Dearest, dearest Dagmar. Would you mind *terribly much* getting me a cup of water?" asked Princess Belinda.

"Of course I mind *terribly much*," said Dagmar. So the princess climbed down and fetched her own water.

That night Dagmar refused to cook dinner or wash dishes or make up beds. Each time, I told the princess, "Don't let her get away with that." And each time, Belinda wrung her hands and cried.

I gave up and joined the black horse under a tree. "Things aren't working out at all," I muttered to myself.

"Things are working out fine," the black horse replied.

I was amazed. Another talking horse! "Are you from Elfland?" I asked.

"Hardly. My mistress and I come from the goblin king's palace in the mountains."

So that explained it. Dagmar was a goblin. No wonder she was so angry and rude.

In the morning, Dagmar made Belinda take off her beautiful golden dress and put on rags. She smeared Belinda's face and hair with mud. "There! No one will ever know you're a princess. If you tell on me, I'll chop you into little pieces. And if *you* tell on me, Falada, I'll have your head cut off." Neither Belinda nor I doubted her for a second.

Dagmar put on the golden dress. When we got to the neighboring kingdom, the old king and his son Humbert came out to greet us. Prince Humbert was delighted with Dagmar. "You're more beautiful than I expected," he cried.

"And you're dumber than I expected," said Dagmar with a sweet smile. Prince Humbert didn't even care that she had insulted him. He had fallen head over heels in love with her. He was the kind of prince who liked being pushed around.

"What shall we do with your serving maid?" asked the old king.

"Oh, her! She's so foolish, she's only good for herding geese," sneered Dagmar.

So Belinda was taken off to a goose farm, and I was chained to a millstone at a mill. Round and round I trudged, grinding grain into flour. My hooves wore down from all the walking. My tail became tangled and full of burrs, and my bones stuck out under my dusty, dirty skin. I looked *worse* than a mangy plow horse on a turnip farm.

Every day Belinda came by with a herd of geese. With her—I could hardly believe it—was Conrad, who had got me into trouble in the first place. His mother had hired him out to the goose farmer. "Hello, Falada. You look awful," the little monster said happily.

"Geese, geese, hiss and fight. Give Conrad a nasty bite," I chanted. I might be banished, but I was still a fairy horse. I knew a little magic. The geese flapped their wings and nipped Conrad's behind. He ran off screaming loud enough to be heard in the goblin king's palace in the mountains.

"Poor Falada, you look so unhappy," sighed Princess Belinda.

"You, too," I said.

"Alas, alas, if mother knew, I fear her heart would break in two," the princess said. "I'd better get these geese to the meadow before they get into more mischief." She herded them onward with a little switch cut from a willow tree.

As time passed, I noticed a change in Belinda. She no longer wrung her hands and wept. In fact, Belinda was learning a great many things from the goose farmer and the goose farmer's wife. Now she could bake bread and grow vegetables. She could shear a sheep and take an egg away from a hen without getting pecked. The more Belinda learned, the more confident she became.

Every day she came past the mill yard and brought me a bunch of carrots or an apple. I, in turn, taught her how to get rid of Conrad. He had a habit of pulling out strands of her long, golden hair to make fishing lures. Now, when he crept up on her, she chanted, "Blow, wind, with all your might. Blow Conrad's hat right out of *sight.*" He spent the rest of the afternoon running all over the meadow after his hat.

Finally, though, Conrad got angry. He waited outside the back door of the palace until the old king came out to sun himself in the garden. "Sir! Sir!" the boy called. "Please listen to me, sir!"

The old king had twelve sons and liked children. "Come here, lad," he said kindly. "What's your problem?"

"It's that nasty goose girl," said Conrad. "Every day she does a magic trick. She has the wind blow my hat all over the meadow. She talks to a horse, too, *and it talks back.* I think she's a witch, sir."

"Well, well. A talking horse. That's something I have to see," said the old king.

Early the next morning he came to the mill yard and sat on a stone. He was dressed like a farmer, but I knew exactly what he was. You don't grow up in Elfland without learning who's a king and who isn't.

Quite soon Belinda came by with her herd of geese. Conrad was bouncing up and down with pure glee. He saw the old king on the stone. "Poor Falada, you look so unhappy," sighed the princess.

"You, too," I replied.

"Alas, alas, if mother knew, I fear her heart would break in two."

Then the devil got into me. *"Geese, geese, hiss and fight. Give Conrad a nasty bite,"* I chanted. Straight off, the geese flapped their wings and nipped Conrad's behind. He ran off screaming loud enough to be heard in the goblin king's palace in the mountains.

The old king laughed so hard, he almost fell off his stone. "That's something you don't see every day," he wheezed. "Come on now, you two. Tell me how a fairy horse and a most unusual goose girl landed in my backyard."

But both Belinda and I were afraid to speak. We knew Prince Humbert was married to a goblin. Belinda didn't want to be chopped into pieces, and I didn't want my head cut off. "Well, sir, it's difficult to say," I began.

"We promised not to tell," said Belinda.

The old king looked from one of us to the other. "I see you are afraid. Well, well. I don't know what to do about that."

Suddenly Belinda straightened her backbone. "I'm through with being a coward," she said. "I've stayed up all night with the lambs when they were sick. I've brought horses to the barn during a thunderstorm. *They* were frightened, but I didn't have time for it."

"Spoken like a true princess," said the old king, smiling.

So then Belinda told him about the trip through the forest and how she was forced to change clothes with the goblin. The old king stood up in a towering rage. He strode off to the palace, calling for his guards, his soldiers and his executioner.

But by the time he got there, Dagmar was gone. In

the way goblins have of knowing when to flee, Dagmar had saddled up her handsome black horse and taken off for the mountains as fast as she could go. Oh, and she took Prince Humbert with her. He was still in love with her, goblin or not. Besides, he liked the way she ordered him around.

Princess Belinda married his little brother Prince Herkimer instead. He was second in line and had a much better character.

I was allowed to return to Elfland. As I crossed over the border, my cracked hooves became smooth again. My hair turned from gray to silver, and my skin became sleek and fat. "It's great to be back," I sighed. When I got to the queen's palace, I saw she had visitors.

They were Dagmar, Prince Humbert, and that wickedly handsome black horse. Dagmar had changed, too, when she crossed over the border to Elfland. She looked exactly like a goblin, which meant she was pea green and had a fine pair of tusks on either side of her nose.

"Things worked out after all," I told the black horse.

"Well, of course," he snorted. "Your job was to take the princess to her new kingdom. *My* job was to see she got some sense before she became a queen. You weren't the only one who was given a task." And we went off to the garden together before anyone could ask us for a ride.

Nancy Farmer grew up in a hotel on the Mexican border. She relates that "the hotel patrons—retired railroad men, cowboys, circus performers, and bank robbers on vacation—stayed up all night, gossiping and playing cards. They were so entertaining, I never got to bed before 3 A.M. and fell asleep in school the next day. I was a terrible student. In sixth grade I learned how to play hooky. I ran away so often, my teachers used to say, 'Who are you?' whenever I showed up.

"But I read mountains of books. I can't think of a fairy tale I *didn't* like. One of my favorites was 'Sleeping Beauty.' Every time I got to the part where the princess pricks her hand on the spindle, I cried, 'Don't take presents from old hags you find lurking in deserted towers! Didn't your mother teach you anything?' I was upset by fairy stories (and there are lots of them) where innocent animals were killed so the heroine could live happily ever after. In particular, I thought Falada the horse got a raw deal. How long did her head stay nailed over the gate? Who did she talk to? How did she eat?"

As an adult, Farmer ran a chicken farm in India, controlled insects on traffic islands in California, monitored water purity for villages in central Africa, and, last of all, wrote children's books. Her novels are *Do You Know Me*; *The Ear, the Eye and the Arm*; *The Warm Place*; and *A Girl Named Disaster*; plus one picture book, *Runnery Granary*. *The Ear, the Eye and the Arm* won a Newbery Honor for 1994, and *A Girl Named Disaster* won a Newbery Honor for 1997 and was a finalist for the National Book Award.

A Wolf at the Door

by Tanith Lee

It was summer during the Ice Age, so Glasina wasn't at school. She spent her holidays with her father and mother in a large house by the sea, whose water in summer unfroze and turned to liquid, although the shore was still deep in snow. The sea and the sky were blue in summer, and the ice cliffs behind the house shone and sparkled. The tall trees in the snowfields put out leaves like glass, which tinkled. They had changed over the centuries of the Ice Age in order to survive, and their trunks were like thick sticks of hard, green sugar. Lions lived along the shore near the house, and they had had to change, too. The lions had developed long, heavy, grayish fur, and huge orange manes (to show they were still fierce), which from the front made them look like chrysanthemums.

For the first fortnight of the summer holidays, Glasina's mother, who was a teacher, was still away teaching in the south. But Glasina's father was an artist, and he always worked at home in the house by the sea.

On the fifth day of her holiday, Glasina was walking along the snowy shore by the dark blue sea. She had her camera, and took pictures of the seals playing in the water, and of the lions, some of whom were fishing off the ice floes. The lions were used to Glasina, since she and her parents fed them sometimes.

After she had walked about a mile, and taken about twenty photographs, Glasina sat down on a snowdrift, and simply smiled and sighed at the joy of being on holiday. Then, when she turned her head, she saw a black wolf was trotting along the sea's edge, toward her.

Now Glasina knew that wolves were not often dangerous; if you acted sensibly, they would never attack you unless they were starving. But this wolf could be hungry, for it looked very thin, and its pale eyes gleamed. Glasina stood up and pointed her camera at the wolf, who might not be sure what it was.

"Stay where you are," said Glasina, "or I'll shoot."

"Shoot away," said the wolf carelessly. "Though I don't look my best."

Glasina lowered the camera. Because of the Ice Age, to help them survive most of the animals had learned how to talk, but usually they could only manage a few words. For example, the lions could only say things such as, *Hallo, wot ya got?* and *More!* This wolf, though, was different.

"How are you?" Glasina therefore said politely.

"Fine," said the wolf. "And that's a lie."

"Yes," said Glasina. "Have you had a difficult winter, wolf?"

"Terrible," said the wolf. It came and sat down nearby. "Is that your house?" it inquired.

"Well, it's my parents' house, but I live there."

"Wow," said the wolf. "Do you mean you're still at school? I thought you were at *least* eighteen."

Glasina was fourteen, and she wasn't silly, either. The wolf was obviously trying to get on her good side. On the other hand, her father and mother would expect her to be kind to the wolf, and considerate.

"If you'd like to come with me," said Glasina, "my father or I can get the food machine to make you something to eat."

"Oh, wonderful," said the wolf, rolling over in the snow with delight. "And I'd give *anything* for a bath! Do you know," it went on, hurrying at Glasina's heels, "I haven't slept in a proper bed for weeks."

"How's the wolf today?" asked Glasina's father three mornings later.

"Still in bed," said Glasina, "with the covers up over its ears. It's spilt coffee on the sheets again, too, and last night it left the bath taps running. The housework machine's still clearing up."

"I'm not happy about this," said Glasina's father, whose hands were red and blue from his latest painting.

"And your mother won't like it at all when she gets home."

Glasina had already taken a photo of the wolf in bed in the guest room in case it left before her mother returned and her mother didn't believe what had happened, and how it had broken two coffee mugs and two teacups, and about the egg stain on the living room wall—the wolf had been explaining how it had run away from some polar bears and brought down its foot in the fried eggs for emphasis. There were also some T-shirts the wolf had wanted to wear, one of which was Glasina's mother's favorite, and the wolf had torn all the T-shirts across the back when it was dancing to Glasina's music tapes, leaping and waving its paws.

"What shall we do?" said Glasina uneasily.

"To be honest," said her father, "I don't know. I mean," he added later as they walked along the shore to avoid the horribly loud way the wolf was by then playing their music center (it always found the tapes they liked the least and said it liked those the best). "It seems to have wandered for miles across the snow, hungry and lonely and forlorn. It doesn't seem to have any family, or any friends . . . although, I must say, I'm not all that amazed by *that*. Its behavior as a human being is dreadful, but it doesn't seem to know how to be a wolf." He frowned. "Which is what worries me the most."

"I've been thinking about that, too," said Glasina.

"You hear these stories," said her father.

They stood and stared out to sea gloomily. It was a beautiful day, sunny and bright, and the water looked like sapphire jelly, but this didn't cheer them up. Nor did the sight of one of the lions standing on the ice at the sea's edge. The lion, too, seemed anxious, or only bored. She was a lioness, so she didn't have a mane and didn't look like a chrysanthemum.

"It's such a responsibility," said Glasina's father. "And, besides, what about you?"

"I wanted to go to college," said Glasina sadly.

"Of course, he couldn't claim you for at least three years—"

Glasina felt like crying, but she bravely didn't. Her father, however, rubbed red and blue paint all over his face without realizing it.

What they were afraid of was that the wolf was really a young man under a spell. According to the stories, if Glasina kissed the wolf, the spell would break, and it would become a young man again. But if he was as annoying as a human being as he was as a wolf, Glasina wasn't keen on the idea. She would, naturally, as his rescuer, be expected to fall in love with him and set up house with him in due course, in the correct tradition. It always happened like that in the stories. And Glasina hadn't planned her life this way. She wanted to learn things, travel, teach, and paint and take pictures. On the other hand, how could she allow a young man to go on being trapped in a wolf body once she'd guessed what was wrong?

"I suppose," said Glasina at last, "I'll have to do it."

"I'm so sorry," said her father. "I wish I could think of another way. Perhaps we should wait until your mother gets here—"

But just then there was a crash of crockery from the house as another coffee mug dropped from the wolf's clumsy paws.

"At least if he's a young man," said Glasina, "he'll be able to hold a mug properly. I'd better go and kiss him now."

The wolf was coming out of the house as they arrived. It was wearing a Walkman, although the ear-pieces didn't fit in its ears, and any minute everything seemed likely to fall off into the snow and get broken.

Glasina strode up to the wolf, with her father marching behind. Behind him loped the lioness, who had recognized them and kept saying insistently, "Hallo, wot ya got?"

"Wolf," said Glasina, "I've considered carefully, and you'd better understand I don't want to. But I will."

"And just you watch yourself when she does," shouted her blue-and-red-faced father angrily at the wolf.

"Wot ya got?" the lioness put in, and barged past them.

Glasina kissed the wolf on the cheek.

The lioness kissed the wolf on the other cheek.

Tanith Lee

The Walkman fell off and got broken.

The wolf disappeared.

Glasina and her father looked round nervously, and there was a lion with a chrysanthemum mane, gazing at the lioness in surprise. "Funny," it said. "I thought I was meant to be a human being—oh, well. Knew I had friends here somewhere. Confused by the spell . . . anyone can make a mistake." Then it trod on the Walkman, nuzzled the lioness, and said fiercely to Glasina's father, "Hallo, wot ya got?"

"I'll get you a lovely big steak," said Glasina's father, beaming.

"And I'll take your photo," said Glasina. To her relief, both lions only looked puzzled.

Tanith Lee, who lives on the coast of England, has written a number of novels for children and young adults, including *The Dragon Hoard*; *Princess Hynchatti*; *Prince on a White Horse*; *Islands in the Sky*; *Black Unicorn*; *Gold Unicorn*; and *Red Unicorn*; and *Law of the Wolf Tower*, first of the Wolf Law trilogy.

She says, "Wolves are part of the landscape for so many fairy tales—moving pieces of the Forest Dark and Terrible. As a child, they scared me, but I loved them, too (the love persists). My mother started my trend of turning such stories around, even inside out, and the oddity of humor that true drama somehow invites. (Something wonderful and very serious is so often the best material for the send-up.) I was always very intrigued by the *changes*, too—the frog who is really a prince, the cat who is a princess . . . maybe we are all something also, something other than what the world sees when it looks at us. How many people, for example, look at a child and see 'only' a child."

Ali Baba and the Forty Aliens

by Janeen Webb

Alberto Barbarino hated his name. He blamed his parents. They should have *known* that naming him after his uncle Al would cause confusion. His uncle was big Al, so Alberto was little Al, or Ali for short. And with *Barbarino*'s being the best-known Italian restaurant in the whole Ballarat goldfields district, when he got to school it didn't take long for the kids in his class to start calling him Ali Baba, after that stupid story the teacher read to them. The nickname stuck. And here he was, ten years old and nearly an adult, still called Ali Baba, still refusing to waste his time with the kids who called him that. He didn't need them, with their skateboards and their trendy bikes and their private jokes. He had better things to do.

Ali was pretty much a loner. He read all the *Sandman* comics and talked his mother into buying him a supply of gothic black T-shirts and black jeans. He had a black jean jacket, too, though he was saving up to replace it with a leather one. Black, of course. An oversized pair of Doc Martens and a dangling silver earring in the shape of an ankh completed his outfit. With his glossy black hair spiked up with gel, and his wraparound black sunglasses making his pale skin look even paler against the black clothes, he looked pretty cool.

His older brother, Dean, said he looked creepy. Ali didn't care. He stayed away from the noise and bustle of the family restaurant where everyone was shouting and his horrible brother was forever giving him errands to run. He headed for the hills, pedaling his battered bike to the old goldfields country on the outskirts of town. He mostly avoided the historical tourist park, where busloads of crumpled visitors paid to go into a fenced-off area to get what the glossy brochures called the "Australian gold rush experience." This meant that people dressed up in 1850s costumes showed the tourists how to pan for gold in the creek, and when the tourists got hot and bored, they were taken to the tourist shop to buy little bottles with specks of gold in them. Ali thought it was stupid, especially the way the visitors wandered around the park with their cameras looking for kangaroos and koalas. Okay, so there were kangaroos hereabouts in the scrub, but they avoided the tourists, too, and Ali knew that no one making *that* much noise was ever going to see one!

So Ali left them to it, and pedaled farther out of town to the overgrown parts of the goldfields, where the roads turned into dangerous little tracks that buses and cars couldn't drive on. Ali loved the silence of the old diggings, with their mullock heaps and abandoned mines and weirdly shaped rusting machinery. He spent most of his free time out there, fossicking among the ruins or panning in the creek. And he did find valuables from time to time—little nuggets or flecks of alluvial gold, which he sold to the tourist shop when he had enough to make it worthwhile. He even went out to the diggings at night, hoping for ghosts. But he never saw one, not even when he found the lumps that marked bush graves of long-forgotten people. Maybe they were too tired after all that digging to be bothered haunting their graves.

Ali thought he knew all the old mine sites. But this Saturday morning he stumbled across one mine he could have sworn wasn't there the week before. Or ever before, come to think of it. There was something wrong about the entrance to this particular disused gold mine. Sure it looked like it had been dug out the hard way, by pick and shovel. And it had the usual rough-hewn wooden framework, the usual rusted-through bit of corrugated iron across the entrance, the usual KEEP OUT sign slapped on it in drippy paint. But something looked

Ali Baba and the Forty Aliens

wrong. It was too neat. There were crumpled cola cans and paper wrappers lying about, typical rubbish you'd expect someone careless to leave after a picnic. But the grass was trampled flatter than a couple of picnickers with a blanket could have left it. And the bush was quiet. Too quiet. Like the birds and animals were giving it a wide berth. And it smelled wrong—the dusty bush smell was overlaid with some chemical tang Ali couldn't put a name to.

He decided to investigate. He had his flashlight. He told himself he'd just take a peek. He wouldn't go too far in. He bent to pull aside the old iron cover across the entrance. It wouldn't budge. It looked flimsy, like all the others, but Ali couldn't make it move at all. He climbed up onto the earth mounded above the entrance tunnel and tried to loosen the iron from the top. Nothing happened. He gave it a good hard kick, which hurt his foot. But the cover didn't even vibrate. Ali's frustration was growing—he climbed back down and tried attacking the old iron with a heavy piece of timber from the abandoned pile. Nothing. Not even a dent. The tin even sounded wrong, kind of muffled. The entrance was sealed. And Ali couldn't see what was sealing it.

Then it happened. One minute he was alone in the little bush clearing, next there was the sound of feet. A lot of feet. Ali was terrified. He felt the blood drain from his pale face, felt his heart thumping loudly in his chest. He barely had time to scramble up the nearest tree

Janeen Webb

before the first of the intruders came into view. Ali counted forty of them, and they were all carrying packs and bundles of various shapes and sizes.

Ali knew they were aliens. They couldn't be anything else. They weren't bug-eyed monsters or robots or anything; they looked right, but they felt wrong. Like those models you make up from pictures and diagrams that never quite come out looking like the real thing. These guys looked like humans, but they didn't act like humans. They weren't talking or looking about, just heading straight for the mine. They carried their heavy packages without effort, without even breaking into a sweat. Maybe they couldn't sweat.

The chemical smell was getting a lot stronger, and Ali hoped he wouldn't choke or cry, or faint from the effort of staying still in his tree. He didn't think forty aliens would be very gentle if they caught him spying.

The aliens walked right up to the mine entrance. The leader faced the barrier that had been giving Ali so much trouble, and softly said, "Keep In."

That old corrugated iron didn't make a sound—it just disappeared. Now you see it, now you don't. And Ali watched openmouthed as the aliens walked *through* it and into the mine tunnel beyond. The entrance stayed open a few minutes, shimmering a little. There was a faint ozone smell in the air.

Then the door reappeared, solid as ever.

Ali waited in his tree, too scared to come down. Just

as he was thinking he'd have to make a run for it, the door dematerialized again. He saw the strangers walk back into the clearing, without their bundles. When the last member of the group appeared, the leader turned and murmured, "Keep Out." And the barrier was back. The aliens left, as strangely as they had come, vanishing into the bush.

Ali was shaking as he climbed down, but was fascinated, too. He wondered if the password would work for him. There was only one way to find out. He faced the entrance and said, "Keep In."

The ozone smell came back, and the doorway opened. Ali was inside before he could think about it. He'd expected it to be dark, but he found himself in a softly lit chamber. The walls were lined with shelves of experimental-looking tubes and specimen jars and equipment. Maybe the aliens were collecting samples. He hoped they didn't include any live ones. A familiar gleam attracted his gaze, and Ali found himself looking at a whole basket full of very small gold nuggets. There was another basket of natural crystals of various types, and even more baskets of minerals he couldn't identify.

Ordinarily Ali wouldn't take what wasn't his, but he figured this stuff didn't properly belong to the aliens, either. And no one in authority would believe his story if he told them—which he wouldn't. The aliens would never miss a few bits and pieces out of this huge hoard.

So Ali decided to help himself. He was not greedy:

He quickly filled his pockets with the smaller nuggets, and hurried back outside. He turned to the entrance and breathed the words, "Keep Out," watching in relief as the doorway resumed its abandoned gold mine disguise.

Back at the restaurant, Ali sidled into the preparation area and borrrowed the kitchen scales to weigh his treasure. Then he hid the gold at the bottom of his underwear drawer and quickly returned the scales. He planned to sell the gold a little at a time, until he had enough to buy his leather jacket without inviting suspicion.

But the weighing pan had been a bit sticky, and a couple of flecks of gold stayed stuck on the bottom. And the person who had noticed was Dean, who was helping out in the kitchen because Saturday night was so busy.

And that's where the trouble started. Dean sauntered into Ali's room and said, "So how come you got so much gold, you got to weigh it? Who'd you steal it from?"

His voice was low and nasty. Ali felt his face growing hot. He tried to sound casual. "You spied on me. I found it at the diggings, if you must know," he said.

Dean's answer was to grab Ali and push him hard against the wall. His breath was hot and sour in Ali's face as he said, "Listen, creep, I know you're up to something, and if you don't let me in on it, I'll tell Dad he should take a look in your underwear drawer. Understand?"

Ali admitted defeat. He didn't expect Dean to believe

him about the aliens, but the gold was a powerful incentive. Dean was already dreaming about cars and clothes and how impressed those stuck-up girls would be.

Next morning, a reluctant Ali took Dean out to the alien's gold mine. It looked just the same as it had yesterday, and that lingering chemical odor told Ali that the aliens had been back. He wondered if they'd noticed anything.

He faced the door and muttered, "Keep In," half hoping it wouldn't open. But it did, and Dean was through the entrance like a shot. He was making a lot of noise. Dean *was* greedy—he'd brought a couple of backpacks to fill with whatever looked valuable, despite Ali's objection that he'd never be able to carry them back to the edge of the scrub, where they had to leave their bikes.

Ali tried one more time to warn Dean not to stay too long, and not to take too much. Dean's only response was, "If you're so scared, you can piss off home."

So Ali left, feeling miserable and betrayed.

And that was the last time he ever saw his brother.

When Dean didn't come home that night, Ali told his parents the truth. Then he told it again to the police, and again to the search and rescue team. They didn't believe the stuff about aliens and magic doors, so Ali didn't push it. But the rest was plausible enough. The small amount of gold that Ali showed them could easily have come from a disused mine, and the police reckoned

Janeen Webb

Ali might have stumbled across the spot where one of the old fossickers who worked the diggings was storing his findings. They expected some old guy to turn up and claim he'd been robbed.

Volunteers combed the bush for days, looking for Dean. His bike was right there where he'd left it, untouched. Ali imagined they'd find his brother trussed up in one of those alien specimen jars, or worse.

But they never found him, or the exact same mine entrance that Ali described. The trouble was, it *had* looked just like all the others, and everyone thought that Ali was too upset to remember exactly where it was.

There was a lot of fuss on TV for a few days, and all kinds of experts said how dangerous the old diggings were, full of hidden mine shafts that a kid could fall down and never be found. Ali's distraught family and the local volunteers kept searching long after the experts went home. In the end, the authorities just labeled Dean's disappearance "misadventure." And left it at that.

But the kids at school wouldn't let it drop. Alberto Barbarino was a star. He was interviewed on TV, and he had press clippings and everything. Suddenly everyone wanted to talk to Ali. And Ali surprised them all by being willing to retell his story dozens of times, though he still left out the parts about the aliens. He found he kind of liked having a lot of new friends, and being on the inside of the private jokes that he used to hate so much. And he didn't even notice that he was too busy hanging out with his friends to go back to the old diggings very often.

He got to keep the gold. No one else claimed it. Finders keepers.

And he bought his black leather jacket.

But he doesn't wear it much.

Janeen Webb is a writer and academic who teaches literature at Australian Catholic University, Melbourne, Australia. When she was growing up in Newcastle, New South Wales, she spent most of her time reading, and surfing at the local beach. She always loved fairy tales, especially the ones where young people outsmart the grown-ups. She especially loved the *Tales from the Thousand and One Nights*, which is why she wrote her Ali Baba story for this book.

She is cowinner (with Jack Dann) of the Aurealis Award for best short story for "Niagara Falling," and "Death at the Blue Elephant" was on the final ballot for both the HQ Short Story prize and the Aurealis Award in the fantasy section. Both stories were chosen for *The Year's Best Australian Science Fiction and Fantasy, Volume 2* edited by Jonathan Strahan and Jeremy Byrne. Webb is also coeditor of the ground-breaking Australian anthology, *Dreaming Down Under*.

Her most recent nonfiction book is *Aliens and Savages: Fiction, Politics and Prejudice in Australia*, cowritten by Andrew Enstice.

Swans

by Kelly Link

My name is Emma Bear, and I am eleven years old. I
live on Black Ankle Road beside the Licking River. I
live in a palace. My father is a king. I have a fairy godfather. This summer I read *The True Confessions of
Charlotte Doyle* and learned how to make blue dye from
a flower called woad. I have six brothers. My mother is
dead. I'm in the seventh grade. My father remarried this
summer. My favorite class is home ec. I love to sew. I
make all my own clothes. My mother taught me how to
sew. I can also knit, crochet, and quilt.

Yesterday my stepmother pointed her pinkie finger at
my brothers and turned them all into swans. They were
being too noisy. I'm never too noisy. I don't talk at all.

This year I was failing choir. I opened my mouth to
sing, and nothing came out. I hadn't been able to say a
word since my mother died. In my other classes, it was
okay. Homework was okay. Math was okay, and English.
Art was okay. I could write down answers on the black-

board. I carried around a pad of paper and a pen. You'd be surprised how often you don't actually have to say anything. Mostly if I just nodded, it was okay. But choir doesn't work that way. You can't sing by writing on a pad of paper. But nothing came out of my mouth when I opened it.

Last year I had lots of friends. This year I didn't have any. What happened in between? My mother died. I stopped talking. No more friends. Really, I've been too busy to have friends, I suppose.

When I first stopped talking, no one noticed. Not until Mom's funeral, when we were all supposed to stand up and say something. I stood up, but nothing came out when I opened my mouth. First my father sent me to see a psychologist. I just sat on her couch. I looked at pictures, and wrote down what they looked like. They all looked like flowers, or birds, or schnauzers. Then my fairy godfather came to the palace.

My fairy godfather is a little man with red hair. His name is Rumpelstiltskin. He was a friend of my mother's. He'd been away on business for a few months—he'd missed the funeral. His eyes were all red, and he cursed a lot. He'd loved my mother a lot. He sat with me for a long time, brushing my hair, and patting my hand.

Finally he said, "Well, you certainly don't have to talk until you want to. Keffluffle. Excuse my French. What a mess this is, Emma."

I nodded. I wrote down on my pad of paper, *I miss her*.

"Fudge, I do, too," my godfather said. "Excuse the French."

He tapped me on the nose gently. "You know your father is going to have to get married again."

I wrote, *I'll have an evil stepmother?*

"That evil stepmother stuff is just a pile of horsepucky," he said, "excuse me. It's just baloney. Whoever he marries will be just as afraid of you and your brothers as you are of her. You keep that in mind."

To my father, he said, "Emma just needs a piece of time. When she needs to say something, she'll open her mouth and say it."

He hugged my father, and he hugged me. He said, "I have a commission for you, Emma. I have a godchild who is going to a ball. All she's got to wear are rags. She needs a fancy dress. Not pink, I think. It wouldn't match. She's got lovely red hair, just like me. Maybe a nice sea-foam green. Right down to the ankles. Lots of lace."

I wrote, *When do you need it?*

"When she turns seventeen," he said. "That's not for a bit. I'll send you her measurements. Okay?"

Okay, I wrote and kissed him good-bye.

When my mother was young, she was famous. She could spin straw into gold. Her name was Cleanthea. A

Kelly Link

year ago, she went jogging in the rain, and then she caught cold, and then she died.

My mother's quilts were famous. Famous quilts have their own names. She made crazy quilts, which are just bits of scraps sewn together, and then decorated and embroidered with fancy stitches—wheat stitches, briar stitches, flowers, birds, little frogs, and snowflakes. She made Log Cabin quilts and Wedding Ring quilts, and she also made up her own patterns. Her quilts had names like Going Down to the River and Snakes Fall in Love and Watering the Garden. People paid hundreds of dollars for them. Every bed in the castle has a quilt on it that my mother made.

Each of my brothers had a quilt that my mother made just for them. She made my brother Julian a *Star Wars* quilt, with X-Wing Fighters and Death Stars. She made my oldest brother an Elvis quilt. Up close it's just strips and patches of purple cloth, all different patterns. But when you back away, you can see that all the bits of different colors of purple make up Elvis's face—his eyes, his lips, his hair. For my youngest brother, she made a Cats Eat Birds quilt. She sewed real feathers into the cats' mouths, and little red cloth-patch birds into their stomachs.

She never finished my quilt. We were working on it together. I'm still working on it now. I don't really want to finish it. In fact, it's gotten a little bit big for my bed. When I spread it out, it's almost as big as a swimming pool. Eventually, it will fill up my whole room, I guess. Every night now I sleep on a different bed in the castle, under a different quilt. I pretend that each quilt is a quilt that I have never seen before, that she has just finished making, just for me.

I should tell you about my father and my brothers. I should also tell you about my stepmother. My father is very tall and handsome, and also very busy with things like affairs of state and cutting ribbons at the grand openings of grocery stores and presenting awards to writers and musicians and artists and also going to soccer games and football games so that photographers can take his picture. That was how he met my stepmother. He was at the zoo, which had just been given a rare species of bird. He was supposed to be photographed with the bird on his shoulder.

When he arrived, however, the keepers were distraught. The bird had disappeared. Even worse, a naked woman had been found wandering around the grounds. She wouldn't say who she was, or where she came from. No one could find her clothes. The keepers were afraid that she might be a terrorist, or an anarchist, come to blow up the zoo, or kill my father. It would be bad publicity for everyone.

"Nonsense," my father said. He asked to meet the woman. The zookeepers protested, saying that this was a bad idea. My father insisted. And so my father's picture

Kelly Link

appeared in the papers, holding out his hand to a woman dressed in a long white T-shirt and a pair of flip-flops that one of the keepers got out of the lost and found. The picture in the paper was blurry, but if you looked closely you could see the look in my father's eyes. He looked like he'd been hit on the head. He looked like he was falling in love, which he was.

The woman, my stepmother, looked small and fragile in the photograph, like a Christmas tree ornament. She had long, feathered hair. The T-shirt hung on her like a tent, and the flip-flops were too big for her.

We still don't know much about my stepmother. She was from a faraway country, we thought, because she had a slight but unrecognizable accent. She was a little bit cross-eyed, like a Siamese cat. She never brushed her hair. It stuck up in points behind her ears, like horns. She was very beautiful, but she hated noise. My brothers made too much noise. That's why she turned them into swans.

They came and stood on the lawn this morning, and I fed them dried corn and bits of burnt buttered toast. They came back early, while my stepmother was still sleeping. They honked at me very quietly. I think they were afraid if they were loud, she'd turn them into something even worse. Snails, maybe, or toads.

Some of the other girls at school thought I was lucky to have so many brothers. Some of them said how handsome my brothers were. I never really thought so. My brothers used to pull my hair and short-sheet my bed, and they never helped with my homework unless I gave them my allowance. They liked to sit on top of me and tickle me until I cried. But when my mother died, they all cried. I couldn't.

My brothers' names are George, Theodore, Russell, Anthony, William, and Julian. George is the oldest. Theodore is the nicest. Anthony is the tallest. Russell has freckles, and he is allergic to milk. William and Julian are twins, and two years younger than me. They liked to wear each other's clothes and pretend that Julian was William, and William was Julian. The thing is, all of them look alike now that they're birds. They all look like twins.

My father told us that my stepmother didn't like noise. They got married at the beginning of the summer. We got to throw rice. We'd only seen my stepmother twice before—once in the newspaper picture, and once when my father brought her home for dinner. There were a lot of important people at that dinner. We ate in the kitchen, but afterward we stood in the secret passageway and spied through the painting that has the eyes cut out.

My future stepmother didn't eat much dinner, but she had three helpings of dessert. This is when I first became suspicious that she was magic—a witch, or else under an enchantment. Witches and people under

Kelly Link

spells, magic people, always have sweet tooths. My fairy godfather carries around sugar cubes in his pockets and stirs dozens of them in his coffee, or else just eats them plain, like a horse. And he never gets cavities.

When my father and stepmother came back from their honeymoon, we were all standing on the palace steps. We had all just had baths. The palace steps had just been washed.

My father and stepmother were holding hands. When they saw us, my stepmother let go of my father's hand and slipped inside the palace. I was holding up a big sign that said, WELCOME HOME, DAD. There wasn't any room on the sign for STEPMOTHER.

"Hey," my brother George said, "what did you bring me?"

"Anthony stole my rocket launcher," Russell said.

"It wasn't me," Anthony said, "it was Theodore."

"It was NOT me," Theodore said, and William and Julian said, "Emma made us brush our teeth every night."

Everyone began yelling. My father yelled loudest of all.

"I'd really appreciate it if you all tried to be quiet and didn't yell all at once. Your stepmother has a bad headache, and besides, she's very shy, and not at all used to loud children," he said, looking at my brothers. Then he looked at me. "Emma," he said, "are you still not talking?"

I took out my notepad and wrote *yes* on it. He sighed. "Does that mean 'yes, you are talking now,' or 'yes, you still aren't talking'?"

I didn't say anything. I just smiled and nodded. "Maybe you'd like to show your new stepmother around the castle," he said.

My stepmother was in the library, reclining on a sofa with a damp cloth over her eyes. I stood there for a bit, and then I tapped my foot some. She didn't move. Finally I reached down and touched her shoulder. Her eyelids fluttered.

I held up my pad of paper. I wrote, *I'm Emma. I don't talk.*

She sat up and looked at me. She wasn't very big. When she stood up, I bet that we would have been the same height, almost, except she was wearing pointy black shoes with tall heels to make her look taller.

I wrote, *Dad asked me to show you the castle.*

I showed her around the castle. I showed her the kitchen with the roasting spit that the dogs turn, and the microwave, and the coffeemaker. I showed her the ballroom, which is haunted, and the dungeon, which my father had converted into an indoor swimming pool and squash court, and I showed her the bowling alley which is also haunted, and the stables, and the upstairs bathroom, which has modern plumbing. Then I took her to my mother's room. The quilt on the bed was Roses and

Cabbages Growing Up Together, all pieced together from old green velvet hunting coats and rose-colored satin gloves.

My new stepmother sat down on the bed. She bounced experimentally, holding her head. She stared at me with her slightly crossed eyes. "A nice bed," she said in a soft, gravelly voice. "Thanks, Emma."

My mother made this quilt, I wrote. *Her quilts are very valuable. Please be careful when you are sleeping.* Then I left her there on my mother's bed. The next day she turned George into a swan. He was practicing his saxophone.

George is my father's heir. George doesn't want to be king. George wants to be a saxophonist in a heavy metal band. I was listening to him in the ballroom. He isn't very good yet, but he likes to have an audience. I sit and listen to him, and he pays me five dollars. He says someday it will be the other way round.

I was embroidering the back of a blouse with blue silk thread. I was trying to embroider a horse, but it looked more like a crocodile, or maybe a dachshund.

My stepmother had been swimming in the pool. She was still in her bathing suit. She came into the ballroom and left puddly footprints all over the waxed and polished black walnut floor. "Excuse me," she said. George ignored her. He kept on honking and tootling. He smirked at me. "Excuse me," our stepmother said, a little bit louder, and then she pointed her pinkie finger at him. She flicked her pinkie up at him, and he turned into a swan. The swan—George—honked. He sounded surprised. Then he spread out his wings and flew away through an open window.

I opened my mouth, but of course nothing came out. I stared at my stepmother, and she shrugged apologetically. Then she turned and left, still dripping. Later that afternoon when Anthony set off Russell's rocket over the frog pond, my stepmother turned him into a swan, too. I was up in the tree house watching.

You're probably wondering why I didn't tell someone. My dad, for instance. Well, for one thing, it was kind of fun. My brothers looked so surprised. Besides, at dinner no one missed Anthony or George. My brothers are always off somewhere, camping with friends, or else sleeping over at someone else's house, or else keeping vigil in the haunted bowling alley. The ghost always shows up in the bowling alley at midnight, with his head in his hand. The pins scream when he throws his head down the lane.

My stepmother had three helpings of pineapple upside-down cake. After dinner, she turned Theodore and Russell into swans. They were banging down the grand staircase on tin trays. I have to admit this is a lot of fun. I've done it myself. Not turning people into swans, I mean, sliding down on trays.

I had to open up a window for Theodore and Russell. They honked reproachfully at me as I pushed

Kelly Link

them out over the windowsill. But once they opened up their wings, they looked so graceful, so strong. They flew up into the sky, curving and diving and hanging on a current of air, dipping their long necks.

How do you do that? I wrote down on my pad. My stepmother was sitting down on the staircase, looking almost ashamed.

"I don't know," she said. "It just seems to happen. It's just so noisy."

Can you turn them back? I wrote.

"What an excellent inquiry," she said. "I do not know. Perhaps and we shall see."

William and Julian refused, as usual, to brush their teeth before bedtime. Loudly. I told them, *Be quiet, or else.*

"Or else what?" Julian screamed at me, his face red with temper.

New stepmother will turn you into a swan.

"Liar," William said loudly. He said it again, even louder, experimentally. My stepmother, wearing pink flannel pajamas, was standing there, just outside the bathroom door. She stuck her head in, looking pained. Julian and William pretended to be afraid. They screamed and giggled. Then they pretended to be swans, flapping their arms. My stepmother waved her finger at them, and they sprouted wings. They sprouted feathers and beaks, and blinked their black beady eyes at her.

I filled up the bathtub with water, and put them in it. It was the first time they ever seemed to enjoy a bath. Even better, they didn't have any teeth to brush.

Then I put them outside, because I wasn't sure if they were house-trained.

The next morning I woke under my favorite quilt, the Rapunzel quilt, with the gray tower, and the witch, and the prince climbing up the long yellow braids. I ate breakfast and then I went outside and fed my brothers. I'd never had pets before. Now I had six. I tried to decide what I liked better, birds or brothers.

When I went back to get more toast, my father was sitting in the kitchen, reading the morning paper. He was wearing the striped purple bathrobe I'd made him for Christmas three years ago. Mom had helped with the cuffs. The hem was a little bit frayed. "Good morning, Emma," he said. "Still not speaking? Where are the rest of you, anyway?"

I wrote down, *New stepmom turned them into swans.*

"Ha," he said. "You're a funny girl, Emma. Don't forget. Today I'm dedicating the new school gymnasium. We'll see you about two-ish."

First there were speeches. I sat with the rest of my grade, in the bleachers, and looked at my new stepmother. I was thinking that the smart thing would have been to buy her earplugs. Whenever my principal, Mr. Wolf, put his mouth too close to the microphone, there was a squeal of feedback. My stepmother was looking pale. Her lips were pressed tightly together. She sat behind Mr. Wolf on the stage, beside my father.

Sorley Meadows, who wears colored lip gloss, was sitting next to me. She dug her pointy elbow into my side. "Your stepmother is, like, tiny," she said. "She looks like a little kid."

I ignored her. My father sat with his back straight, and his mouth fixed in a dignified, royal smile. My father can sleep with his eyes open. That's what my mother used to say. She used to poke him at state occasions, just to see if he was still awake.

Mr. Wolf finished his speech, and we all clapped. Then the marching band came in. My father woke up. My stepmother put her hand out, as if she were going to conduct them.

Really, the band isn't very good. But they are enthusiastic. My stepmother stood up. She stuck out her pinkie finger, and instead of a marching band there was suddenly a lot of large white hissing swans.

I jumped down out of the bleachers. How mortifying. Students and teachers all began to stand up. "She turned them into birds," someone said.

My father looked at my stepmother with a new sort of look. It was still a sort of being hit on the head sort of look, but a different sort of being hit on the head look. Mr. Wolf turned toward my father and my stepmother. "Your Royal Majesty, my dear mademoiselle," he said, "please do not be alarmed. This is, no doubt, some student prank."

He lifted the little silver whistle around his neck and blew on it. "Everyone," he said. "Please be quiet! Please sit back down."

My stepmother did not sit back down. She pointed at Mr. Wolf. Mrs. Heliotrope, the French teacher, screamed suddenly. Mr. Wolf was a swan. So was Mrs. Heliotrope. And as I watched, suddenly the new gynasium was full of birds. Sorley Meadows was a swan. John Riley, who is someone I once had a crush on until I saw him picking his nose in the cloakroom, was a swan. Emma Valerie Snope, who used to be my best friend because we had the same name, was a swan. Marisa Valdez, the prettiest girl in the seventh grade, was a swan.

My father grabbed my stepmother's arm. "What is going on here?" he said to her. She turned him into a swan.

In that whole gymnasium, it was just me and my stepmother and a lot of swans. There were feathers floating all over in the air. It looked like a henhouse. I pulled out my pad of paper. I jumped up on the stage and walked over to her. She had just turned my whole school into a bunch of birds. She had just turned my father into a bird. She put her hand down absentmindedly and patted him on the top of his white feathery head. He darted his head away, and snapped at her.

Kelly Link

I was so angry, I stabbed right through the pad of paper with my ballpoint. The tip of the pen broke off. I threw the pad of paper down.

I opened my mouth. I wasn't sure what was going to come out. Maybe a yell. Maybe a curse. Maybe a squawk. What if she turned me into a bird, too? "WHAT?" I said. "WHAT?"

It was the first word I had said in a whole year. I saw it hit her. Her eyes got so big. She threw her arm out, pointing her pinkie finger at me. I was pointing at her. "WHAT?" I said again. I saw her pinkie finger become a feather. Her arms got downy. Her nose got longer, and sharp. She flapped her wings at me.

She wasn't a swan. She was some other kind of bird. I don't know what kind. She was like an owl, but bigger, or maybe a great auk, or a kiwi. Her feathers looked fiery and metallic. She had a long tail, like a peacock. She fanned it out. She looked extremely relieved. She cocked her head to one side and looked at me, and then she flew out of the gymnasium.

"WHAT?" I screamed after her. "WAIT!" What a mess. She'd turned my family, my entire school into birds, and then she flew away? Was this fair? What was I supposed to do? "I want to be a swan, too! I want my mom!"

I sat down on the stage and cried. I really missed my mom.

Then I went to the school library and did a little

research. A lot of the swans came with me. They don't seem to be house-trained, so I spread out newspaper on the floor for them.

My fairy godfather is never around when you need him. This is why it's important to develop good research skills, and know how to find your way around a library. If you can't depend on your fairy godfather, at least you can depend on the card catalog. I found the section of books on enchantments, and read for a bit. The swans settled down in the library, honking softly. It was kind of pleasant.

It seems that to break my stepmother's pinkie spell, I need to make shirts for all of the birds and throw the shirts over their necks. I need to sew these shirts out of nettle cloth, which doesn't sound very pleasant. Nettles burn when you pick them. Really, I think linen, or cotton is probably more practical. And I think I have a better idea than a bunch of silly shirts that no one is probably going to want to wear again, anyway. And how are you supposed to sew a shirt for a bird? Is there a pattern? Down in the castle storerooms, there are a lot of trunks filled with my mother's quilting supplies.

I miss my mother.

Excuse me. I just can't seem to stop talking. My voice is all hoarse and croaky. I sound like a crow. I probably wouldn't have gotten a good grade in choir, anyway. Mrs. Orlovsky, the choir teacher, is the swan over there,

Kelly Link

on top of the librarian's desk. Her head is tucked under her wing. At least I think it's Mrs. Orlovsky. Maybe it's Mr. Beatty, the librarian. My father is perched up on the windowsill. He's looking out the window, but I can't see anything out there. Just sky.

I think I'm going to finish the quilt that my mother and I started. It's going to be a lot bigger than either of us was planning on making it. When I finish, it should be big enough even to cover the floor of the gymnasium.

It's a blue quilt, a crazy quilt. Silk, corduroy, denim, satin, velvet. Sapphire, midnight blue, navy, marine, royal blue, sky blue. I'm going to patch in white birds with wide white wings on one side, and on the other side I'm going to patch in little white shirts. When I finish, I'm going to roll it up, and then throw it over all the swans I can find. I'm going to turn them back into people. This quilt is going to be as beautiful as sky. It's going to be as soft as feathers. It's going to be just like magic.

Kelly Link writes, "When I was very little, I was obsessed with the big bad wolf. I didn't care that much for the three little pigs. I liked the huffing and puffing. In kindergarten I was Little Red Riding Hood in the class play, and the next year I was the troll under the bridge in *The Three Billy Goats Gruff.* I got to wear a white beard made out of white cotton balls.

"When I was old enough to read to myself, I loved *The Tinderbox,* where the soldier meets the three dogs whose eyes are as big as saucers, as dinner plates, as spinning wheels. I also loved *The Goose Girl,* although I was never satisfied with the ending. Before the princess becomes a goose girl, she has a talking horse. Afterward, she has a prince, but no horse. I did not feel that a prince was anywhere near as good as a talking horse. I still don't. Now I love the Russian fairy tales, where the witch Baba Yaga lives in a house that walks around on chicken legs. Now that's as good as a talking horse.

"I wanted to retell the story of the girl who makes shirts out of nettles for her brothers, who have been turned into swans by their wicked stepmother. I thought that in my version, the girl might want to be a swan as well. I would. But Emma Bear is much more practical than I am. She's also much better at sewing."

Link lives outside Boston, Massachusetts.

The Kingdom of Melting Glances

by Katherine Vaz

The shape of a bright red lily was on Rosa's cheek. A shadow of a lily had once fallen across her face and blushed to touch a girl so beautiful and decided to cling to her forever. This miraculous bloom made her as special as a walking garden, but her sisters laughed and called her "Lily Face"—full of bites and buzzing! Rosa thought that they were actually mosquitoes that had grown enormous.

Rosa's parents had met each other years before in Portugal, by the sea. One day, when she was a pretty young girl, Mother sat down at The Wall of Melting Glances near the waves, which roared up like teeth made of liquid glass. Father, a young man longing for adventure, approached, and when he looked at Mother, and she looked back at him, their bones melted, their hearts changed to red, thump-thumping puddles, and their skin melted.

It was a good thing that a wall was there, or else these two would have trickled right across the burning sand to drown in the waves! Little boats, with eyes painted on the prows, watched with approval and bobbed up and down on the surf as if they were over-joyed to see that once again The Wall of Melting Glances had worked its spell.

The lives of Mother and Father continued melting together. They moved to the Gold Country of California, the dry, yellow-green valley below the mountains. There was no buried treasure anymore in the town of Gold Hills, of course. Only restaurants called "Prospector's Diner" or "Eureka Café," and antique shops called "Treasure Bin." Or "Mother Lode." Sometimes tourists would go into a place and pretend to pan for gold in a fake stream or look at pictures of scruffy men with mustaches who had come to these foothills in the past. Nowadays, there were lots and lots of nice but ordinary homes. The only gold coin to be discovered was the round, golden sun that shone angrily every day, from the first scream of the loggers' trucks and traffic to the close of day, when the loggers and commuters returned in a silvery stream of cars.

Mother missed the magic wall where she had fallen in love with Father, and she ached for water, sweet or sour, dripping or crashing, the sound and fishy smell and blue-green look of it. She took to her bed ready to dry up like an autumn leaf.

Father, his heart breaking, remembered the story of

the Scandinavian princess who had long ago married a Portuguese prince. The prince took his new bride to southern Portugal, where she was shriveling and dying because she missed the cool, white snow of her homeland. The prince loved her so much that he planted almond trees, and their white blossoms covered the ground like snow. His princess recovered.

Father planted hydrangeas, which are globe-shaped flowers that drink water like thirsty children. They are so full of water that they're really sponges pretending to be flowers. The petals are bright pink and purple. Father climbed onto the roof with an armful of hydrangeas and shook them so that they dropped a pink-and-purple waterfall past Mother's window.

Joy returned to her.

Mother and Father soon had three daughters—Isabel, Ana, and Rosa-with-the-lily-on-her-face.

Isabel and Ana were cruel to Rosa and dry like twigs. Their words were brittle, and they never bathed. Rosa, meanwhile, loved to find streams in the Gold Country and go swimming beneath the apple and fig trees.

One day the sisters discovered that their parents had melted completely away. Isabel, Ana, and Rosa waded into their parents' room, into water up to their knees. The ceiling and walls were damp, and the water was seeping out under the door to run down the street.

"They've decided to go back to the sea without us!" said Isabel, kicking at the water. "What nerve!"

"They left us with a rotting house!" said Ana. "I can smell the mildew already!"

"That's you that you're smelling!" said Isabel.

"They've finally melted from loving each other so much," said Rosa, "and this water is all of them and their tears of joy." She cupped her hands together and drank up some of her melted parents.

Isabel and Ana crackled and almost snapped in two from laughing. Now they were free to torment their youngest sister more than ever.

"Lily Face, Lily Face!"

"Hey, water-lily, hey dilly-dilly."

Rosa stopped going to Gold Hills High School because everyone began to dance in front of her like a talking insect, with her sisters the biggest praying-mantis cheerleaders of them all with glowing red eyes and green-twiggy limbs. Yes, she knew she had the mark of a big red lily on her face! And yes, no matter how much anyone teased her, she still believed that her parents had melted in a flood of love!

Rosa stopped swimming in streams because the buzzing and teasing followed her there. She set a basin of cold water on her parents' windowsill, because she could not survive without little lakes or streams, even if they had to be make-believe ones. She watered the hydrangeas and looked out at the cloudless, huge sky of the Gold Country.

She knew that ghosts wandered across the gentle

Katherine Vaz

curves of the valley, ghosts of the gold miners who had come here to seek their fortunes but who had now disappeared. Deep in the ground, their skeletons tried to dance under the weight of so much dirt. Rosa wished she knew the stories of the fortune-seekers. She wanted to unbury their pickaxes, their buckets and dirt-plastered blue jeans and weighing pans. And if she could, she would step in and settle the quarrels that had led to fights in the saloons . . . but that was all dissolved and vanished, sunk into the town and below the housing developments of Gold Hills the way that water sinks invisibly into a field of yellow grass.

She wept for her parents, though she knew they were happy.

One afternoon, a hummingbird lit down into the basin of water she kept at the window and beat his wings faster than most people can think a thought. He churned like a miniature water mill and splashed the lily on Rosa's face until she smiled. "There!" said the bird. "Why so sad?"

"Because I'm all alone," said Rosa.

"I was drawn to the lily on your face to drink from it, and then I saw that you had made a private swimming pool for me!"

"Yes," said Rosa, cheering up. "May I take hold of your wings and fly away with you?"

"Naturally," said the hummingbird.

But right as Rosa was preparing to take hold of the

bird's fluttery fairy-wings, her sisters saw what was happening and rushed in to slap the bird away.

They had no idea how swift hummingbirds are.

He sang out, "I'll return tomorrow!" to Rosa before he escaped.

"Will you deny me every comfort?" shouted Rosa at her sisters.

"If anyone should fly away on wings of joy, it should be us!" yelled the twig-sisters.

"A bird should collect you both to build a rotting nest!" shouted Rosa.

That night she set out a basin for the hummingbird once again. While Rosa slept—with her dreams the color of irises, lilies, roses, and sunflowers—Isabel and Ana tiptoed in and put razor blades all through the water.

Sharp razor blades! The twig-sisters went off to sleep a sound sleep, with only a blank where most people have dreams!

When the hummingbird returned in the moonlight and began to splash and bathe, the razor blades cut him terribly. He made a high-pitched sound that no human could hear. He flew away as best he could, badly injured, one wing almost completely cut off. Though his heart was only the size of a pinhead, it rattled like an alarm clock inside him. The next morning, when Rosa ran to the basin, she saw the blood in the water and wept so much that the water turned from red to pink.

Isabel and Ana pretended to know nothing, but Rosa

Katherine Vaz

was not fooled. She said to herself, I must be brave enough to leave this place and find him. If my princely bird is wounded, I shall nurse him back to health. If he is dead—and here she stopped to sob again—then I shall give him a proper burial.

Rosa remembered her mother saying that Portuguese people once believed that certain hours of the day are "open" or full of invisible doors, that a person can slip into another world if he or she believes in magic. Sometimes these open hours are at dawn, when the sun is still half asleep; sometimes at noon, when the sun tires for a moment of the endless day ahead; often at night, when the moon rides high, dropping its white flowers of light onto the landscape.

That evening, with her sisters snoring in another room, Rosa stepped through a silver door of moonlight and saw a thread hanging down from the moon like a white vine. She had scarcely reached up to touch it before it wrapped around her and hoisted her toward the mottled face of the Moon.

"You've got marks on your face, just as I do!" she cried to the Moon.

"Yes," said the Moon. "Mine are so huge, you can see them from Earth!"

"Moon, have you seen a hummingbird injured by razor blades planted by my horrible sisters?"

"No," said the Moon. "He might have been carried away on the Wind. Go, but take this gift."

The Moon wrapped a golden veil around her hair.

Rosa sailed away until a star punctured the moonlight, and she tumbled into the blue curving arms of the Wind.

"Wind, have you seen a hummingbird injured by razor blades planted by my horrible sisters?" she asked the Wind.

"I've tried to rip your sisters' hair out many times," said the Wind, sighing heavily, "but I have not seen the hummingbird. He might have been rescued by the Sun. Go, but take this gift."

The Wind blew a garland of golden grasses around her wrists as bracelets.

A blue shaft of wind carried Rosa along until a burst of sunlight cracked the blueness wide open and dropped her into the Sun's palace.

The gold on all sides shone so brilliantly that it went from gold to white-gold to white. The glare was so strong that sometimes it erased everything in its path, as if a painter had taken a cloth dipped in turpentine and wiped away part of the world. When Rosa stared at the palace floor, its dazzling golden squares made her dizzy. Even the lilies in the sun's garden were covered with gilt.

Rosa heard a sound, and turned her head to watch: A drawbridge made of gold dropped down, over a moat filled with sparkling golden water and golden crocodiles. Rosa could not tell where the sky ended and the teeth of crocodiles began.

Katherine Vaz

The Sun's Mother strolled out of the palace wearing a sun-bleached white dress.

"Have you seen a hummingbird injured by razor blades planted by my horrible sisters?" Rosa asked.

"Yes," said the Sun's Mother, "but he is in the high tower, and my son refuses to let anyone see him."

"Oh, but I must!" shouted Rosa. "Please! I will nurse him back to health!"

"I'm afraid that my son will have to be bribed. As you can see from this house, he has many expenses."

"I don't have anything but this lily on my face!" cried Rosa.

"That won't do," said the Sun's Mother. "But I have a plan. Don't worry!"

The Sun's Mother spun for Rosa a magnificent golden dress with long, wide sleeves to go with her golden veil from the Moon and her golden bracelets from the Wind.

"You must do exactly as I say," said the Sun's Mother. "At tonight's banquet, stuff as much bacon as you can find on the table up your sleeves."

"Bacon?" said Rosa.

"Bacon and grease," said the Sun's Mother.

"As much as possible—?"

"Up your sleeves," said the Sun's Mother, nodding.

At the banquet that night, Rosa was shocked to see her sisters, Isabel and Ana, sitting at the long table for the feast. Huge golden grapes hung from bowls on the table, and golden men and women plucked them and passed around platters of sun-cooked marvels.

"What are you doing here!" Rosa said, shaking beneath her golden veil and inside her golden dress. Her wicked sisters were dressed in drab cotton shifts from the Gold Hills Mall.

The other guests stopped dining and chatting to watch the sisters.

"Mother and Father told us also about the invisible doors in a day that a person can open to ride into another world," said Isabel sniffily. "We deserve to ride away on wings of joy, not you, Lily Face." And with that, she picked up a huge turkey leg and began to gnaw it.

"I will give up eating birds," said Ana, stuffing a huge pork chop into her face.

Rosa could feel her face burning as she did what the Sun's Mother commanded. She crammed bacon, fatty white bacon, thick slabs of greasy wet bacon, up her sleeves. There were so many trays of it!

Everyone was staring at her and choking with laughter.

"She's gone crazy!" announced Isabel.

But on the sly, she and Ana decided to imitate Rosa, for surely this must be some magic spell. They also stuffed bacon up their sleeves.

And where was the Sun? And the Sun's Mother?

A woman in golden velvet blew a trumpet and shouted, "Time for dancing! Everyone!"

Katherine Vaz

Out on the golden dance floor, as the music of the harps and cymbals, trumpets and organs, violins and tubas, harmonicas and guitars began their sunny tunes, Rosa forgot about everything but the golden, glorious sounds. She began to dance, hopping on one foot and the next, twirling about. She did a waltz and tango.

Her sisters did the same, jumping and shouting, flinging their arms into the air, not noticing that the bacon they had hidden up their sleeves was hurling up toward the ceiling and then falling onto the floor—SPLAT!—smearing the floor and making the other dancers slip and slide and trip.

SPLAT! SPLAT!

Bacon flung here and there! Bacon sticking to the bottoms of shoes! Dancers falling face-first into pork fat!

A golden woman screamed, "Are we in a frying pan?"

Rosa stopped dancing, because a miracle was happening. Out of her sleeves, diamonds were falling! She stared in shock. Diamonds, bright as chips of ice! The bacon that had been up her sleeves was turning into diamonds!

Isabel and Ana slipped and slid and were soon covered head to foot with bacon grease. A shout suddenly rang up to the domed ceiling:

"WHO IS RESPONSIBLE FOR THIS PIGSTY?"

The music stopped. The dancing stopped (except for the dancers who could not control their sliding about).

The Sun—like the largest torch imaginable—and

the Sun's Mother had entered the dining room. Isabel and Ana glanced up. They looked as if they were washerwomen down on their hands and knees, scrubbing the floor with bacon.

The Sun was so furious to see his golden floor so greasy that he threw open the main doors and tipped his palace so that the grease-covered people slid out, screeching like barnyard animals. They were tossed out into the empty sky.

Out went the twig-sisters, too.

Rosa's diamonds saved her from sliding away. They made a rough carpet that caught her feet and kept her in place. She stood braced up on the jewels and looked as best she could into the Sun's harsh stare. The Sun stopped tipping the palace, scooped up the diamonds, and said in heated words to Rosa, "What wish would you like me to grant?"

"I would like to nurse the hummingbird in your tower back to health," she said.

"Please try," said the Sun. "The sun is supposed to cheer creatures, but I have failed with him! Intolerable, I tell you!"

"Now, now, dear," said the Sun's Mother. "Calm down."

Rosa flew to the tower.

The hummingbird lay on a bed, bleeding from many wounds. His thin beak had been partly snapped off, and Rosa removed her golden bracelet to prop up his broken wing.

The bird said, in pain, "Have you come to say good-bye?"

"I won't leave you," said Rosa, weeping. "I love you more than all the gold that was ever in Gold Hills, more than the gold in the Sun's palace. I love you more than all the water that bathes every sea creature. I give you the lily on my face so that you may drink of my sweetness."

Saying this, she turned the lily on her face, red as the red of the bird's wounds, toward him.

He was so overcome by her love that his gaze melted into the lily and into her, and when she glanced at him, her tears melted right on her eyes. He wept with gratitude, and she wept with worry, and soon they sailed out of the tower on the salty river they cried together.

The salty river made by their tears was vast enough to pour from the Sun's tower all the way back to Gold Hills.

And salt cures wounds.

The hummingbird healed, and Rosa was changed into a lily, because it was the best, magical part of her. She took root as a lily in a garden outside Gold Hills.

Every day, many times a day, the hummingbird kissed her. Because, after all, in Portuguese the word for "hummingbird" is *beija-flor*, which means "kiss-flower."

Rosa-the-Lily was so happy, and so was her hummingbird, that a golden glow remained around them. Because of this, the ghosts of the gold miners came out looking. They discovered Rosa-the-Lily and the hummingbird and told them their tall frontier tales. She told them that she'd been in a palace all of gold, but it blinded her. She preferred to live on Earth, where she did not have to blink and squint.

The hydrangeas planted nearby began to babble their own stories . . . and that is how Rosa learned that she'd joined the garden where her parents, Mother and Father, now lived as water-flowers.

As for Isabel and Ana, they were slippery with bacon grease as they fell from the sky, but they could not stop the stars from cutting them into little pieces. Each piece of the chopped-up sisters turned into a mosquito, like a tiny, buzzing, red devil.

Melting glances do not work to get rid of them, so go ahead and swat mosquitoes if you see them.

Glance deeply at lilies and into water, and you will feel a strange happiness. Your heart will beat like a hummingbird's. You will want to melt into the bright water that you see full of lilies; you will want to sink toward the roots and stories hidden in the earth.

(From the Portuguese legends "A Paraboìnha de Oiro" and "A Cara de Boi," with much refiguring and many additions.)

Katherine Vaz

Katherine Vaz writes, "I have read straight through all of the *Oz* books in my mother's collection, and I'm still a huge fan of the *Babar* series. "The Kingdom of Melting Glances" borrows elements from two Portuguese folktales that feature bacon fat, princes as birds, and razor blades. I was going to leave out the razor blades, but my ten-year-old nephew, Daniel Duarte, my official consultant for the story in this collection, assured me that they made the bad sisters thrillingly more evil. So the razor blades are back in!"

Vaz is a writer and academic who teaches literature at the University of California at Davis. She is the author of two novels and the short story collection *Fado*, which won the Drue Heinz Literature Prize. Her writing often draws upon her Portugese-American background. She lives in Davis, California.

Hansel's Eyes

by Garth Nix

Hansel was ten and his sister, Gretel, was eleven when their stepmother decided to get rid of them. They didn't catch on at first, because the Hagmom (their secret name for her) had always hated them. So leaving them behind at the supermarket or forgetting to pick them up after school was no big deal.

It was only when their father got in on the "disappearing the kids" act that they realized it was serious. Although he was a weak man, they thought he might still love them enough to stand up to the Hagmom.

They realized he didn't the day he took them out into the woods. Hansel wanted to do the whole Boy Scout thing and take a water bottle and a pile of other stuff, but their dad said they wouldn't need it. It'd only be a short walk.

Then he dumped them. They'd just gotten out of the car when he took off. They didn't try to chase him. They knew the signs. The Hagmom had hypnotized him again or whatever she did to make him do things.

"Guess she's going to get a nasty surprise when we get back," said Hansel, taking out the map he'd stuffed down the front of his shirt. Gretel silently handed him the compass she'd tucked into her sock.

It took them three hours to get home, first walking, then in a highway patrol cruiser, and finally in their dad's car. They were almost back when the Hagmom rang on the cell phone. Hansel and Gretel could hear her screaming. But when they finally got home, she smiled and kissed the air near their cheeks.

"She's planning something," said Gretel. "Something bad."

Hansel agreed, and they both slept in their clothes, with some maps, the compass, and candy bars stuffed down their shirts.

Gretel dreamed a terrible dream. She saw the Hagmom creep into their room, quiet as a cat in her velvet slippers. She had a big yellow sponge in her hand, a sponge that smelled sweet, but too sweet to be anything but awful. She went to Hansel's bunk and pushed the sponge against his nose and face. His arms and legs thrashed for a second, then he fell back like he was dead.

Gretel tried and tried to wake from the dream, but when she finally opened her eyes, there was the yellow sponge and the Hagmom's smiling face and then the dream was gone and there was nothing but total, absolute darkness.

When Gretel did wake up, she wasn't at home. She was lying in an alley. Her head hurt, and she could hardly open her eyes because the sun seemed too bright.

"Chloroform," whispered Hansel. "The Hagmom drugged us and got Dad to dump us."

"I feel sick," said Gretel. She forced herself to stand and noticed that there was nothing tucked into her shirt, or Hansel's, either. The candy bars and the compass were gone.

"This looks bad," said Hansel, shielding his eyes with his hand and taking in the piles of trash, the broken windows, and the lingering, charcoal smell of past fires. "We're in the old part of the city, that got fenced off after the riots."

"She must hope someone will kill us," said Gretel. She scowled and picked up a jagged piece of glass, winding an old rag around it so she could use it like a knife.

"Probably," agreed Hansel, who wasn't fooled. He knew Gretel was scared, and so was he.

"Let's look around," Gretel said. Doing something would be better than just standing still, letting the fear grow inside them.

They walked in silence, much closer together than usual, their elbows almost bumping. The alley opened into a wide street that wasn't any better. The only sign of life was a flock of pigeons.

But around the next corner, Hansel backed up so

Garth Nix

suddenly that Gretel's glass knife almost went into his side. She was so upset, she threw it away. The sound of shattering glass echoed through the empty streets and sent the pigeons flying.

"I almost stabbed you, you moron!" exclaimed Gretel. "Why did you stop?"

"There's a shop," said Hansel. "A brand-new one."

"Let me see," said Gretel. She looked around the corner for a long time, till Hansel got impatient and tugged at her collar, cutting off her breath.

"It is a shop," she said. "A Sony PlayStation shop. That's what's in the windows. Lots of games."

"Weird," said Hansel. "I mean, there's nothing here. No one to buy anything."

Gretel frowned. Somehow the shop frightened her, but the more she tried not to think of that, the more scared she got.

"Maybe it got left by accident," added Hansel. "You know, when they just fenced the whole area off after the fires."

"Maybe . . . ," said Gretel.

"Let's check it out," said Hansel. He could sense Gretel's uneasiness, but to him the shop seemed like a good sign.

"I don't want to," said Gretel, shaking her head.

"Well, I'm going," said Hansel. After he'd gone six or seven steps, Gretel caught up with him. Hansel smiled to himself. Gretel could never stay behind.

The shop was strange. The windows were so clear that you could see right inside, to the rows of PlayStations all set up ready to go, connected to really big television screens. There was even a Coke machine and a snack machine at the back.

Hansel touched the door with one finger, a bit hesitantly. Half of him wanted it to be locked, and half of him wanted it to give a little under his hand. But it did more than that. It slid open automatically, and a cool breeze of air-conditioned air blew across his face.

He stepped inside. Gretel reluctantly followed. The door shut behind them, and instantly all the screens came on and were running games. Then the Coke machine clunked out a couple of cans of Coke, and the snack machine whirred and hummed and a whole bunch of candy bars and chocolate piled up out the slot.

"Excellent!" exclaimed Hansel happily, and he went over and picked up a Coke. Gretel put out her hand to stop him, but it was too late.

"Hansel, I don't like this," said Gretel, moving back to the door. There was something strange about all this—the flicker of the television screens reaching out to her, beckoning her to play, trying to draw them both in . . .

Hansel ignored her, as if she had ceased to exist. He swigged from the can and started playing a game. Gretel ran over and tugged at his arm, but his eyes never left the screen.

Garth Nix

"Hansel!" Gretel screamed. "We have to get out of here!"

"Why?" asked a soft voice.

Gretel shivered. The voice sounded human enough, but it instantly gave her the mental picture of a spider, welcoming flies. Flies it meant to suck dry and hang like trophies in its web.

She turned around slowly, telling herself it couldn't really be a spider, trying to blank out the image of a hideous eight-legged, fat-bellied, fanged monstrosity.

When she saw it was only a woman, she didn't feel any better. A woman in her mid-forties, maybe, in a plain black dress, showing her bare arms. Long, sinewy arms that ended in narrow hands and long, grasping fingers. Gretel couldn't look directly at her face, just glimpsing bright red lipstick, a hungry mouth, and the darkest of sunglasses.

"So you don't want to play the games like your brother, Hansel," said the woman. "But you can feel their power, can't you, Gretel?"

Gretel couldn't move. Her whole body was filled up with fear because this woman was a spider, Gretel thought, a hunting spider in human shape, and she and Hansel were well and truly caught. Without thinking, she blurted out, "Spider!"

"A spider?" laughed the woman, her red mouth spreading wide, lips peeling back to reveal nicotine-stained teeth. "I'm not a spider, Gretel. I'm a shadow against the moon, a dark shape in the night doorway, a catch-as-catch-can . . . witch!"

"A witch," whispered Gretel. "What are you going to do with us?"

"I'm going to give you a choice that I have never given before," whispered the witch. "You have some smattering of power, Gretel. You dream true, and strong enough that my machines cannot catch you in their dreaming. The seed of a witch lies in your heart, and I will tend it and make it grow. You will be my apprentice and learn the secrets of my power, the secrets of the night and the moon, of the twilight and the dawn. Magic, Gretel, magic! Power and freedom and dominion over beasts and men!

"Or you can take the other path," she continued, leaning in close till her breath washed into Gretel's nose, foul breath that smelled of cigarettes and whisky. "The path that ends in the end of Gretel. Pulled apart for your heart, and lungs and liver and kidneys. Transplant organs are so in demand, particularly for sick little children with very rich parents! Strange, they never ask me where the organs come from."

"And Hansel?" whispered Gretel, without thinking of her own danger, or the seed in her heart that begged to be made a witch. "What about Hansel?"

"Ah, Hansel," cried the witch. She clicked her fingers, and Hansel walked over to them like a zombie, his fingers still twitching from the game.

"I have a particular plan for Hansel," crooned the witch. "Hansel with the beautiful, beautiful blue eyes."

She tilted Hansel's head back so his eyes caught the light, glimmering blue. Then she took off her sunglasses, and Gretel saw that the witch's own eyes were shriveled like raisins and thick with fat white lines like webs.

"Hansel's eyes go to a very special customer," whispered the witch. "And the rest of him? That depends on Gretel. If she's a good apprentice, the boy shall live. Better blind than dead, don't you think?" She snapped out her arm on the last word and grabbed Gretel, stopping her movement toward the door.

"You can't go without my leave, Gretel," said the witch. "Not when there's so much still for you to see. Ah, to see again, all crisp and clean, with eyes so blue and bright. Lazarus!"

An animal padded out from the rear of the shop and came up to the witch's hand. It was a cat, of sorts. It stood almost to the witch's waist, and it was multicolored, and terribly scarred, lines of bare skin running between patches of different-colored fur like a horrible jigsaw. Even its ears were different colors, and its tail seemed to be made of seven quite distinct rings of fur. Gretel felt sick as she realized it was a patchwork beast, sewn together from many different cats, and given life by the witch's magic.

Then Gretel noticed that whenever the witch turned her head, so did Lazarus. If she looked up, the cat looked up. If she turned her head left, it turned left. Clearly, the witch saw the world through the cat's eyes.

With the cat at her side, the witch pushed Gretel ahead of her, and whistled for Hansel to follow. They went through the back of the shop, then down a long stairway, deep into the earth. At the bottom, the witch unlocked the door with a key of polished bone.

Beyond the door was a huge cave, ill lit by seven soot-darkened lanterns. One side of the cave was lined with empty cages, each just big enough to house a standing child.

There was also an industrial cold room—a shed-sized refrigerator that had a row of toothy icicles hanging from the gutters of its sloping roof—that dominated the other side of the cave. Next to the cold room was a slab of marble that served as a table. Behind it, hanging from hooks in the damp stone of the cave wall, were a dozen knives and cruel-looking instruments of steel.

"Into the cage, young Hansel," commanded the witch, and Hansel did as he was told, without a word. The patchwork cat slunk after him, and shot the bolt home with a slap of its paw.

"Now, Gretel," said the witch. "Will you become a witch or be broken into bits?"

Gretel looked at Hansel in his cage, and then at the marble slab and the knives. There seemed to be no choice. At least if she chose the path of witchery, Hansel would only . . . only . . . lose his eyes. And perhaps they would get a chance to escape. "I will learn to be a witch," she said finally. "If you promise to take no more of Hansel than his eyes."

The witch laughed and took Gretel's hands in a bony grip, ignoring the girl's shudder. Then she started to dance, swinging Gretel around and around, with Lazarus leaping and screeching between them.

As she danced, the witch sang:

> *"Gretel's chosen the witch's way,*
> *And Hansel will be the one to pay.*
> *Sister sees more and brother less*
> *Hansel and Gretel, what a mess!*

Then she suddenly stopped and let go. Gretel spun across the cave and crashed into the door of one of the cages.

"You'll live down here," said the witch. "There's food in the cold room, and a bathroom in the last cage. I will instruct you on your duties each morning. If you try to escape, you will be punished."

Gretel nodded, but she couldn't help looking across at the knives sparkling on the wall. The witch and Lazarus looked, too, and the witch laughed again. "No steel can cut me, or rod mark my back," she said. "But if you wish to test that, it is Hansel I will punish."

Then the witch left, with Lazarus padding alongside her.

Gretel immediately went to Hansel, but he was still in the grip of the Playstation spell, eyes and fingers locked in some phantom game.

Next she tried the door, but sparks flew up and burned her when she stuck a knife in the lock. The door to the cold room opened easily enough, though, frosted air and bright fluorescent light spilling out. It was much colder inside than a normal refrigerator. One side of the room was stacked high with chiller boxes, each labeled with a red cross and a bright sticker that said, URGENT: HUMAN TRANSPLANT. Gretel tried not to look at them, or think about what they contained. The other side was stacked with all kinds of frozen food. Gretel took some spinach. She hated it, but spinach was the most opposite food to meat she could imagine. She didn't even want to think about eating meat.

The next day marked the first of many in the cave. The witch gave Gretel chores to do, mostly cleaning or packing up boxes from the cold room in special messenger bags the witch brought down. Then the witch would teach Gretel magic, like the spell that would keep herself and Hansel warm.

Always, Gretel lived with the fear that the witch would choose that day to bring down another child to be cut up on the marble slab, or to take Hansel's eyes. But the witch always came alone, and merely looked at Hansel through Lazarus's eyes and muttered, "Not ready."

So Gretel worked and learned, fed Hansel and

Garth Nix

whispered to him. She constantly told him not to get better, to pretend that he was still under the spell. Either Hansel listened and pretended, even to her, or he really was still entranced.

Days went by, then weeks, and Gretel realized that she enjoyed learning magic too much. She looked forward to her lessons, and sometimes she would forget about Hansel for hours, forget that he would soon lose his eyes.

When she realized that she might forget Hansel all together, Gretel decided that she had to kill the witch. She told Hansel that night, whispering her fears to him and trying to think of a plan. But nothing came to her, for now Gretel had learned enough to know the witch really couldn't be cut by metal, or struck down by a blow.

The next morning, Hansel spoke in his sleep while the witch was in the cave. Gretel cried out from where she was scrubbing the floor, to try and cover it up, but it was too late. The witch came over and glared through the bars.

"So you've been shamming," she said. "But now I shall take your left eye, for the spell to graft it to my own socket must be fueled by your fear. And your sister will help me."

"No, I won't!" cried Gretel. But the witch just laughed and blew on Gretel's chest. The breath sank into her heart, and the ember of witchcraft that was there blazed up and grew, spreading through her body. Higher and higher it rose, till Gretel grew small inside her own head and could feel herself move around only at the witch's whim.

Then the witch took Hansel from the cage and bound him with red rope. She laid him on the marble slab, and Lazarus jumped up so she could see. Gretel brought her herbs, and the wand of ivory, the wand of jet, and the wand of horn. Finally, the witch chanted her spell. Gretel's mind went away completely then. When she came back to herself, Hansel was in his cage, one eye bandaged with a thick pad of cobwebs. He looked at Gretel through his other, tear-filled eye.

"She's going to take the other one tomorrow," he whispered.

"No," said Gretel, sobbing. "No."

"I know it isn't really you helping her," said Hansel. "But what can you do?"

"I don't know," said Gretel. "We have to kill her—but she'll punish you if we try and we fail."

"I wish it was a dream," said Hansel. "Dreams end, and you wake up. But I'm not asleep, am I? It's too cold, and my eye . . . it hurts."

Gretel opened the cage to hug him and cast the spell that would warm them. But she was thinking about cold—and the witch. "If we could trap the witch and Lazarus in the cold room somehow, they might freeze to death," she said slowly. "But we'd have to make it much colder, so she won't have time to cast a spell."

They went to look at the cold room, and found that it was set as cold as it would go. But Hansel found a barrel of liquid nitrogen at the back, and that gave him an idea.

An hour later, they'd rigged their instant witch-freezing trap. Using one of the knives, Hansel unscrewed the inside handle of the door so there was no way to get out. Then they balanced the barrel on top of a pile of boxes, just past the door. Finally, they poured water everywhere to completely ice up the floor.

Then they took turns sleeping, till Gretel heard the click of the witch's key in the door. She sprang up and went to the cold room. Leaving the door ajar, she carefully stood on the ice and took the lid off the liquid nitrogen. Then she stepped back outside, pinching her nose and gasping. "Something's wrong, Mistress!" she exclaimed. "Everything's gone rotten."

"What!" cried the witch, dashing across the cave, her one blue eye glittering. Lazarus ran at her heels from habit, though she no longer needed his sight.

Gretel stood aside as she ran past, then gave her a hefty push. The witch skidded on the ice, crashed into the boxes, and fell flat on her back just as the barrel toppled over. An instant later, her final scream was smothered in a cloud of freezing vapor.

But, Lazarus, quicker than any normal cat, did a backflip in midair, even as Gretel slammed the door. Ancient stitches gave way, and the cat started coming apart, accompanied by an explosion of the magical silver dust that filled it and gave it life.

Gretel relaxed for an instant as the dust obscured the beast, then screamed as the front part of Lazarus jumped out at her, teeth snapping. She kicked at it, but the cat was too swift, its great jaws meeting around her ankle. Gretel screamed again, and then Hansel was there, shaking the strange dust out of the broken body as if he were emptying a vacuum cleaner. In a few seconds there was nothing left of Lazarus but its head and an empty skin. Even then it wouldn't let go, till Hansel forced its mouth open with a broomstick and pushed the snarling remnant across the floor and into one of the cages.

Gretel hopped across and watched it biting the bars, its green eyes still filled with magical life and hatred. "Hansel," she said. "Your own eye is frozen with the witch. But I think I can remember the spell—and there is an eye for the taking here."

So it was that when they entered the cold room later to take the key of bone from the frozen, twisted body of the witch, Hansel saw the world through one eye of blue and one of green.

Later, when they found their way home, it was the sight of that green eye that gave the Hagmom a heart attack and made her die. But their father was still a weak man, and within a year he thought to marry another woman who had no love for his children. Only this time, the new Hagmom faced a Gretel who was more than half a witch, and a Hansel who had gained strange powers from his magic cat's-eye.

But that is all another story. . . .

Garth Nix

Garth Nix is the author of the children's fantasy novel *The Ragwitch*, and two novels for an older audience, *Sabriel* and *Shade's Children*. He first encountered Grimms' fairy tales when they were read to him at the age of five or six. He spent the next two years attempting to spin straw into gold, turn pumpkins into carriages, and find a bearskin to put on—all without success. He chose Hansel and Gretel for retelling, as it was always a favorite, probably because his mother made him a fantastic gingerbread house for his eighth birthday, complete with a witch made out of sweets. He chose to set the retold story in a city because he has always found being lost in cities much more terrifying than being lost in the woods—or, in his case, the bush of Australia. Garth lives in Sydney, but has been lost in many different countries.

Becoming Charise

by Kathe Koja

In the back of the school bus, hunched next to a window smeared and cloudy with breath, sketchbook open on her knees: Charise. Sitting alone; again; always. Imagining the world.

"Hey, Nerdstein," Tibb Gleason said, shoving her shoulder, ruining her pencil's line. "Draw a picture of this."

Charise bit her lip, erased the mark, started drawing again. Not the world around her, the world as it was, but her world, the way she imagined things could be. A world where no one hurt animals, or polluted the water and skies. A world where no one hurt anyone, where no one called names, where girls could wear oversized red sweatshirts printed with pictures of Albert Einstein and not get called a nerd. Or a geek. Or worse. All the time.

Charise wondered if Einstein had ever been called a nerd.

She had read everything she could find about Albert Einstein: how he had decided, at age twelve, to solve the riddle of the "huge world" all around him. How he was such a crappy student, he left school at fifteen. How four papers he wrote, scientific papers, did more to solve that riddle than anyone before or since. Charise thought he might be a kind of saint, a saint of knowing, if there was such a thing. Charise loved knowing things, how things worked, what they did; she knew that Knowing was the first step to Becoming.

"I want to Become," she told her Aunt Tamara. Breakfast, the windows dark around them; raisin bagels and orange juice fluorescent in her glass. Beneath the chair, her mutt terrier, Dino, waited for the usual crumbs.

Aunt Tamara poured herself some orange juice, sliced a bagel with one swift swipe. "Become what? You could be an artist, with all that drawing you do. Or maybe a scientist. Or an engineer—"

"I don't mean that," Charise said. "I mean . . . I just want to Become." Become what I am, she wanted to say, but didn't know how. Like a caterpillar is a butterfly, somewhere inside its genes; like an atom splits. Like a piece of paper and a Number Two pencil are a drawing, when they meet a particular hand and eye, when all of it finally gets together, to Become what it somehow was, all along, forever . . . Aunt Tamara was smiling at her.

"You want another bagel?"

Dino put up his pointy little ears; Charise shook her head. "I gotta go."

"I'll see you after work," Aunt Tamara said.

On the bus, Charise had to squeeze past some seventh graders, big girls in bright parkas, pink and green. In seventh grade they did a science unit on Einstein; that was something to wait for, a bright marker on the dull road of the days. Maybe it would be different if she were somewhere else, a different road, but Jackson was a school like a cheese sandwich was a meal; it would get you by, but that was all. Not a hot pepperoni pizza, like, say, the Bayley Academy. Charise had heard about Bayley: A couple kids from Jackson—smart kids; lucky kids—had gone there. It lived in her mind like a moon, bright and unreachable, something to consider at night.

But today was orange juice and bagels and the bus, the jostling halls of Jackson, trying not to mind that she had no locker partner, trying to get through the day.

It had always been hard for Charise to fit in. Too wild for the smart kids, too smart for the wild kids, as if school were one kind of puzzle, and she was a piece from another box. Don't you want to go out and play? Aunt Tamara used to ask her as she sat with cookies or a Coke, legs hooked around the kitchen chair, Dino alert beneath. Or maybe ask a friend over?

I don't have any friends, she said in her head, but to Aunt Tamara she would say, "Not today," or, "Not right now." In grade school most of the kids had seemed silly,

Kathe Koja

babyish, but, still, it hurt to stand and watch as they played soccer or four-square, or walked home together after school. She kept hoping that one day things might be different—"You wait," Aunt Tamara kept telling her, "things will change for you, you'll see"—but, still, they were the same. And the hurt was the same, a dark, dry ache not in her center but deeper, as if she were a kind of funnel, and the emptiness before the bottom was part of the hurting, too.

I'm just different, Charise told herself, biting her lip. I bet Einstein was different, too.

At Jackson there were three groups of kids. The largest was the Regulars, the middle-of-the-roaders, who moved past Charise in the stream of the hall like boats around a buoy, avoiding her without effort, without even seeing she was there. In the lunchroom, hunched over her sketchbook at the end of the unpopular kids' table, where Clarissa and DeeDee and DeJuan played their endless games of Hearts or Bump Rummy, she sometimes heard, "Hey, Geekstein!" from one of the Regulars, calling out to make the others laugh: mean, but not too mean, the way they might use a magnifying glass to burn up ants on the sidewalk, never thinking it might hurt the ants to be killed.

But the kids who did think, the smart kids, were always busy with stuff like student council, or the school newspaper, or the debate group, things Charise didn't want to do. And, anyway, they didn't want to hang out with her, either; they respected her for her brains, but that was all. Respect is different from being friends: You can respect someone you don't even like.

And the third group, the outsiders, the wild kids like Tibb Gleason—they always sat in the back, sniggering to each other and writing swear words in their books, or on the desks for other kids to find later. They ignored Charise unless they needed a quiz answer, then called her a bitch if she wouldn't give it to them.

Which she wouldn't. "You want to know the answer?" she would whisper, very low, so her lips barely moved and the teacher couldn't see. "Then study." Why should they sponge off her hard work? Every night she took home books, she went to the library, she went on the Net on her Aunt Tamara's computer: "What are you doing?" Aunt Tamara would call from the living room, where she sat with her own books, her night school work. "Are you online?"

"I'm downloading some stuff," Charise would call back. "For school." Mostly it wasn't for school, it was for herself, things she wanted to know about, but Aunt Tamara didn't mind. She said learning was learning. Mr. Mahfouz said the same thing.

Mr. Mahfouz was the sixth-grade science teacher. Some kids called him Mr. MahFool, but most of the kids liked him: He told jokes, he brought in laser games and giant Slinkys, he didn't care if you laughed or shouted out. Sometimes he wore funny T-shirts under his sport coat, or a baseball cap with a cardinal on it, for some sports team he liked. All sports were a closed book to Charise, but Mr. Mahfouz talked about the physics of baseball; he could find science in anything. Even TV.

"Your mission," he told the class that day, "is to find science on TV. Or in a TV: Cut it up, dissect it, see what you get. And then tell me all about it in a report. No less than five pages, at least three illustrations. That means pictures, guys."

Most of the kids watched nature shows; a few rented videos and brought them in. Mark Carver, who was editor of the school paper, did a newspaper story, with three photographs, of him and his friends "dissecting" a TV with a screwdriver. Charise did her report on the science of TV—what made it work, why you saw a picture when you clicked the remote. "This is dynamite," Mr. Mahfouz said, and put up her report in the showcase at the front of the room. "Charise, come see me after class."

"Dynamite you, Geekstein," said Tibb Gleason when Charise sat down again.

When the day was over, she came back to Mr. Mahfouz, who sat behind his desk, sorting papers. Lockers click-and-banging, a faraway shout in the hall; the school grew quiet as she waited. Finally, Mr. Mahfouz said "Finished," setting the papers aside. "Sorry it took so long. . . . You know, your report was really excellent, Charise. Even for you."

Charise nodded, watchful. She knew more was coming.

"Do you like it here, at Jackson?" Did she like it? What kind of a question was that? "Reason I ask," he said, "is there's a couple of placements opening up at Bayley—the Bayley Academy, ever heard of it?—and I'd like to sponsor you for one of them." From the papers on his desk he chose two, along with a brochure, slick and glossy like a magazine. "Take that home, let your folks have a look at it and, if you're interested, we'll talk some more."

THE BAYLEY ACADEMY OF ARTS & SCIENCE: slim black letters on a cool blue background, lots of stuff about academic excellence, a world of learning. And lots of pictures: of kids in a laboratory, kids on a stage, kids with computers; lots of computers. This was no cheese sandwich. It was a big, juicy pizza with everything, the kind of place Einstein would have loved.

Charise kept the brochure hidden in her backpack, as if it might be taken from her, or vanish like a magic trick; she read it like the Bible, she read it for a week, looking at the kids, the labs, the computers—

"I'd like to sponsor you . . ."

no more Tibb Gleason, no more Geekstein

a world of learning

Aunt Tamara you have to say yes

—until at last, at Friday dinner, trying her best to sound casual: "From Mr. Mahfouz," Charise said, sliding the brochure across the table. "He said to show it to you; he said he'd sponsor me if I wanted."

Fork in hand but she could not eat, could not swallow, could barely breathe as she watched Aunt Tamara read the whole thing, even the papers inside. Dino shuffled beneath her chair; the dinner grew cold. Finally, Aunt Tamara looked up, without a smile. "Honey," she said, in a voice like lead, "smart as you are, I don't know if this is the place for you. The kids would be—very different from what you're used to."

Charise felt her heart beating, a hard, red drum: like an atom, splitting. Her mouth was open, but Aunt Tamara was still talking. "—way across town, there's no school bus to get you there, and I have to be at work by—"

From inside the drum, the atom, her voice dry and far away: "I could ride my bike."

"It's across town, Charise. And what about wintertime?"

"I could, I could take a regular bus, I could walk—" but Aunt Tamara was shaking her head, she was closing the brochure, she was saying, "Charise, honey, I'm sorry," but Charise was already gone, away, slamming her bedroom door, crouching on the floor with her arms clenched around her body till she was dark and hard and small; like a rock: like a seed. She was crying, but she didn't know it.

I want to Become. I want to Become.

She would ride her bike, take a bus, walk if she had to, walk every mile there and back. She would go to Bayley, she would become Einstein, she would—

"Charise?"

Hard and dark: her arms were cramping: her legs had fallen asleep. Aunt Tamara's knock was as gentle as her voice: "Charise, please, open the door."

"No," she said, but now she knew she was crying, felt the tears like lines on her face, felt their salt and cloudy heat; their elements, Mr. Mahfouz would say. She cried until she thought she was empty, then cried a little more. The door nudged open a crack: Dino, come to lie beside her in the darkness. She was still crying when at last she fell asleep.

"Your aunt called me," said Mr. Mahfouz as soon as Charise walked into class; he looked sad. "Can you stop in after school for a minute?"

"Sure." No tears today, Charise kept her face still, kept her hands in her pockets as Mr. Mahfouz talked: Your aunt said, so and so and so on, watching her face as he spoke. "I have to tell you," he said at last, slumping a little in his rolling chair, "I'm pretty disappointed. What about you?" His face looked tired, like a helium balloon the day after the party, as if something good had gone out of him.

"Yeah," Charise said, "I am." She shrugged a little, a thin motion. "So what."

"So I guess we'll have to do the best we can, you and me." Mr. Mahfouz sighed. "You know the story of the ugly duckling?"

She nodded, sharp, almost rude with the weight of her heart inside her. All she wanted now was for him to stop talking so she could get away, get her coat, get out of this crappy school for today, at least . . . but Mr. Mahfouz was waiting for an answer, so, "Yeah," she said, looking not at him but out the window, into the gray slant of afternoon sun. "He grew up to be a swan, or something. So what."

"So he never was a duckling in the first place," Mr. Mahfouz said. His voice was calm now, and very precise, the way it was when he was explaining something, something he expected them to get. Her to get. "He was going to become a swan. No matter where he went, no matter what he did—it was in his genes, Charise, you understand what I'm saying?"

"I understand," she said, still wanting to get away, wishing she was in her room, wishing she could find Einstein and tell him her problems, tell him how much she wished she could

become

what she was meant to be, what she was inside—

a swan.

Like a pencil and some paper is a picture; like a caterpillar is a butterfly. Like she was what she was, Charise, part of a puzzle that was not the puzzle she knew, but still part of something bigger: a different puzzle, somewhere else. Maybe at Bayley, or maybe not. Did it matter? In the end, it probably didn't matter.

Becoming Charise

It was in his genes, Charise, you understand what I'm saying?

"Charise?" said Mr. Mahfouz, leaning forward, arms on the desk, and, "Yes," she said, because she got it now, she knew why he was smiling; she was smiling, too. Not a big smile but a bright one, like a little moon a million miles away, getting bigger as you get closer to it, and, "You know," said Mr. Mahfouz, "you can always try again next year. For Bayley, I mean. Your aunt might—"

"Einstein dropped out of school," Charise said. Now her smile was a grin.

Mr. Mahfouz laughed. "You don't have to do everything Einstein did," he said.

On the bus, Tibb Gleason stuck his foot out in the aisle, but Charise stepped over it as if it wasn't there; quack, quack, she thought. Quack you, Tibb Gleason. Plopping down into the seat, she took out her sketchbook and spent the ride home drawing: The world she wanted, Einstein's "huge world," and herself, grown up, in the middle, with big white wings like a swan's.

Kathe Koja says: "I chose to retell this story because I have been the Ugly Duckling more than once: I know how it hurts, and I know that you have to be who you are, no matter what. I hope this story helps another duckling, somewhere else."

Koja is the author of several adult novels, including *The Cipher*, which was cowinner of the Bram Stoker Award for Superior Achievement in a First Novel; *Skin*; and *Strange Angels*. She lives in Michigan with her husband, artist Rick Lieder, and her son, Aaron.

The Seven Stage a Comeback

by Gregory Maguire

1. So that's how it is, fellows.
   The man with the crazed expression
   Clawed open her coffin,
   Kissed her awake,
   And carried her off.
   There goes our lovely daughter.
   All we have left of her
   Is the apple that tumbled from her lips
   And the glass box we nested her in.

2. We're better off without her.
   I always told you that.
   And you, and you, and you two, too.
   (*You*, I rarely spoke to. Mop up your nose.)
   Wasn't she always on us about something?

"Can't you tidy the woodpile some?"
"Hasn't anyone ever heard of a thing called soap?"
"I don't trust little men with beards."
And then with the sighs.
The expressive eyes.
Followed by floods of agitated song.
Frankly, when she ate that poisoned apple—
Oh, yes, I was sad, I cried—
But you want to know what else?
I thought: *At last. A little peace and quiet around here.*

3. So why are your eyes all rimmed with red?
You loved her as we all did.
Her with her lips like October apples,
Her hair like the wind on April nights.
Or did you just like having someone to complain
about?
You kept your vigil as I did. As we all did.

4. And all that's left is the apple and the coffin.
The fruit and the glass.
And our troubled hearts.
Let's worry a solution out of this.
What could we do?
Put the bit of the apple in the glass coffin
And close it up again?
The coffin keeps things pretty fresh.
And for a good, long time, too, it seems.
You never know when we'll need a bit of poison
apple again.

5. Let's take the coffin on our backs
   And wander o'er the mountain tracks.
   Sing ho! for the life of a dwarf.

6. This isn't the time for singing.
   But it's not a bad idea.
   I say let's muscle it out. Come on.
   Let's get this baby home.
   All together now, on a count of three—
   One, two—alley-oop and upsy-daisy.
   You, carry the iron-head hammer.
   Mind how you swing it, dolt.
   And stop with that racket.

7. Ohhhhhhh, ohhhhhhh, ohhhhhhh, ohhhhhhh,
   ohhhhhhh, ohhhhhhh, ohhhhhhh.

1. So listen, guys. Put down your beer steins.
   Life hasn't been kind to us.
   We find an orphan girl, we take her in.
   Locate some moldy blankets to keep her warm.
   Porridge in the morning, porridge in the evening.
   A little dwarf folk music to cheer her up.
   It was a humble life, but it was ours,
   And freely we gave it to her.
   No wonder we're still upset.
   No wonder we can't focus.
   On our plates, our gray beard hardens.
   In the cold cauldron, our soup grows a skin of scum.

Gregory Maguire

We have to shape up. We're falling to pieces here.

2. Easy come, easy go.
   We're better off without her.
   Remember, I always said that.

3. You are the one who speaks with the sharpest tongue,
   But you're the one who moans her name in your sleep.
   Face it. We all miss her.
   When's the last time any one of us laughed out loud?
   Sorrow has a name, and its name is loneliness.
   Sorrow has a shape, and its shape is absence.
   Sorrow is a sickness like any other.
   We don't manage to do what we should.
   We never go out with our iron-head hammer
   To bash the jewels out of secret caves.
   Our hearts are bashed instead.
   But what can we do?

4. We could go find her where she is.
   We could beg her to come back.
   We could bring the glass coffin.
   We could lay her where she was.

5. Let's take the coffin on our backs
   And wander o'er the mountain tracks.
   Sing ho! for the life of a dwarf.

6. Please, would you stop your singing, please?
   It's hard to think.
   Though I'm not one for kidnapping old friends,
   She did leave us high and dry.

The Seven Stage a Comeback

She married that traveling prince.
They could be nine kingdoms away by now.
It has been months already.
I doubt we could ever find her.
But I'm a one for putting on boots
And marching impressively right off a cliff.
Better than sitting around with tears in our beards!
Let me hunt for a map, a compass.
We need cloaks, and staffs, and gumption.
Up from your sloth, you miserable slugs.
Pocket your bread and cork your ale.
Tighten your belts and lace your boots.
Somebody grab the iron-head hammer,
Somebody bring the silver guitar.
You, are you weeping again, you fool?

7. Ohhhhhh,   ohhhhhh.   Ohhhhhh,   ohhhhhh.
Ohhhhhh, ohhhhhh.

✦ ✦ ✦

1. Good-bye to the house in the autumn woods.
Good-bye to our hermit hideaway.
There's no life left for us at home.
This little house, this moldy tomb—
Not our tomb, but the grave and marker
Of what we lost when she went away.
Now hoist the coffin on your backs,
And off we go.

2. We're better off without her.

Gregory Maguire

We're better off without her.
We're better off without her.

3. So you say. So you keep saying.
   But you walk faster than the rest of us.
   Now the air is cold, the wind is high,
   The light is wet, the clouds come in.
   I feel a sadness in my bones.
   It never was to come to this.
   We took her in when she was lost,
   But then we lost her in our turn.
   And are we losing ourselves as well?

4. We'll find our beauty where she rests,
   And coax her home.
   What's wrong with that?
   The least she owes us is a little loyalty.
   She never should have eaten the apple, one,
   Nor, two, attracted the first available prince.
   Ours is not to harm or hurt her.
   Just to keep her safely with us.

5. We have the coffin on our backs
   And wander o'er the mountain tracks.
   Sing ho! for the life of a dwarf.

6. Keep the pace, steady she goes.
   If we suffer one turned ankle,
   One hurt shoulder, one slipped hip,
   Down goes the coffin, and crash goes the glass.
   Out goes the apple bit, bouncing away,
   Into the million brown leaves of the forest floor.

The Seven Stage a Comeback   141

Lost as lost, now and forevermore.
And all our hopes will be lost as well.
You, are you weeping again, you fool?
7. Ohhhhh, ohhhhh. Ohhhhh, ohhhhh.
   Ohhhhh, ohhhhh.

1. The wind on the mountain chills my heart.
2. We're better off without her.
3. She's hoping we rescue her, I know.
4. I fear the clouds are seeded with snow.
5. Sing ho! for the life of a dwarf. Brr.
6. I'll smash your head with the iron-head hammer
   If you don't stop your infernal racket.
7. Ohhh. Ohhh. Ohhh. Ohhh.

1. Now here, a fallen tree. We'll cross
   This rushing icy mountain stream.
   Don't drop the coffin into the flood,
   For there it would sink, and clear as light,
   We'd search in vain and never see it.
   Steady your feet, and steady your hearts.
2. We're better off without her.
   But should we come across her . . .
   I'll be the one to ask her.
   How she could ever leave us.
   I'll laugh at any answer.

Gregory Maguire

We're better off without her.
3. We aren't her abductors.
Just friend who come a-calling.
We'll ask her to rejoin us.
The coffin waits.
4. The coffin waits.
5. The coffin weighs upon our backs
And makes too steep these snowy tracks.
Sing ho! for the life of a dwarf.
6. I see the ice that prickles in the nose
And crusts the corners of our jeweled eyes
Invades the reaches of our dwarfish hearts.
I fear what we're about.
I cannot stop.
We are bewitched; no more, no less.
Her beauty calls us, and we can't escape.
Let's save our breath in this bitter cold.
Mind how you swing that hammer, clumsy oaf!
7. Ohh, ohh, ohh.

1. Here in the inn-yard, huddled about a fire,
A tankard of watered beer, we take our rest,
The winter months have brought us a hopeful spring.
Today we learn that the girl we seek
Lives just beyond the ridge, in a noble home.
No dragons to guard the moat, no spells to break.

The Seven Stage a Comeback

No soldiers lurking upon the shingled roofs.
Nothing to stop us from going the final steps.
Here we'll commit what crime we may,
And live to rue, or praise, the day.

7. Oh, oh, oh, oh, oh.

2. We're better off without her.
Let's give her the poisoned sleep
And lock her within her windows.
What's dead cannot live to leave us again.
We love her too much to allow her to live.

7. Oh, oh, oh, oh.

3. We're smaller than human men, with smaller hearts.
Our strength is in mighty arms, for smashing rocks,
Our strength is for swinging hammers with iron heads.
We aren't built to know what's right or wrong.
We're hardly more than pagan animals.
We met her when she was young, we took her in,
As much to serve us at our filthy home
As out of any wish to do charity.
Let's finish the job we started, and shed no tears
For being smaller creatures than we'd like.
Up to the mansion, then, to take her back,
There to cherish her incorruptible corpse.

7. Oh, oh, oh.

4. The apple awaits to do its lethal job.
The glassy walls of the coffin are polished clear,
Its hinges oiled silent by dwarfish spit.

Gregory Maguire

Now we to our work, and she, our beauty—
She to her work, again, at last, forever.

7. Oh, oh.

5. Let's lift the coffin from our backs
And see what sleeper it attracts.
Sing ho! for the life of a dwarf.

7. Oh.

6. We're decided then; the deed is clear.
The time is now.
We leave to claim our prize.

7. ——

1. There she sits, in an orchard of apple trees.
Who could have thought she would be more
beautiful
Than memory could picture?

2. We're better off without—we're better off—
we're better—

3. You stutter out of shock, and so do I.
Hush, lest she hears us before we make our
approach.
Her hair is longer, see how the wind enjoys it!
See how her smile blossoms; she looks aside,
Shyly, at mending collected inside the basket
That rests in the fragrant grass near her pretty feet.

4. She always loved the household task.
She sang when she worked.

Who can forget her voice?
But once I wondered, bringing the silver guitar,
If she sang to keep her spirits high.
As if we were not the world she truly wanted,
However good our porridge, sweet our music.
Now let us creep up closer to observe.

5. Sing ho, sing ho, sing ho.
    Off with the girl and away we go.

6. She smiles upon the laundry with radiant look,
    She stirs the cloth as if something lies gently within,
    A bruisable apple, a blossom, a porcelain toy.
    Now is the time. There is nobody else around.
    At the count of three, we leap from these thickets, see,
    Surround her—confound her—accuse her—reclaim her—
    One—two—

7. Three
    Is the number we never expected to see.
    Yes, you will listen, all of you! Hear me out.
    It is not just the prince and the princess we disturb.
    That basket of washing is laughing at its mother.
    There is a child within. Are you wholly blind?
    I'll swing this iron-head hammer at your skulls.
    I'll smash the coffin seven directions to heaven.
    Dwarfish mischief we make, and dwarfish music,
    But mischief and music never come closer together
    Than in the laugh of an infant adoring its mother.

Gregory Maguire

1. We come from distant regions, cold and wild,
    To bring you dwarfish music for your child.
2. We come to visit you, and we will try
    To sing the babe a pretty lullaby.
3. We come to see what loneliness is worth;
    It brings new life upon the ancient earth.
4. We smash the coffin of your former days
    Seeing the happiness that spills in your gaze.
5. No coffin is left to lift upon our backs
    And carry home along the mountain tracks.
    Sing ho! for the life of a dwarf.
6. Now standing in splintered glass, in scented grass,
    We sing you all our love, before we pass.
7. All of us loved her as much as we could grieve.
    As hard as we could do, each in our way.
    Now hand me the silver guitar, and I will play
    The final notes before we take our leave.

She thinks:

After this horrible winter, how sweet the air feels!

How silly I'm being. Fanciful, flighty! But I can't help it. It's almost as if the wind were strumming invisible harps.

And the light is a pretty thing today. Pinkish, rosy. It must be the sun streaming down through the apple blossoms.

Reminds me of a dream I must have had. As if I had

lived somewhere else, once upon a time. I never did, of course. I was always here, awake, and in my life. With my loved one just within the sound of my voice, and my baby here at my feet. Smiling as if at some mysterious joke. Smiling as if the happily ever after of stories begins right now, at the very start of life.

Gregory Maguire

Gregory Maguire has written twelve novels for children, including The Hamlet Chronicles: *Seven Spiders Spinning, Six Haunted Hairdos, Five Alien Elves*, and so on. His novels for adults include *Wicked: The Life and Times of the Wicked Witch of the West* and *Confessions of an Ugly Stepsister*. He writes, "When I was seven I came across the stories about Baba Yaga printed in the children's magazine called *Jack and Jill*. Twenty years later I published *The Dream Stealer*, a children's novel with Baba Yaga as a character. I've always liked the witches in fairy tales best—better than dragons or unicorns. But dwarves and trolls and the like are pretty cool, too, so that's what attracted me to Snow White. I've suspected for some time that I have a dwarf colony out behind the garage, but maybe it's moles." Maguire's typewriter, garage, and dwarves-or-moles are in Concord, Massachusetts.

The Twelve Dancing Princesses

by Patricia A. McKillip

One day long ago in a faraway country, a young soldier, walking home from a battle he had fought for the king, found himself lost in a forest. The road he followed dwindled away, leaving him standing among silent trees, with the sun just setting at his back, and the moon just rising ahead of him. Caught alone and astray between night and day, he thought to himself, There are worse things that could be. He had seen many of them on the battlefield. He was alone because he had watched his best friend die; he had given his last few coins to another soldier trying to walk home with only one foot. But he himself, though worn and bloodied with battle, had kept all his bones, and his eyes, and he even had a little bread and cheese in his pack to eat. He settled himself into a tangle of tree roots, where he could watch the moon, and took out his simple meal. He had opened his mouth to take the first bite when a voice at his elbow said, "One bite is a feast to those who have nothing."

He turned, wondering who had crept up so noiselessly to sit beside him. It was a very old woman. Her bones bumped under the surface of her brown, sagging skin like the tree roots under the earth. Her pale eyes, which now held only a memory of the blue they had been, were fixed on the heel of bread, the rind of cheese in his hand. He sighed, for he was very hungry. But so must she be, scuttling like an animal among the trees, with no one to care for her. There are worse things, he thought, than having a little less of something.

So he said, tearing the bread and cheese apart and giving her half, "Then feast with me."

"You are kind, young soldier," she said in her high wavery voice, and bit into her scanty supper as if it might vanish before she could finish it. After she had swallowed her last bite and searched for crumbs, she spoke again. "What is your name?"

"Val," he answered.

"A good name for a soldier. Did you win the battle?"

Val shrugged. "So they say. I could not see, from where I stood, that winning was much better than losing."

"And now what will you do?"

"I don't know. My younger brother has married and

taken care of the family farm and our parents while I have been fighting. I will find my way back and show them that I'm still alive, and then find something to do in the world. After all, someone with nothing has nothing to lose."

"You have a fair and honest face," the old woman said. "That's something." Her pale eyes caught moonlight and glinted, so suddenly and strangely, that he started. "How would you like to be king?"

He swallowed a laugh along with a lump of bread. "Better than being a beggar."

"Then follow this road through the forest. It will take you into the next kingdom, where the king and queen there are desperate for help. They have twelve beautiful daughters—"

"Twelve!"

"None of them will marry; they will laugh at every suitor. The king locks them in their room every night; and every morning he finds them sleeping so soundly, they will not wake until noon, and at the foot of every bed, a pair of satin shoes so worn with dancing, they must be thrown away. But no one knows how the princesses get out of the room, or where they go to dance. The king has promised his kingdom and a daughter to any man who can solve this mystery."

"Any man," Val repeated, and felt a touch of wonder in his heart, where before there had been nothing. "Even me."

Patricia A. McKillip

"Even you. But you must be careful. The king is half mad with worry and fear for his daughters. He will kill any man who fails, even princes who might one day marry his daughters."

The young soldier pondered that. "Well," he said softly. "I have faced death before. No one ever offered to make me king if I survived." He stood up. "There's moon enough to see by, tonight. Where is the road to that kingdom?"

"Under your feet," she answered, and there it was, washed with light and winding among the trees. Val stared at the old woman; her face rippled into a thousand wrinkles as she smiled.

"Two things. One: Drink nothing that the princesses give you. And two"—she touched the dusty cloak at his back—"this will make you invisible when you follow them at night. It pays," she added, as he slid his pack strap over his shoulder, "to be kind to crones."

"So I hope," he breathed, and stepped onto the moonlit road, wondering if he would find death at its end, or love.

Death, he thought instantly, when he met the father of the twelve princesses. The king, wearing black velvet and silver mail, was tall and gaunt, with long, iron-gray hair and a lean, furrowed face. His eyes were black and terrible with frustration and despair. He wore a sword so long and heavy, it would have dragged on the ground at Val's side. He kept one hand always on it; Val wondered if he used it to slay the princes who failed him.

But he spoke to the young soldier with courtesy. Val found himself soaking in a fragrant bath while a barber cut his hair. Then he dressed in fine, elegant clothes, though he refused, for no reasons he gave, to part with his torn, dusty cloak. He sat down to a meal so wondrously cooked that he could scarcely name what he ate. When night fell, the king took him to the princesses' bedchamber.

The doors to the long chamber opened to such color, such rich wood and fabric, such movement of slender, jeweled hands and glowing hair, and bright, curious eyes, so many sweet, laughing voices, that Val froze on the threshold, mute with astonishment that any place so lovely and full of grace could exist in the world he knew. "My daughters," the king said as they floated toward him, breasting the air like swans in their lacy, flowing nightgowns. "The queen named them after flowers. Aster, Bluet, Columbine, Delphinium, Eglantine, Fleur, Gardenia, Heather, Iris, Jonquil, Lily, and Mignonette. She could not find an appropriate flower for K."

"Kumquat," one with long, golden hair giggled behind her hands.

"Knotweed," another said with an explosion of laughter into her nearest sister's shoulder. Then they were all silent, their eyes of amber, emerald, sapphire, unblinking and wide, watching Val like a circle of cats, he thought, watching a sparrow.

Patricia A. McKillip

He said, scarcely hearing himself, while his own eyes were charmed from face to face, "There are folk names for flowers, sometimes, that queens may not know. Kestrel's Eye, farmers call a kind of sunflower, for its smallness and the color of its center."

"Kestrel," a princess with a mass of dark, curly hair and golden eyes repeated. Her beauty held more dignity and assurance than her sisters'; her eyes, smiling at the handsome young stranger, seemed full of secrets. "A pretty word. You might have been Kestrel, then, Lily, and Mignonette would have been you, if our mother had known."

She was the oldest, Val guessed, and was proved right when the youngest protested, "But, Aster, I am Mignonette; I do not want to be Lily."

"Don't worry, goose, you may stay yourself." She yawned, then, and stepped forward to kiss their grim father. "How tired I am, suddenly! I could sleep for a month!"

"I wish you all would," the king murmured, bending as one by one they brushed his face with kisses. They only laughed at him and vanished behind the hangings of lace and gauze around their beds; they were as silent then as if they had already begun to dream.

The king showed Val a small room at the end of the bedchamber, where he could pretend to sleep as he waited for the princesses to reveal the mystery of their dancing. "Many men have come here," the king said, "seeking to win my kingdom, thinking it a trifling matter to outwit my daughters and take my crown. They are all dead, now, even the jesting, lighthearted princes. My daughters show no mercy, and neither do I. But if you fail, I will be sorry."

Val bowed his head. "So will I," he answered. "How strange it seems that yesterday I had nothing to lose, and today I have everything. Except love."

"That alone drives me mad," the king said harshly. "They can love no one. Nothing. They laugh at the young men I put to death. As if they are spellbound. . . ." He turned, begging rather than warning as he closed the door. "Do not fail."

Val sat down on the bed, which was the first he had seen in many months, and the last he dared sleep in. He had just pulled off his boots when the door opened, and the eldest, Aster, appeared, carrying a cup of wine. She handed it to Val. "We always share a cup with guests, for friendship's sake. My father forgot to tell us your name."

"My name is Val. Thank you for the wine." He pretended to take a sip while he wondered blankly how to pretend to finish the cup under her watchful eyes.

"A proper name for a prince."

"I suppose it is, but I am a soldier, returning home after battle."

Her brows rose. "And you stopped here, to try for a crown on your way. You should have kept going. There is nothing for you here but what you escaped in battle."

He smiled, holding her eyes, while he poured the wine into a boot standing at his knee. "There are better memories here," he said, and tilted the cup against his mouth as if he were draining it dry.

He stretched out on the bed when Aster left, and did not move when he heard the door open again. "Look at him," one of them mocked. "Sleeping as if he were already dead."

"I put a stronger potion into the wine," another answered. "His eyes were far too clear."

Then he heard laughter in the princess' bedchamber, and the sound of cupboards, chests, and cases being opened. He waited, watching them while he pretended to snore. They dressed themselves in bright silks, and lace and creamy velvet gowns; they tied the ribbons of new satin dancing slippers around their ankles. They took rings and earrings and strands of pearls out of their jewel cases, and they spun one another's hair into amazing confections threaded with ribbons. Val had thought them beautiful before; now they seemed enchanted, exquisite, unreal, as if he had drunk the wine and were dreaming them. He was so entranced, he forgot to snore. Aster came to look sharply at him through the open door, but another sister only laughed.

"He sleeps so deeply, he has forgotten how to breathe."

Aster went to a bed in the middle of the chamber. She knocked three times on the carved headboard, and the entire bed abruptly disappeared, leaving a dark, oblong hole in the floor. Like a grave, Val thought, feeling his heart beat at the strangeness of it. In a long, graceful line, beginning with A and ending with M, the princesses descended into the earth.

The wet pool of wine at the bottom of one boot cleared Val's amazed thoughts a little as he pulled them on; he remembered to fling his worn cloak over his shoulders before he left. He glanced into one of the many mirrors in the bedchamber as he hurried after Mignonette. *There is no soldier,* the mirror told him. *The room is empty.*

Fearing that the hole in the earth might close behind the princesses, he followed too closely. His first step down the broad, winding steps caught the hem of Mignonette's gown.

She said, startled, "Who is there? Aster, Lily, someone pulled at my dress."

All their faces looked back toward Val, a lovely, silent chain of princesses stretching down the steps. Aster turned away first, picking up her own silks. "Don't be a goose, Mignonette; you caught your skirt on a splinter."

"The steps are marble," Mignonette muttered. "And I have a bad feeling about tonight."

But no one answered her. Val saw a shining ahead, like a thousand touches of starlight. When they reached the bottom of the stairs, the princesses began to walk down a wide road lined with trees. The leaves on the trees were moonlight, it seemed to Val; they were silver fire. They were silver, he realized finally, with such wonder that he could scarcely breathe. He reached up to touch such beauty, and then, beginning to think again, he broke off a twig bearing four or five leaves to show to the king.

The tree gave a splintering crack as if a branch had fallen; Mignonette whirled again. "What is that noise?" she cried. "You all must have heard it!"

Val held his breath. Her sisters glanced indifferently around them. "It was the wind," one said. "It was fireworks from the dance," another offered.

"It sounded," Aster said lightly, "like a heart breaking."

They turned then onto another broad, tree-lined road. Val closed his eyes and opened them again, but what he saw did not change: All the leaves on these trees were made of gold. Like tears of gold they glowed and shimmered and melted down the branches; they flowed into Val's outstretched hand. Again he broke the slenderest of twigs; again the tree made a sound as if it had been split by lightning.

"Another broken heart," Aster said after Mignonette had screamed and complained, and her sisters had bade her to stop fussing so, they would never get to the dance. Only Val heard her whisper, as she trudged after them, "I have a bad feeling about tonight."

On the third road he broke off a cluster of leaves

made of diamonds. They burned of white fire in the moonlight, a light so pure and cold, it hurt his eyes. Mignonette stamped her foot and wailed at the sound the tree made, but her sisters, impatient now, only hurried toward the lake at the end of the road. Only Aster slowed to walk with her. Her voice was as calm as ever as she spoke to Mignonette, but she searched the diamond-studded dark behind them now and then, as if she sensed their invisible follower.

"I have a bad feeling about tonight," Mignonette said stubbornly.

Aster only answered, "We are almost there. One more night and we will never have to leave again."

On the shore of the lake, twelve boats waited for them. Out of each boat rose a shadowy figure to take the hand of the princess who came to him and help her into the boat. Val paused almost too long, trying to see the faces of the richly dressed men who were pushing the boats into the water. He whispered, suddenly sick at heart, "I have a bad feeling about tonight."

He realized then that the boats were floating away from him. He stepped hastily into the last one; it rocked a little until he caught his balance. Mignonette, whose boat he had the misfortune to enter, promptly raised her voice, calling to her sisters, "I think someone got into the boat with me!"

Her sisters' laughter fell as airily as windblown petals around them; even the man who rowed her smiled.

Patricia A. McKillip

"Don't fret, my Mignonette. I could row a dozen invisible guests across the water." His mouth did not move, Val saw, when he spoke. His eyes were closed. And yet he rowed steadily and straight toward the brightly lit castle on the other side of the lake. Torches burned on all its towers and walls; its casements opened wide; candlelight and music spilled from them. Val, his heart hammering, his hands as cold as if he waited for the beginning of a battle, did not dare move until Mignonette left the boat. The man, pulling it ashore, commented puzzledly, "It does seem heavier than usual."

"You see!" Mignonette began. But he only put his arm around her as she stepped ashore, and kissed her with his mouth that never moved.

"Never mind, my smallest love," he said. "Tomorrow you will have nothing to fear ever again."

Val, following them into the castle, saw the light from the torches at the gate fall over their faces. He stopped abruptly, his bones turned to iron, and his blood turned to ice at what he saw. "This," he heard himself whisper, "is the worst thing that could be."

Still, he forced himself into the castle, to watch the dance.

In the vast hall where the music played, the walls glowed with rare, polished wood. Traceries of gold leaf outlined the carvings on the ceiling. Candles in gold and silver and diamond holders stood everywhere, illumining the princesses' enchanting, sparkling faces. They began to dance at once, smiling into the faces of their princes, who may once have been handsome but who, to Val's unenchanted eyes, had been dead a day too long. Their lips were grim, motionless gashes in their blood-less faces; their eyes never opened. The room was crowded with watchers, all holding empty wine cups and tapping a foot to the music. The music, fierce and merciless, never let the dancers rest; it sent them breath-less and spinning around the floor. Ribbons came undone, hems tore, pearls broke and scattered every-where. Still, the princesses danced, their smiles never wavering at the faces of the dead who danced with them. Their satin slippers grew soiled and scuffed; the thin fabric wore through, until their bare feet blistered against the gleaming floor. Still, they danced, driven by blind musicians who had no reason to rest; they had left their lives elsewhere.

"What a celebration there will be tomorrow night!" Val heard many times as he waited. "The wedding of twelve princesses, and a dance that will never end!"

As the lake grew gray with dawn, the music finally stopped. In silence, drooping with exhaustion in their boats, the princesses were returned to the far shore, where they kissed the frozen faces of their princes and bade them farewell until tomorrow. Val walked ahead of them this time so that he could reach his bed and pretend to sleep before they came back. He kept pace with Aster. She looked a wilted flower, he thought; her eyes seemed

Patricia A. McKillip

troubled, now, but by what she could not imagine. She stumbled a little, on pebbles or the bright, sharp metal of fallen leaves, wincing where her shoes had worn through to her bare feet. He wanted to take her hand, help her walk, comfort her, but he guessed that, in such a place, he could be less alive to her than the dead.

When he saw the stairs, he paused to take off his boots so that he could run up without being heard. As he passed Aster, a boot tilted in his hand, spilling a little red wine on the steps. He saw Aster's eyes widen at it, her step falter. But she did not speak to her sisters. Nor did she say anything when, moments later, she found him sleeping in his bed. Another sister said tiredly, "At least he'll die before we wake. And then no one will have to die for us again."

He waited until they were all hidden in their beds, and nothing moved in the room but morning light. Then he rose, and crept out, with his boots in one hand and the magical leaves in the other, to speak to the king.

The king was pacing outside his daughters' bed-chamber; he had not slept that night, either. His hand tightening and loosening and tightening again on his great sword, he gazed wordlessly at Val out of his light-less eyes until Val spoke.

"They go down to the underworld," Val said. "They dance with the dead." He showed the king the three sprays of leaves, silver, gold and diamond, that could only have come from such an enchanted place. His hand trembled with weariness and horror; so did his voice.

"Tomorrow night, they will wed their dead princes, and you will never see them again."

The king, with a shout of rage and grief, tore the leaves from Val's hand and flung open the bedchamber doors. Exhausted, astonished faces appeared from between the hangings in every bed. The king showed them the leaves; sunlight flared from them, turned gold and silver and diamond into fire. "What are these?" he demanded. "Where are they from? You tell me, daughters. Tell me where to go get them. And then I will know where to go to find you."

They stared at the leaves. Little by little, as if before they had only dreamed themselves awake, their faces came alive to terror and confusion. From beneath their beds came the sound of a great, splintering crack, as if a tree had been struck by lightning, or a heart had broken.

Mignonette was the first to burst into tears. "No, it isn't real," she sobbed. "It was a dream! You can't have taken those leaves from a dream!"

"Val followed you," the king said while all around him his daughters wept as if their hearts had broken. "He brought these back with him to show me."

"How could it have been real?" Aster whispered, shivering in her bed while tears slipped down her face. "We were—we pledged ourselves in marriage to—we danced with—"

"Dead princes," Val said. She stared at him, her face as white as alabaster. "Which dead princes?" she asked

Patricia A. McKillip

him. "The ones our father killed because of us?"

"I don't know," he answered gently, though he shuddered, too, at the thought.

She closed her eyes against a nightmare. "You might have died, too, Val, if you had not kept watch."

"I knew someone followed us," Mignonette sobbed to her sisters. "I tried to tell you. And you would not believe me!"

"You were all enchanted," Val said.

Aster opened her eyes again, looked at him. "Did I know you were there?" she wondered softly. "Or did I only wish it?"

There was another sound, the clang of the king's great sword as he drew it from the scabbard and flung it to the floor. Then he took the crown from his head and held it out to Val. "Take my kingdom," he said with great relief. "You have broken the spell over my house, and over me. I no longer want to rule; there are too many innocent dead among my memories."

"Well," Val said uncertainly, turning the crown, which looked too big for him, over in his hands. "There are worse things that could be."

He lifted his eyes, looked at Aster, for comfort, and for friendship. She smiled a little, through her tears, and he saw that she agreed with him: There were worse things that could be than what he had: a kingdom and a choice of flowers from A to M.

Patricia A. McKillip writes: "I read all kinds of fairytales when I was young. I loved the eerie and wonderful illustrations by Fritz Kredel in the copy of *Grimms' Fairytales* my parents gave me. They made the tales seem from a differ᠎ t world, strange and frightening and comical, where ᴗᴗnkeys talked and parents tried to kill their children, where love turned into terror, and terror into a life lived 'happily ever after.'

"I chose to retell 'The Twelve Dancing Princesses' because it has elements that stirred my imagination: an unlikely hero, twelve troublesome princesses instead of one; a subterranean world, which might be the place where dreams begin, or maybe where they end. It all depends on how you tell the story."

McKillip is the author of many magical books for children and adults, and has won both the World Fantasy Award and the Mythopoeic Award. Her novels include *Riddle-Master: The Complete Trilogy*, *The Sorceress and the Cygnet*, *The Moon and the Face*, and *Song for the Basilisk*.

She lives in the Catskill Mountains of upper New York state.

GREENKID

BY JANE YOLEN

We were sitting under a rowan with Dad's field glasses, Merendy and me. I was instructing her in the finer points of bird watching, which meant I was trying not to give either of us warbler neck. That's what comes when you stare up into the trees too long trying to distinguish one kind of fall warbler from another.

The woods had been exceptionally quiet for such a lovely September day. Hardly any movement in the canopy or underbrush, and it wasn't even noon, when things usually quiet down.

Above us, seen through the overlacing of tree limbs and leaves, was a slate blue sky, with clouds as flat and gray as aircraft carriers racing across.

D-Day, I thought. Or at least I hoped. *Landings ahead.*

I was thinking of Merendy, of course. Not expecting much. To be truthful, not actually knowing what to expect. My heart was hammering, though, which might have been what was scaring away the birds. *Look out, birds, boy falling in love here!* it was calling.

That's a joke. Really.

"Something moved. Over there." Merendy pointed one gorgeous pinkie in the direction of a tangle of bramble and witch hazel, because I had warned her about large movements and frightening the birds.

"Where?" I whispered. Whispering was important, and not just to keep from scaring the warblers off. I had just turned fourteen, and my voice—a late bloomer like the rest of me—had started to squeak at irregular intervals. It's hard enough to impress a girl who's just moved into the neighborhood if you're an eighth grader and she's in ninth, worse with a voice that sounds as if a good dose of 3 in 1 oil is not only necessary but past due. And I had to impress her fast. School started in a week, and after that someone that beautiful was going to be off-limits for the likes of me. She was high school material for sure.

"There," she whispered.

I didn't see anything where Merendy was pointing, but in our woods—deep and entwined—that doesn't mean anything. To see in the woods—to *really* see—takes a "long patience," which is how my biology teacher says a man named Buffon defined genius.

I'm not a genius in any other way, but in matters of the woods I do have a particular patient flair. To my certain knowledge we have foxes and raccoons, turkeys and deer, coyotes and an occasional bear.

I didn't know if Merendy had ever seen any of those before. She's from some kingdom or other in the east of Scotland, I think. Her father teaches at the university. He always stays in his study when I visit, calling out orders in a strange, strained language I don't understand. Merendy and her mother speak the same quick, consonant-filled tongue to one another, but a pleasantly accented and very formal English to me.

Since there are only the two houses on our little mountain and school hadn't yet started, I had Merendy all to myself. I wasn't going to ruin it with my squeaky voice.

"There," Merendy said again without a bit of annoyance in her voice.

This time I saw the movement too. I put my finger to my lips.

"Hush," I whispered.

She giggled, a sound like water over stone. And then she was still.

The forest seemed to breathe around us, a fresh woody odor. A ribbon of mist wound gently through the trees, making the sharper edges melt away.

I glanced at Merendy's profile, her straight nose, the slight pursing of her untinted lips, that glorious fall of white-gold hair. Then I looked back where the movement had been.

There! A slight tremble in a branch, but low down, so I didn't have to worry about bear.

Then the brambles and witch hazel parted, and—to my horror and surprise—a child toddled out onto the grass. A boy child.

Quite definitely a boy child.

I could tell because he was totally naked.

"Do not look!" Merendy cried out. It was not a cry of embarrassment but fear.

I stood. "Don't be silly," I said. "We have to get him back to the house. He must be freezing. And lost. And . . ."

She stood too, her back to the toddler. She stared at me with wide lake-blue eyes. "He is a Jack o' the Green, a trickster and a villain. We must leave this place. Now! While we still have the time."

"Are you out of your mind?" I told her, my voice cracking badly on the last word. "He's a baby."

But I spoke to her back, for she had already run off toward her house, that glorious white-gold hair like a wave across her shoulders.

I turned around to the little boy. "You sure better be worth it," I said, guessing that was the last I would see of Merendy except, perhaps, at the bus stop or across a crowded school cafeteria, or encircled by an admiring football team. I took five steps over to him and lifted him into my arms.

He stared at me, his eyes the light green of peeled grapes. Then he laughed, his little gums the same grape green.

Jack o' the Green Merendy had called him, whatever that meant.

Well, he was certainly a kind of green. Which definitely tipped the odd meter.

"Jack?" I said.

He laughed again and twined his little fingers in my hair.

"Ouch!" I cried, all oddnesses forgotten with the pain.

This time his laughter, high and delighted, filled the woods, and all around the birds suddenly began to sing.

I took him home, and he seemed to get heavier the longer I walked. I suppose all little kids are like that. Great big lumps of meat surrounded by charm.

Overhead warblers were wheeling and diving as if they were swallows. And a lone crow followed us from tree to tree, crying out raucously.

When I got to my house, the crow flew in front of us and landed on the lintel over the door.

If I had a strong imagination, I might have said that it cried out, "Nevermore." But it did no such thing. It just sat on the lintel and, when I pushed through the door, it decorated me with its own brand of punishment, a white splotch on the shoulder of my dad's Grateful Dead T-shirt.

The child—Jack—laughed out loud.

"Mom!" I called, and tried to dump the kid on the floor, only he clung to me leechlike and would not let go. "Help!"

The door slammed behind us, and I heard the crow flap away, cawing.

"Mom!"

She came at my call. I must have sounded really panicked. Normally her writing time is sacrosanct. Her word, not mine. It meant I had to be bleeding from an important orifice before she looked up from her keyboard.

"Good grief," she said. For a writer she had a pretty small vocabulary when it came to swears. "What are you doing with that child, Sandy?"

"Found him," I said. "Naked. In the woods."

While she took this in, she also opened her arms, and the kid—Jack I was already calling him in my mind— seemed to leap from my arms to hers.

Along the way he managed to rip my good shirt with one foot, kick over Dad's favorite Arts and Crafts jar with the other, and slobber in Mom's hair, turning a streak of it a strange green.

"You sweet thing," said Mom, oblivious to the havoc Jack had just wreaked with his one small jump through the air. "Who's your mother?"

"Mama," said Jack, and twined his arms around her neck.

"Umph!" she looked at me with dazed eyes. "He's heavier than I expected."

I wasn't surprised. He was also as large as a five-year-old. *Definitely time to put pants on that kid,* I thought. I went into my bedroom, found some boxers I used as shorts, and brought them out to the living room.

Mom was on the sofa and little Jack was on her lap. They were playing pat-a-cake, or something, their hands slapping together in a complicated rhythm that seemed much too sophisticated for such a little guy.

I came between them in the middle of one *pat* and one *cake* and managed to wrestle the pants onto him. He glared at me with his gooseberry green eyes and tugged at the pants, but could not seem to get them off, which was definitely strange since they were miles too big.

"Go away," he said.

I shrugged and turned, and the phone began to ring, which startled us both.

He screamed and put his hands over his ears.

I answered the phone.

"Do not let the Green Child into your house." It was Merendy.

"Too late," I said.

"Do not feed him. Do not tell him your name."

"Too late," I said again. "On the name thing. We haven't fed him yet."

"Your name or your nickname?"

"Oh." I thought hard. Mom had called me Sandy. But my real name is Sandor Christopher Vander. "Nick."

"Good." She hung up.

I looked over at the sofa. Mom and Jack were no longer there. Hearing giggles from the kitchen, I ran in.

Mom was stuffing Jack's mouth with Twinkies.

Twinkies? This was a sugar-free house. This was a Tofu "R" Us house. This was a We Would Be Vegans If We Didn't Like Eggs So Much house. Where in the world had the Twinkies come from?

"Mom?" I yelled.

She looked up at me with glazed eyes. Jack slipped from her grasp, now the size of at least a seven-year-old with that gappy lost-tooth look. He still was wearing the shorts, and there was a smear of cream across his lips.

"Sandy?" he said.

I felt my knees give. "Yes?" I answered.

"Cookies."

Well, I ransacked the kitchen for cookies and found a stash of Mrs. Fields. Dad must have fallen off the tofu wagon. At this point there was a sugar jar cracked open on the floor and tracks through the crunchy brown stuff. Mom's hanging herbs had been trampled through the mess. And seven free-range eggs had somehow been smashed there as well. Plus Dad's favorite flowered blue platter.

The phone rang again.

I picked it up. This time it was very heavy. I spoke into the mouthpiece. Or maybe I spoke into the earpiece.

"Too late," I said, my voice sounding like whale song, low and slow.

"No names," the phone told me.

I whale-songed back. "No."

"No names."

It was Merendy's father.

"Yes, sir," I said. "I mean no, sir. No names."

He hung up. I dropped the phone right into the egg and sugar and herbal mess.

Jack laughed at me. He was over ten years old, I bet. Mom was no longer holding him up, though she was still holding on. I felt the laughter sawing through me, cutting my cords. I collapsed on the floor.

"Jack!" I said.

"Sandy," he said back.

We were best friends. I would follow him anywhere. Idly, I ran my finger through the egg mess and then stuck the finger in my mouth. Vague thoughts of salmonella and other diseases wafted through my brain.

"Salmonella," I said. "Kissed a fella. Walking with her black umbrella." I giggled.

Mom giggled.

Jack, now a teenager, the muscle kind who would take Merendy away from me, just grinned. He deserved her, not me. He had the magic, the charm, the power. I was a nerd. A nerdlet.

"Take her," I said. "Take my girl." I was about to name her. "Take Mer . . . ," and something stopped me. Some little bit of memory.

No names.

I giggled.

"Mer . . . ," Jack said, coming over and staring at me, nose to nose. Green eyes to . . . "Got it!" He laughed and cartwheeled out our front door, going down the mountain toward Merendy's house.

The minute he was gone, I woke as if from a terrible nightmare. Saw the mess on the floor, saw Mom's stricken look. Thought about Merendy and the Jack.

"No farking way!" I shouted, and ran after him, leaving Mom to clean the place alone.

He had gone through the woods as if the paved road was too human a route for him. But it wasn't the quicker way. The road was. So we arrived at Merendy's door at the same time.

"Jack!" I roared, my voice cracking.

He turned and smiled. Definitely a high school senior. Football team. Basketball team. Track team. Class president.

"Sandy," he said, and raised a finger in warning.

"Not my name!" I cried, and head-butted him in the belly, which was clearly not what he was expecting.

He went down on his back and was about to get up, when Merendy's dad appeared at the door.

He raised his hand and spread his fingers in what looked like a Spock V, only the ring finger was flexed— which is just about impossible. I know, because I tried it later. He said something that seemed to rhyme, only not in English.

Jack's head snapped back, little black bugs streaming out of his mouth. Then he said a word that was probably a swear but in a foreign language, so who knows. And then—poof!—he was gone.

All that was left were my boxers.

"Burn them," Dr. O'Bron said. "With a branch of rowan."

"Rowan?"

"I will get it for him, Father." Merendy was suddenly at the door, looking impossibly beautiful.

"I . . . I . . ." The words stuck in my mouth. "I didn't tell him your name."

"You do not know it," said Merendy. Then she smiled to take the sting of her words away. "But I bless you for trying." She made a small sign with her fingers, and a feeling of total bliss came over me.

That was when I knew none of the seniors would have a chance with her either. That we would remain friends for as long as she stayed in our world. That I would love her till the day I died. And all that other fairy tale stuff as well.

It was enough.

❧

JANE YOLEN, author of more than two hundred thirty books for children, young adults, and adults, has been called the "Hans Christian Andersen of America." Of this story she says, "I have had a fascination for the Greenman for many years. There are all kinds of stories about this god of the woods, who is a kind of British Pan figure. He is pictured as both a trickster and a god of vegetation. When I was in the middle of writing this story, I was in Scotland and had just visited a famous chapel that has hundreds of carvings of Greenmen. What an inspiration! But as I am an American, I decided to move him across the ocean to a place near where I live, in western Massachusetts. The actual setting is the house of my good friend, Patricia MacLachlan, author of *Sarah, Plain and Tall*."

❧

JANE YOLEN divides her time between homes in western Massachusetts and Scotland. Her most recent books are *Hippolyta and the Curse of the Amazons, The Bagpiper's Ghost, Wild Wings: Poems for Young People, The Firebird, Bedtime for Bunny,* and *Off We Go!,* a board book. Her Web site is www.janeyolen.com.

GOLDEN FUR

BY MIDORI SNYDER

ᚲ

It happened once that a king went to war, and when he did, he lost first his fortune, then his crown, and last his life. But before he died, he sent his queen and infant son into hiding so that they might be spared. The queen and her son, Khan, lived alone with only two trusted servants on the edge of a great desert, where the sand shimmered golden in the sun and purple by the twilight.

"So like the palace," the queen sighed at a desert sunset, sand devils twisting into gold spires. "But see how I have faded," she said, looking at her garments that once were dyed a royal plum and now were threadbare and bleached. The queen undid the silver pins that held her hair and let the wind and sand drift through the graying silk.

Khan did not miss palace life for he scarcely knew it, and he found his riches in the desert. As a boy he hunted for the red snakes that sheltered in the cool shade of the rocks; he climbed the slender palms and retrieved handfuls of dates. He watched the hawks hunting in the distance, their wide wings spread to catch the wind. He brought home to his mother the pin scrub roses that bloomed with a sweet, dusty scent just after a rain. And in the night he marveled at the stars scattered like diamonds across the sky.

One morning the queen did not rise from her bed, and one of the servants called him to her side. "My son, I am not well, for this life in the desert without your father has grieved me more than I can say. You are almost a man now, and so I am ready at last to join him. The servants will beg you to return home, but do not, for that would be dangerous. Your father's enemy sits on the throne, and his men still search for you. You must cross the desert and find your future elsewhere." He bowed his head and she kissed him farewell. Then she sighed, turned toward the horizon, and died.

The servants wept and begged the prince to return with them to the king's land. But Khan heeded his mother's warning and could not be swayed. He gave them food for the journey, a small bag of the queen's jewels as payment, an old horse, and three blankets.

After they had left, Khan packed for himself—a skin of water from the well, dates and apricots, and seed cakes. Khan waited until the cool twilight, and then he saddled his horse. He rode into the desert, following the stars as they wheeled merrily in the sky. One star in particular attracted him, for it glowed more brightly than all the rest. He followed it until he grew weary and then, rolling in a blanket, slept beneath its watchful eye. He rose early in the morning and saw the star just before it faded with the rising sun. Setting his horse in that direction, he continued his journey.

It was on the third day that Khan arrived at the gates of a huge castle. It rose out of the desert like a giant's back tooth. The blue domes had faded to gray, and the mosaic towers had cracks. But no matter how loudly he called, there was no answer from within. Khan rode the horse around the base of the silent castle until at the back he found a patch of green grass growing near a spring. Three palms provided shade from the sun.

Khan and his horse were very thirsty after their journey, their water skin nearly empty. Man and horse alike dipped their heads into the cool water and dank. Then Khan let his horse feed on the grass while he unpacked the last of his food. He sighed at the two apricots and the half a seed cake remaining in his bag. They weren't much to fill the emptiness of his stomach. In the early twilight he looked up and saw his star trapped like a flickering moth between the castle towers. "Well," he said, "it looks as though I am here."

He was startled by a scurrying noise, and from a little hole between the rocks of the castle wall a small golden-furred creature emerged. Her whiskers quivered on either side of her pink nose. She squeezed herself through the rocks, and then, sitting on the flat stone beside him, she began to wash. Though tired, Khan delighted in the sight of the little creature. She was graceful as her tiny paws washed first her face, then scrubbed behind each shell ear; last she arched her neck to lick down her back. As she smoothed her ruffled fur, it shone in the setting sun like a spoonful of honey. She finished her cleaning, crossing her paws before her. Two black-bead eyes looked up at him.

Khan laughed, and though it was little enough for himself, he gave her his last seed cake. She took it between her paws, nibbling at the edges. And then all at once, she broke the cake in two and stuffed it into her cheeks. Khan laughed again as her small, narrow head became round and fat.

"I thank you, young lord," she squeaked. "You have a generous nature."

"Though it benefits you, small one, I fear it has done me little good," he replied sadly. "I have reached the end of my journey but am worse off than when I began."

The creature rocked back on her hind legs and wiped at the crumbs in her whiskers. "Not so," she disagreed. "In exchange for the meal you have shared with me, I shall tell you the secret of this castle. Behind these stone walls there waits a princess. It is said that she is very beautiful and wealthy, a ring on every finger."

"But why, then, does she live here? Away from everyone?" Khan asked.

"She is a prisoner of the Guardians, dangerous and long-toothed monsters," the small creature answered gravely. "But perhaps you will succeed in winning her freedom. A bride and a kingdom would be yours to gain. Are you willing to try?"

"Perhaps. What if I should fail?"

The creature *tsked* between two long front teeth. "You would die, as the others before you. But a man with a noble heart and a wise head cannot fail."

Khan leaned his back against the castle wall and considered. Above him the star twinkled brightly. "I shall try," he agreed.

"Sleep now, then. I, Golden Fur, shall watch over you and your horse."

Khan was amused at Golden Fur's offer to guard them, as small as she was. Yet when he lay down on his blanket, weary with hunger and travel, he found he could not keep his eyes open. It wasn't long before he dreamed of a woman with raven colored hair and almond-scented skin. In her black eyes, the stars gleamed.

Khan woke as the first rays of the sun slanted over the castle walls. Beside him was a tray with bread, fruit, and white cheese. Tiny etched glasses held tea spiced with mint. Golden Fur sat washing her face, her paws crisscrossing over her pink nose.

She waited until Khan had eaten his fill. Then she spoke. "Come closer."

Khan bent to listen.

"The gates will be opened to you today. Once you are

183

inside, the Guardians will surround you. Be brave, for they are fierce to look at, their claws like daggers, but they will not harm you as long you do not draw your sword. They will ask you to dine. Use your wits, mark where they sit." Then she yawned widely. "And now I shall sleep, for I am a night creature." She crawled into the pocket of his cloak and curled into a ball.

Khan went to the gates, and just as Golden Fur had said, they were opened to receive him. But no sooner had he set foot inside the courtyard than he was surrounded by the Guardians. There were four of them, and though they were longhaired beasts, they were richly dressed and reared back on two legs, towering over him. They had flat faces, their eyes emerald disks, and their tufted ears pricked forward from a ruff of silvery fur. They howled and hissed at him, and though their sharp teeth and gleaming claws frightened him, he did not draw his sword. They circled him, tails twitching, until, satisfied by his stillness, they sat back on their haunches and licked their terrible claws.

"Join us at our table," the largest Guardian rumbled in a deep voice.

"You honor me," Khan replied humbly.

"Well, at least this one has manners," the second Guardian whispered to the third.

"Mannered or not, they all taste the same," snarled the fourth, and a cold drop of sweat prickled down Khan's back.

They entered the Great Hall, where a fire roared in the hearth. Serving women rested on their haunches, pulling thin sheets of bread off the baking stones. Low tables were set with golden plates filled with rice, pine nuts, cinnamon, and raisins. Crystal goblets brimmed with steaming sweet tea. Silken pillows and thick carpets covered the floors. On the walls hung tapestries bearing scenes of royal hunts, the hawks flying over the scrubby forests of the desert hills.

Khan sat, being careful to note how the Guardians arranged themselves at the low tables.

"Well, my prince," rumbled the largest Guardian, "you shall cut the capon." The Guardian passed Khan a tray on which sat a whole roasted bird with plump breasts and brown crackling skin. The head was decorated with cherries and plumes of peacock feathers.

Khan carved first the head and, placing it on a golden plate, gave it to the largest Guardian, seated at the first table on his right hand. "To the father goes the head, for he must guide the family well," he murmured.

Then Khan carved the back and presented it to the Guardian with two gold earrings in the tips of her ears, seated at a smaller table to his left. Henna stained her whiskers red. "To the mother goes the back, for she shoulders the cares of her family and sees to their needs."

Next he carved the legs and passed them to a Guardian with silver-capped teeth seated to the right of the largest Guardian. "To the son go the legs, for he must run to follow his parents' commands."

Khan took the two wings and gave those to the Guardian with only one earring in the tip of her ear. "To the daughter go wings that she may fly away from her family to marriage."

"And you, my prince," rumbled the largest Guardian, "will you not eat?"

Khan was hungry, the sight of so much food enticing, but Golden Fur had warned him to keep his wits, and he knew that the food of the Guardians was not meant for mortals. He politely refused. At that the Guardians sprang up from their seats, hissing angrily and baring their sharp teeth. The servants cowered against the walls as the Guardians arched their shoulders and flattened their ears. Khan tensed, expecting the slash of those claws. But in a moment they were gone, disappearing into a cloud of blue smoke.

With them went the room's grandeur. All its rich furnishings were returned to stone. Even the wonderful food dissolved into desert plants with thick leaves and stout thorns. Brown lizards scurried along the walls where once the servants had sat.

Khan left the Great Hall, surprised to discover that outside it was already night. As he sat down by the spring the creature in his pocket stirred. She slipped out and, standing on a stone, began to wash her face.

Then she stopped, and the black eyes twinkled at him. "You have succeeded at the fist task," she said. "But now you must sleep, and I will watch over you."

Khan needed little coaxing, for he was very tired, and soon he lay fast asleep beside the spring. He dreamed again of the woman with raven hair and almond-scented skin. She spoke to him this time, and her voice was musical. She sat beside him and, in the soft breeze, her hair brushed against his face. Khan stirred and then realized it was Golden Fur's whiskers tickling his ear.

"Wake now, good prince," she said urgently. "You must prepare for the second task."

"I dreamed of the princess," Khan said, taking a piece of bread and cheese.

"And how did you find her?" asked Golden Fur.

"She's beautiful."

"Could you love her?"

"Perhaps."

"Good. Then listen again to the wisdom of your heart, and do not be swayed by the Guardians' generosity."

Khan smiled at the pretty creature, offered her his palm, into which she climbed, and then tucked her into his pocket. Khan went to the gates, and as before, they were opened to him. The Guardians appeared, and this time they were friendly, clapping their heavy paws on his shoulders in greeting. Their tails brushed against Khan's legs, sweeping the dust from his boots.

"Come," rumbled the largest Guardian. "Today you will choose a token from our treasure chamber."

The Guardians led Khan to a room, and as he entered he was nearly blinded by the light of so many jewels.

"Perhaps this never-empty chest of gold to keep your love in splendor," suggested the largest Guardian.

"Or a crown to circle her head," said the Guardian with the two earrings in her tufted ears.

"You could protect her against all enemies with this sword," exclaimed the Guardian with the silver-capped teeth. He slashed at the air with a whistling sword of polished steel.

"A gold ring for her finger," sighed the last Guardian with the one earring in her pointed ear. She dangled a ring with a smoky topaz from one claw.

Khan stared in awe at the magnificent wealth of the treasure chamber and felt sorely tempted. Never in his life had he seen such riches. Yet as he walked through the glittering room the jewels seemed cold, like shards of colored ice. He didn't touch them but did as Golden Fur bid him and waited for the wisdom of his heart to choose. He searched among the splendid jewels until at last something caught his eye. "I will take this," he said, holding up a pomegranate, its rind tough as rust-colored leather.

"Is that all?" demanded the largest Guardian.

"It is all I want," the prince replied.

The Guardians howled and spat, flames igniting in their emerald eyes. But as before, they disappeared into a cloud of blue smoke. The bright jewels became rocks, the sword a twisted stick, and the chest of gold held withered leaves. Only the pomegranate in his hand remained.

Khan left the castle and saw again that it was night. He sat by the spring, waiting for Golden Fur to wake. She wriggled free of his pocket and sat on a stone to wash her face. When she was done, she crossed her paws and sniffed the air.

"You have the pomegranate," she said. "Open it and see what is inside."

Khan pried away the leathery rind and saw that the rows of seeds were carved from chips of rubies.

"Those are tears shed by the princess," said Golden Fur.

Khan gathered them into a cloth.

"Do they not please you?" Golden Fur asked.

"I would rather be poor than gain wealth by her unhappiness," Khan sighed.

He lay down to sleep, and soon he was dreaming of the princess. Her long black hair flowed over her shoulder, and her starlit eyes captivated his heart. In his dream they walked through a flowering garden, sharing their innermost thoughts. Khan bent his head to kiss the princess, but instead of her lips he felt the soft tickling of Golden Fur's whiskers on his cheek.

"Rise, my prince, for today is the last trial."

Khan woke and saw a tray of bread and cheese. He ate sparingly and drank a small sip of the water.

"I dreamed of the princess again," he said.

"And how did you find her?"

"More beautiful than before," he replied.

"Do you love her?"

"Yes," Khan answered. "I think I do." He rose, eager to be done with the final task. "What must I do?" he asked Golden Fur.

She lowered her head, her whiskers quivering. "There is nothing I can say, for no other suitor has yet come so far."

Khan gathered Golden Fur into his palm. He smelled the sweet scent of almonds on her fur. "Don't worry, small one." He tucked her into his pocket, and with the bold courage that comes from love he strode through the castle gates.

The Guardians were there to meet him, seated on jeweled thrones. Over their shoulders they wore mantles made from golden fur. The largest Guardian, his black-tipped ears flat against his skull, rose to greet Khan.

"For your final task, my prince, we demand that you bring us one more pelt of fur to complete my mantle." The Guardian held up his cloak and showed Khan the bare spot at the hem about the size of Golden Fur's back. "Do this, and the princess and her kingdom are yours. Fail, and we will tear you apart with our claws."

Khan's blood ran cold. In his pocket Golden Fur trembled. Slowly Khan began to search the rooms of the castle, wondering what he should do. The Guardians followed close behind him, their claws clicking against the stones, their breath hot on his neck.

When he came to the last room, Khan realized it was useless to pretend any longer. He turned to the Guardians with a heavy heart. There were no other creatures with golden fur but the one hiding in his pocket, and he knew as he faced the Guardians that he would not betray her. He thought of the princess and her sad smile, and though he loved her, he hoped she would understand.

"Well?" hissed the largest Guardian.

"I cannot find the creature you seek," Khan answered simply.

"Are you sure?" asked the second Guardian. She lifted her nose and sniffed the air. "I can smell it close by," she growled.

"No," Khan said, tightening his hand on the hilt of his sword.

Without warning, Golden Fur wriggled out of his pocket. She scampered quickly across the tiled floor.

The largest Guardian drew back one huge paw, claws extended to strike. Khan threw himself between the great paw and Golden Fur. The sharp claws cut deep, scoring five crimson lines across his chest. Khan fell, the pain blinding him to all but the sight of Golden Fur trapped between the claws of the second Guardian, her earrings jingling as she ducked her head to nip at the creature beneath her paw.

"No!" Khan shouted and, despite his pain, released his sword and struck the largest Guardian in the chest as the monster pounced. To Khan's amazement his sword passed through the Guardian with ease, and the Guardian's hollow head, still snarling, rolled across the floor. Blue smoke steamed from the depths of the headless body. The Guardian with silver-capped teeth attacked Khan, and with a renewed courage Khan countered with his sword, sparks flying as the edge of his sword slid against the polished claws. But as before, Khan's sword slashed through the body of the howling Guardian, and his form split apart like the two halves of a gourd. Scorpions and centipedes rushed from the empty husk.

"Release Golden Fur," Khan shouted as he stood, his

legs trembling and weak, and faced the third Guardian. She hunched her shoulders, her fur bristled, and her twitching tail whipped up a storm of dust, blinding him. Khan raised his arm to shield his face from the driving sand and saw, just in time, the emerald disks of her eyes as she lunged for him. He slipped to the side and drove his sword into her pelt. Steam hissed and coiled in the sand, and she crumpled like old paper before his astonished eyes. The last Guardian fled the hall, but as she leaped across the threshold, she burst into flames and were quickly turned into black ash.

And then around him, as swiftly as the desert dissolves one dune into another, the castle and all its domes and towers crumbled into fine sand and was tossed into the wind.

There was no one left except himself and Golden Fur curled in a ball on the edge of a small oasis. Khan heard the anxious whinnying of his horse, and he called to the stallion not to fear. His legs were weak and he sank to his knees, the blood from his wounds staining the front of his shirt. He picked up Golden Fur gently. She lifted her small head, her black-bead eyes damp with tiny glistening tears that turned red as pomegranate seeds.

"Ah, Prince," she said, "your courage has saved me. Take us to the spring."

Moving slowly and in great pain, Khan carried Golden Fur to the spring and laid her down in the dry grass.

"Drink," instructed Golden Fur.

He cupped his hands and took a drink of water. At once the pain in his chest subsided. He could breathe easily again. The blood stopped flowing, and the gashes knitted whole until the skin of his chest was smooth and unmarked as before.

Golden Fur dipped her head, and her whiskers worried the surface of the water as her tongue lapped a drop. "Free," she said.

Her fur began to split down the back and then fall away. From within the tiny body something large struggled to get out. He stepped back as a coil of golden, rose-scented smoke rose from the small creature. The smoke cleared, and there standing before him was the woman in his dreams. She shook out her long black hair and gave a musical laugh. The stars sparkled in her dark eyes, and the wind carried the scent of almonds. She reached down and, taking the lifeless body of Golden Fur in her palms, breathed across the honey fur. Khan saw the creature stir and come to life again. She twitched her pink nose, pricked her ears, and without a word scampered from the princess's hands, disappearing into a small hole in the sand.

The princess smiled at the astonished young man. "I am the Princess Sofia. My father was once a powerful magician. He died when I was still young, and fearing that my wealth and power would endanger my life, he placed me into the little creature. He made the Guardians from paper, wheat, and water, and breathed life into them that they should protect me. Last he set the tasks, hoping that one day there might be a man worthy of my love. You were the only one generous and brave enough to help a small creature such as Golden Fur."

Khan took her hands and glanced sadly at the desert. "I have no other wealth but my love to offer you," he said. "And I fear that yours has disappeared with the desert wind."

The Princess Sofia laughed. "Love is the only wealth that matters." She turned to the barren dunes and opened wide her arms.

Around them the desert changed, becoming rolling hills of green grass. Flowers bloomed and palms sprouted from rocks, lifting graceful fronds to the blue sky. Water bubbled from the little spring and flowed into a sparkling pond and then a river. A castle shaped itself out of white clouds, the marble towers etched with flowers and calligraphy, the blue domes the color of the sky. A thick carpet of moss and ferns grew around the castle walls, while overhead doves cooed in their nests in the eaves. Falcons launched into the wind from the gold-roofed minarets.

"Look there," said the princess. "Those are my subjects returning." On a road cut into a valley of ripening wheat Khan saw wagons pulled by teams of oxen. Herd boys and farmers shouted, their dogs barking as they guided their sheep and cattle over the hills. A woman waved a bright-colored scarf in greeting. Children skipped beside a musician who marched along the road playing a fiddle as people streamed toward the castle.

Khan and the Princess Sofia were married soon after. For three days there was feasting and dancing. And so huge was the wedding cake that even now there are still crumbs of it to be found at the back of every cupboard.

MIDORI SNYDER writes, "When I was a child one of my favorite books was a large, illustrated version of *The Arabian Nights.* Long before I could read, I was making up stories to go with the enchanting and sometimes terrifying images on the pages: turbaned princes flashing curved swords, almond-eyed women whispering secret advice into the ears of sleeping heroes, feathered and furred creatures, and plates of exotic foods. I also grew up in a house full of cats, and much later, when I couldn't have cats, my daughter kept golden hamsters. One day I read that hamsters originated from the Syrian deserts and, recalling my old fairy tale book, which my daughter was now reading, I imagined them as having escaped from the pages of *The Arabian Nights,* pursued by Persian cats. I wrote this story for my daughter, who likes to invent stories too, and to celebrate all the 'golden furs' who have provided us with such charming company over the years."

MIDORI SNYDER is the author of the young-adult novel *Hannah's Garden* and the fantasy trilogy that includes *New Moon, Sadar's Keep,* and *Beldan's Fire.* She lives with her husband, son, and daughter in Wisconsin, where she teaches high school English.

CHAMBERS OF THE HEART

BY NINA KIRIKI HOFFMAN

My family lived next door to Bluebeard's country mansion all my life. We shared a hedge with him, and we could see the fruit-tree tops in his orchard above the hedge from our orchard.

Bluebeard lived well. All his horses were strong and elegant, his carriages beautifully appointed and maintained. His gardens flourished. Even from a distance, his house sparkled. Yet he made everyone uneasy.

I, the youngest of five children and the one most often alone, spent much of my time pushing hedge branches aside to peer between them. I saw Bluebeard in snatches; I knew that his head was bald, his brows thick and black, and that his eyes, under the shelves of his brows, held dark fire.

His beard, though, as everyone said, was a strange color of blue, lighter than lapis but not so light as the sky, more as though he had dipped it into the sky's reflection in a dark lake.

Like everyone else, I found him strange. On those rare occasions when I saw all of him, I shivered.

When I was young, my family kept our distance from Bluebeard with ease. My father, a merchant, prospered; we had friends all around us and could afford to ignore one neighbor.

After Father died, everything changed. None of us had learned Father's bookkeeping practices. Most of our money evaporated.

My three brothers joined the army. They sent some of their wages home to our mother, my older sister, Anna, and me. We had almost enough money to live on.

Mother made lace. Anna took in laundry and mending from the neighbors. And I, well, I foraged; sneaking was what I had always done best, and now I put it to use.

On my forays I observed several of Bluebeard's wives through the hedge and met two of them.

Our orchard was still bearing well when I met the first. She was chasing a small white dog, with little cries of dismay that her slippers grew wet from the dewy grasses of his garden.

I was picking cherries from one of our trees. The dog hid in my skirts.

The wife wore a hat so large it shielded not only her face but her shoulders from the summer sun. She did not want to stoop to pick up the dog, fearing paw prints on her dress, so I carried the little thing all the way back to her house and set it within the door. She did nothing to restrain it. It ran out again.

She cried.

I fetched the dog for her twice more, the last time asking her for a cord to tie it with. That was the first time I went into Bluebeard's house.

The rug in the living room showed a scene from some warmer country, where people sat outdoors and played musical instruments I had never seen nor heard, though somehow, as I leaned to look, I thought I heard an unknown song. The couches and chairs in that room were covered in cloth so soft it felt warmer and finer to the fingers than animal fur, and the colors were like flowers. Mirrors on the walls caught images of each other so that the room looked like it went on forever, framed in carved crystal. A cabinet against one wall held many small, marvelous bottles and figurines of colored stone, ivory, and pearl. The wife left me there to look. Each object was more delicate and astonishing than the last.

It was the most wonderful room I had ever seen.

Bluebeard's wife ran to the kitchen and returned with a cake sweeter than fresh cherries and laden with buttery frosting. I had never tasted anything so lovely before. The wife let me wrap most of my piece up in a kerchief to take home to Mother and Anna. She kissed my cheek and showed me out.

My hands ached with longing to hold the little wonders I had seen in the cabinet.

I met another wife in the evening, a year or so later. By that time we had had to cut down half our orchard for wood; my brothers had no wages from the army to send home, for the war had been going on so long no one was being paid.

I had become a daughter my mother had never raised me to be, one who skulked about at night, foraging for fruit from other people's orchards, beans from other people's bushes, eggs from beneath other people's chickens. My older sister held on to the rags of her dignity by taking in laundry and sewing, though the harsh soap roughened her hands. Mother was a little blind by then, or chose not to see how we put food on the table. She knitted endless pairs of stockings from wool my sister bought with laundry money and never asked where they went when she had finished them.

No one knew for sure what had happened to the wife with the little dog. Rumor said that she, like Bluebeard's other wives, had been carried off by disease—that there was something unhealthy in the air near his house, which, after all, backed on the sea marshes. Some of the villagers had seen him mourning her, his best carriage shrouded in black, the horses' heads capped with black ostrich plumes, when he rode out to take care of his business ventures. He did not bury his wives in the church cemetery. Some said he had sent her home to her family for burial.

Other rumors whispered of darker fates for Bluebeard's wives.

The new wife was pale and had a gloomy face. She was searching for herbs that bloomed at night, she said. Did I know where the Angel of Death mushroom grew?

"Is a mushroom truly an herb?" I asked her.

"Perhaps not, but it might work like one," she said. "My mind is troubled, and I want to make myself a tincture to help me sleep. The recipe comes from my godmother."

The pockets of my apron were full of apples plucked from Bluebeard's trees. I pulled the folds of my patched skirt forward to hide the bulges and led the wife into the Wastes, where high tide brought salt water so that no good crops would sprout, but one sometimes found shipwrecked things. There was a little hummock higher than the marshlands where curious things grew. I told her I had seen mushrooms there I didn't dare pick, not knowing if they were useful or deadly.

The wife gave me a strange smile, and I left her there.

It was not so long afterward that Bluebeard came to visit. My sister and I hid upstairs when Mother opened the door, for neither of us wanted to meet him; but our mother's voice was full of welcome, and presently she called up the staircase, telling us to tidy up and come down to meet the gentleman from next door.

Anna and I clutched each other's arms, then took turns dressing each other's hair and sponging spots from each other's best remaining dress. I thought of the rug I had seen in Bluebeard's house, how stepping on it had reminded me of walking on feathers.

We went down to the front parlor, the only room where we laid fires so we could work with a little warmth. Bluebeard stood before the hearth. He was tall and broad shouldered, his clothes darkest blue, his cuffed black boots shiny. Something about him made me turn my head away. I could not look at his face.

"Daughters, here is Mr. Thanos from next door, with such a wonderful offer," said Mother. She smiled. Her mouth looked stiff.

Anna and I curtsied. I fixed my gaze on the hilt of Bluebeard's cutlass. A tiny ivory moon face smiled from the pommel.

"My dears," said Bluebeard, and his voice was softer and gentler than I had imagined. "I have long admired you. I am in need of a wife. Though I hesitate to mention it, I can see that you have fallen on hard times." He glanced toward the table, where lay three withered apples from his trees in a chipped bowl, remnants of last summer's crop. "I can offer you and your mother comfort, food, and luxury. Won't one of you marry me?"

Anna and I clasped each other's hands, stared into each other's eyes. "Anna is the eldest. She most deserves the honor," I said, and my stomach soured.

"Sara is much prettier than I," said Anna. Her cheeks lost color.

I thought of the cabinet full of small stone marvels. "His house is full of wonders," I told Anna.

"Indeed," said Bluebeard. "The finest furs, the most beautiful tapestries, the most intricate carvings, paintings by the best artists in the world. My cook is skilled in the cuisines of seven countries. I have enough coal to last us through twenty winters, enough lands to raise wheat and mutton and fruit forever. My trading ventures bring me tea and spices from all over the world. The one who marries me will want for nothing."

Anna gripped my hands. I turned to stare at Bluebeard, forcing myself to study his face without flinching.

Mother could no longer see to match the colors for the stockings she knitted. We had to lay out the yarns for her. Though she didn't complain, I knew her bones ached with cold most nights; the joints of her hands were swollen and twisted. She would be so much happier if she could curl up beside a fire.

Anna looked at Mother too, then glanced toward Bluebeard. She shuddered and looked away.

"Mr. Thanos?" I said.

"My dear."

"I would be honored to accept your offer of marriage."

In the first month of our marriage I was happier than I had ever been before. Bluebeard was kind to me and let Mother and Anna visit and eat with us every day. He let me open the cabinet in the living room and take out each precious thing, delicately painted snuff bottles from

China, tiny metal, glass, and gemstone gods from distant countries with more arms and faces than humans had, cunning ivory carvings of mice and frogs and birds.

In every room of the house I found more beautiful treasures to admire. One cabinet was full of porcelain-headed dolls with human hair wigs and their velvet, lace-adorned outfits; each doll had its own wardrobe and accessories: tiny shoes that buttoned with hooks, tiny hats decorated with tinier ribbon flowers and the tips of feathers. I wondered if the wife with the dog had played with them.

I wondered what had become of her.

I hugged one of the dolls to me, stroked my hand over her blue velvet skirt. I touched her face. It was cold.

The library was full of leather-covered books with gilt-edged pages and marbled end papers. In some of them I found pressed flowers, the colors ghosts of what they had been when alive. I wondered if the herb-searching wife had left the flowers.

I did not ask those questions.

I found closets full of fancy clothes, the materials sturdier or more delicate or more beautiful than any I had seen before. The colors were rich, the fabrics sumptuous. Some clothes fit me. Some bore faint wisps of perfume from other owners. Bluebeard said I could have any of them altered to suit me. It suited me to have the warmest and the softest altered to fit Anna and Mother.

Bluebeard said that anything I found in the house was mine, one thing at a time. It became a game between us for me to search the house over and choose my favorite thing that day. The next day I would choose another, or the next hour. The house was full of marvelous treasures.

Even in the night, after we blew the lanterns out, he was kind, warm, and gentle.

I received a letter from my brothers. They said they were taking unpaid leave, as there was a lull in the battle. I readied guest rooms for them, imagining their pleasure.

Then my husband said he must travel to attend to his business. "Here are the keys to everything in the house," he said, handing me a great ring with a forest of keys on it.

"Everything?"

"Every door, every lock, every secret."

I held the ring. It was heavy with the power of opening.

"Even the dark door in the cellar?" I asked.

He took the key ring back, separated out the keys until he held a small golden one, its bow shaped like a heart. "This is the key to that door. You may open every door in my house but that one, Sara. I forbid you to open that door. If you do, you will know unending sorrow."

"What is in that room?" I whispered.

He looked away. His beard bristled. "It is the source of my strength, a chamber of my heart. It is the one thing I can never share with you."

I felt a small fire in my chest, a flare of hurt. I had married him to take care of my family, but wouldn't our marriage be better if I learned to love him? How could I love him if I could not know him?

He handed me the key ring and kissed my forehead. "I will probably be gone six weeks," he said. "Invite whomever you wish to the house, and enjoy our treasures. Order whatever you like from my warehouses; tell the cook to fix whatever you favor."

So my husband left me. Anna and Mother moved into the house with me, and we had friends from the village come for dinner. We invited musicians to perform and our neighbors to dance and play cards. The chef made wonderful confections.

I could not get the thought of that dark door out of my mind.

My husband was good to me. Could I not obey this one request of his?

But what could be in that room? What gave him his strength? What was so dear to his heart he had to hide it from everyone but himself? What was it he felt he could never share?

For four days I resisted. I made myself stay away from the cellar. There were so many other things to look at and play with. I took the gold key off the key ring and left it in the drawer beside my bed.

But every night before I fell asleep I thought of the dark door. My sleep was broken by my waking to wonder and fret.

One afternoon while Mother napped and Anna embroidered, I put the gold key in my pocket, took a candle with me, and went down to the cellar to stand before the forbidden door.

I rubbed my fingers over the key, with its heart shaped bow.

What could it hurt?

He need never know.

I would only open the door a crack, take a quick look, close it.

I could learn what it was my husband truly cherished.

I put the key into the lock.

It made such a little noise as I turned it.

I touched the doorknob.

Then I turned the key back to lock the door. Was I not happy? Did I not have everything I needed? He had asked for only this one thing. I should respect his wishes.

I took the key from the lock, dropped it into my pocket, and walked away.

I was almost to the stairs when I turned back.

What could be in that room?

What was the secret of my husband's heart?

I opened the lock, stood with my hand on the door-knob for a long moment. I listened to the house. A board creaked above me.

I swallowed and turned the knob.

I held the candle up as the door creaked slowly open.

It was dark inside, but a smell drifted from the room, warm and sweet, slightly chemical, strangely glittery in my nose. It brushed my throat with the impulse to retch. Hair prickled on the back of my neck.

I opened the door wider.

The floor was dark and gleaming. Against the

windowless walls of the room I saw long pale things.

I blinked. I put my hand over my mouth.

Could they truly be—women?

The bodies of women, their heads on the floor beside their pale forms, faces with their shuttered eyes turned toward me.

The tumbled gold curls of she who had chased her little dog into my yard. The high, troubled forehead of the one who had searched for a mushroom. And others, so many others.

My scream caught in my throat. I fumbled with the door, jerked at the knob. The key slipped from the lock and fell to the dark floor.

The floor was awash with blood.

I stooped and fished the key from the blood, my fingers horribly warm and wet and red, the worst questions rising in my mind: How could they be so fresh when some must be so long dead? How was the blood still wet?

There was a scent of magic, like flower dust, in this death-troubled air.

He had said this was a chamber of his heart and the source of his strength. What contract had my husband signed, and with whom?

I wiped the key on my skirt, pulled the door closed, and locked it.

My hem was wet with blood, and blood spotted my skirt. My fingertips were red with it. My throat ached with strangled screams. I gathered my skirt and fled up the servants' stairs to my dressing room, where I washed my hands and tried to wash my garments.

But this was no earthly blood. Its spots did not fade. I took my ruined clothes through into my bedroom, stoked the fire high, and burned what I could not clean.

I washed the little gold key. I scrubbed it with soap, and later with sand. As soon as I got the blood off one side, spots appeared on the other.

My heart was sick. I could see my future. My husband would return, and the key would betray me. He would kill me as he had all the others.

How could I live in a house that was also a tomb?

Had every other wife gone to look into that room?

I went down to my sister. "We must leave."

"Why?" She threaded her needle with green.

"I have disobeyed my husband. He will kill me."

She stared at me. Then she rose.

"You go upstairs and wake Mother," I said. "I have to pack."

Anna nodded.

I had thrown away wealth and comfort by turning a small gold key. I had found a secret I could not live with, a horror that would haunt me. We could not stay here. We would have to escape, start over somewhere else.

I took the apron with the most pockets and went down-stairs to collect as many small valuable things as I could find so we could sell them and make a new start. Anna would not take things, nor would Mother. I would provide.

I had just wrapped a jade dragon in a handkerchief

when shivers traveled over my back. I turned and found my husband in the doorway of the living room.

"My business went much swifter than I thought," he said, and smiled at me. "It is already concluded, to my advantage!"

"Welcome home," I said.

"What are you doing?"

"Polishing the treasures." I unwrapped the jade dragon and set it back on the shelf.

"Did you enjoy yourself while I was gone?"

"Oh, yes, Husband." I thought of the silent women in the basement, the river of their still-warm blood.

"Where are my keys?"

I pulled the key ring from my belt. He smiled as I handed it back to him, then sorted among the keys. "But one is missing," he said.

"Oh? Perhaps I left it by my bed."

"Go and get it."

In the front hallway I paused at the foot of the stairs. Should I run now? But then I would have to leave Anna and Mother.

I ran upstairs. Anna was leading Mother down the hall. "He is home. Go down the back way," I said, "and flee as quickly as you can."

Anna's face pinched. "Come with us," she whispered.

My heart raced. I had filled some of my pockets. Surely it was better to live than go down and join the other wives in the cellar.

But Bluebeard had horses and carriages. He was huge and strong. How could we outrun him?

I stripped off my apron and handed it to my sister. "Take what's in the pockets," I whispered. "Run as fast as you can. Send help if you can, but make sure you escape above all."

"Sara." Anna gripped my arm.

"Sara," Mother murmured, her face turning as she searched for me with dim eyes.

"I must delay him! Go. Take care of Mother." I kissed each of them and pushed them toward the back stairs.

Anna hurried Mother down the hall, glanced back at me. I gestured for her to go, and finally she did.

"Wife?" Bluebeard called up the stairs.

I went to my room and got the gold key. Then I went down and gave the key to my husband.

"Why is there blood on the key?" he asked.

Cold crept into my fingers and face. I trembled. "I don't know," I whispered.

"You don't know? I know very well. You have gone into the forbidden room." His eyes narrowed. He stared at me, then said, "Oh, Sara, I hoped you would be different. I always hope they will be different, but with you, I thought we had a real chance. Were we not happy together?"

Tears fell from my eyes. I had been happy.

I had been blind.

Even now I could smell the taint of the dark-doored room below us. I could never be happy here again.

Bluebeard unsheathed his cutlass. "Prepare to join my other wives."

Sobs broke from me. "No. Please. Please don't kill me. I only wanted to know you."

"No one may know me and live. You must die."

I hugged myself. "At least give me a little time to say my prayers," I whispered.

"Very well. I will grant you ten minutes, but no more."

I raced upstairs. What if I ran down the back stairs and out the back door? Ran, and never stopped? Had Anna and Mother gotten far enough away? No! I should delay my husband if I could, give them time to escape.

My feet carried me past my chamber door, toward the back stairs. I knew the land. I knew places in the Wastes where no one else had ever been, sanctuaries I could find where others would founder. I reached the head of the stairs and looked down into my husband's face.

He stared up at me, wordless. With dragging feet I went back to my room, then crossed to the window and looked out. But there was no escape from the window except to fall two stories to the ground.

I knelt beside my bed and prayed. I glanced to the bedside table and saw the latest letter from my brothers.

My brothers!

"Are you ready yet?" Bluebeard called. "Come down now or I shall come up to you."

I rose. "Just a little while longer!" I called through the door. Then I ran to the window. I peered toward the road.

All was still.

"Wife, are you ready? Come down or I will come up!"

"Only a moment longer!" Was that a plume of dust on the road in the distance?

"Come down now!"

"I'm coming." I clutched the curtain and stared toward the road, willing my brothers to come.

Yes. It was a plume of dust. Something was cantering toward me.

"Wife. You've taken long enough!"

I heard his footsteps on the stairs. I went out to meet him. He took my arm and jerked me down the stairs, then pushed me to kneel on the cold gray stone floor in the front hall.

"A moment longer," I whispered.

"Make yourself right with God, and then be ready to join my other wives," he said.

I clasped my hands, closed my eyes, prayed that my brothers would arrive in time.

"Good-bye, Sara," said my husband. He raised his sword.

Then thundering knocks came on the door. "Open up!" The door burst open and my brothers rushed into the room.

"Who are you?" roared my husband.

"Sara! What are you doing on the ground?" Michael asked. "What is this man— Hey, fellow! Put up that sword!"

My brothers drew their swords and chased my husband away from me. Somewhere in the back of the house the chase ended. I heard my husband cry out, a bellow of anger that changed to a cry of pain, and then the last sound of a dying creature.

I hugged myself, and then I cried, for the poor sad ladies in the basement, for the life of poverty I had left without a backward look, for the pleasant life I had thought I had with my husband, for the life I would lead now that I knew nothing was safe.

I keep the gold key on a chain around my neck, but always I wear it inside my clothes. The blood is still on it, even though we have buried the dead.

Now I run my husband's businesses and sell my husband's treasures. I have provided a dowry for my sister and captains' commissions for my brothers and fine things for my mother. I live in comfort I dreamed of and craved from the day I first set foot inside Bluebeard's house.

I often find myself fingering the key.

NINA KIRIKI HOFFMAN says, "One of my writing teachers, Algis Budrys, says people read stories because they're searching for survival information.

"I never liked the story of Bluebeard. But in the wake of the September 11 tragedy, this was the tale that gripped my imagination. I wanted to write a story about someone who looked into the dark corridors of another's heart where unimaginably horrible deeds hibernated, someone who stared into that darkness, lost her innocence, and yet survived."

NINA KIRIKI HOFFMAN's books for adults include *The Thread that Binds the Bones, The Silent Strength of Stones, A Red Heart of Memories, Past the Size of Dreaming,* and *A Fistful of Sky.* Some of her stories for younger readers appeared in Bruce Coville anthologies. Viking will publish her first Young Adult book in 2003. She lives in Oregon with three cats and lots of toys.

LITTLE RED AND THE BIG BAD

BY WILL SHETTERLY

ᕱ

You know I'm giving the straight and deep 'cause it's about a friend of a friend. A few weeks back, just 'cross town, a true sweet chiquita, called Red for her fave red hoodie, gets a 911 from her momma's momma. The Grams is bed-bound with a winter bug, but she's jonesing for Sesame Noodles, Hot and Sour Soup, and Kung Pao Tofu from the local Chineserie—'cept their delivery wheels broke down. So Grams is notioning if Red fetches food, they'll feast together.

Red greenlights that. Veggie Asian chow and the Grams are solid in her top ten. So Red puts on her hoodie, leaves a note for the Moms, and BMXes away.

Now, down by the corner is a fine looking beastie boy who thinks he's the Big Bad, and maybe he is. He sees Red exit the eatery with a humongous bag of munch matter and calls, "Hey, Little Red Hoodie Hottie. Got me a tasty treat?"

Red doesn't slow. She just says, "Not if you're not my Grams, and you're not."

This Big Bad wouldn't be so big or so bad if he quit easy. He smiles and follows Red to her chained-up wheels. While Red juggles dinner and digs for her bike lock key, the Bad says, "Take five? Or all ten?" and holds out both hands.

Red warms to his style and his smile—this beastie boy isn't half as smooth as he thinks he is, but half is twice as smooth as this town's seen. Red hands off the bag, the Bad peeps in, and his stomach makes a five-two Richter. He's thinking he's holding the appetizer, and Red's the main course.

Red mounts her wheels, takes back the bag, gives the Bad a gracias, and pedals off down the main drag, riding slow. She doesn't want to be a sweatpig when she gets to Grams's. The day's as sweet as a sugar donut, but Red's not happy. As she rides she calls herself a ho for flirting up a corner boy with Grams so sick. Pumping the right pedal is like pins. Pumping the left is like needles.

The sec Red rounds the corner, the Bad's off on a mountain bike, zipping 'cross town, cruising down alleys, cutting through yards, taking every shortcut he knows and making up seven new ones. 'Cause when he peeped in the chow sack, he saw the foodery's little green delivery slip spelling out Grams's name and address.

The Bad gets to Grams's front door while Red's still blocks away. He leans on the buzzer till a weak, weak voice asks, "Who's there?"

The Bad pitches his voice like Red's. "It's me, Grams! It's major munching time!"

Grams laughs and buzzes him in. She's laughing right until she sees the Bad, and then she's not laughing at all.

Red's the gladdest when she gets to Grams's place. Walking up to the door, she pokes her nose in the bag of Chinese tastiness, snorting peppers and garlic as if she were dipping her face in a spicy sauna. She has to smile. What can be wrong when a great dinner's coming?

In Grams's bedroom, the Bad thinks the same as a tap-tap comes at the door. He hops in the Grams's bed, calls, "Hurry in, my sweet surprise!" and pulls the covers up over his nose.

Red walks in the front room, saying, "You shouldn't leave your door open."

The Bad calls from the back, "It's just to let you in, my munchiliciousness."

Red heads down the hall, saying, "Your voice sounds funny."

The Bad calls, "It's just my sore throat getting sorer. It'll be better once I eat, my little main dish!"

Red brakes at the bedroom door. The place looks nice, if nice is a dark, dark cave. On the shadow that she knows is Grams's bed is a shadow that could be Grams. The shadow says, "Now, come snuggle your poor, cold Grams," and pulls the bedcovers back to invite Red in.

Red sets down the food, gives the shadow some serious squinteye, and wants to turn on every light in the room. Then she hears Grams, near to tears, add, "Or don't you love your Grams?"

Red says, "Sure do, Grams," and hops in bed without a doubt in her head. But when the Bad pulls her close, Red's a little spooked. She says, "Your eyes are way bright, Grams."

"'Cause I'm way glad to see you," says the Bad, pulling her closer.

More spooked, Red says, "Your arms are way strong, Grams."

"'Cause I'm way glad to hold you," says the Bad, pulling her closest.

And as spooked as spooked gets, Red says, "And your teeth are way sharp, Grams."

"'Cause I'm way glad to eat you," says the Bad.

Now, I could say that's when a bold cop hears Red scream, runs in faster than the Bad can bite, shoots down the Bad like the cold, cruel creature he is, finds Grams tied up safe in a closet, and Red and Grams and the cop all get the happy ever after.

Or I could say there's no scream, no handy cop, and the Bad has a happy belly glow for days, thanks to Red and her Grams.

Either way, there's uno problemo with my story: If the Bad dies, how do I know how he gets 'cross town? If Red dies, how do I know how she feels biking to Grams's?

Here's what's sure: One dies. One lives to tell the tale. And the one telling the tale is guessing 'bout the other.

Now, pick the end you like. But before you do, think on this:

The storyteller's still around. Maybe nearer than you think.

And everyone's got to eat.

WILL SHETTERLY writes, "The first version of 'Red Riding Hood' that I heard had great things: a girl goes off on a trip all alone, and a wolf tricks her into getting in bed with him. There's great dialogue: "What big teeth you have, Granny." "The better to eat you with, my dear." But it ended with a woodsman coming in from nowhere to save the girl. And I thought the point of the story was that she was too trusting. She deserved to be eaten.

"When I got older, I started reading about folktales. I learned that in the oldest recorded versions of 'Red Riding Hood,' she ends up Wolf Chow. But by that time, I was a little less bloodthirsty, and I understood why people like happy endings.

"So when I had the chance to write a story for this book, I picked 'Red Riding Hood.' Maybe because the right ending nagged at me. Maybe because it has a girl on an adventure, and a tricky wolf, and cool dialogue—"

WILL SHETTERLY is the author of *Elsewhere, Nevernever, Dogland,* and other works. He lives in Brisbee, Arizona, with his wife, Emma Bull, and their cat, Buddha. His Web site is www.player.org/pub/flash/people/will.html.

The Fish's Story

by Pat York

@

Mira was a lovely girl who lived on the edge of the great Inland Sea with her farmer father, a cranky Auntie, and her little cat, Sasha.

Mira's mama was gone. Years before, she had taken her little sailboat out to catch the great silver fish of the Inland Sea, but a great wind came up and Mama did not return, nor was her boat ever found.

The aunt came to visit after Mama was lost, and she never went home. At first she cooked and cleaned and took the eggs to the village to sell them, but as time went on she stopped working, sat with her knitting, and demanded that Mira do everything.

One day Mira was fishing for their supper from the little wooden dock that jutted into the Inland Sea. Auntie sat on the porch in front of the cottage, pretending to knit, but mostly shouting cranky and disagreeable things down the hill at Mira.

"There are no fish on that side of the dock! Move to the right where the little waves lap, or we shall all go hungry tonight." Or, "Mind your worm, girl; fish don't like soggy bait!"

Mira sighed and did as she was told. Suddenly, when her fresh bait touched the water, it was snatched by something large and heavy and bright silver.

Mira was a fine fisher. She played the fish carefully, never pulling too hard and never giving too much line, and soon the great fish was hers! She pulled it onto the dock with her net and was about to put it into her little wicker creel when the fish opened its mouth and spoke to her. "Fortunate girl, I am no mortal fish, but a magic fish! This has been a painful day for me. You are the second human to catch me. Release me now, as the old fisherman across the bay released me, and I will be forever in your debt."

Mira knew the old fisherman across the bay. He and his old wife lived in a crusty barrel that had once been used to ship vinegar. She squinted across the bay to where the vinegar barrel once stood. Now a snug cottage hugged the hills.

"Good fish, I see that you are indeed a special creature, for you have turned the old fisherman's vinegar barrel into a cottage."

The fish looked troubled and answered, "The fisherman

would have released me, from a good heart, but his wife wanted the cottage."

Mira's heart swelled with pity. "I release you with my whole heart," she said, and gently put the creature back into the dark blue waters of the Inland Sea.

The fish stood on its tail, looking very beautiful on the water. "Pretty maid," it said, "you have done kindness today; may kindness come to you."

The lazy Auntie had by now made her way to the dock, and she heard the fish speaking. She looked across the bay and spied the fisherman's new cottage. She put two and two together and realized there was a fine cottage to be had. But she was a sneak who never said what she thought, but tried to get her way with smooth or spiteful words. Instead of asking for a better house, which was what she wanted, Auntie cried out to Mira, "Don't let that magic fish go, for pity's sake. Ask it for something—if not for your own sake, think of your poor cat!"

Mira hung her head and murmured, "Little fish, I would have let you go and asked for nothing, but for little Sasha's sake, let a fish of the Inland Sea come to my line with ease so that he will eat tonight."

The skies turned blue and little yellow birds fluttered by. "You are a thoughtful mistress to your pet, Mira. It is done."

And with that the fish dove into the sea and was gone.

"Fish! You asked for fish! Look across the bay at that tidy cottage! With its porch and garden and everything just as it should be, how happy would your cat have been in that cottage! How could you be so stupid?"

But what was done was done. Auntie stomped back to the house, and Mira threw her line again into the sea. Before the bait could touch the water, a great fish took it and Mira pulled it in. It was too big for her creel, so she pulled it onto the grass, where little Sasha played with it then ate her fill and fell asleep in a patch of sunshine.

Three more times Mira put her line into the water, and three more times a great fish took the bait and was pulled to shore.

Father was pleased and astounded. "Darling child," he said, "with this fine catch we'll have food for tonight and smoked fish to last us a month!"

But Auntie was not happy at all. She brooded and brooded about the cottage across the bay. Finally she could stand it no more, and she went to Mira's little room in the attic, woke her out of a sound sleep, and said, "You thought of your little cat, and all you could think of was fish. Well, fine. But now think of your poor mother floating in the deep Inland Sea. Would she be happy to see her husband and her daughter and her dear sister living like beggars in this tiny house? Would she not want silks and jewels for those she loved? Would she not want servants by the dozens?"

Mira thought all night about her mother, and in the morning just as the sun was rising she called out to the waters of the Inland Sea,

"Magic fish, magic fish,
Listen to me,
Your friend little Mira
Wants something of thee!"

The water boiled and the air thickened and out from between the waves jumped the fish, looking at her curiously.

"You are not the first caller of my day," the fish said. "That fisherman was by this morning. His wife wasn't content with her cottage; now she wants a mansion. Look across the bay!"

Sure as her eyes were true, there across the bay where their vinegar barrel had once been and then the cottage, there now stood a great mansion of stone with a fine lawn and a great boathouse near the water's edge.

"That is a lovely mansion," Mira said, "but I have been thinking of my beloved mother, who sailed away when I was very small. Father cut a stone with her name and a prayer that she would return, but she never did. Could I have a yellow rose bush for that stone?"

"Go to your mother's stone," the fish said ever so gently. "It is done." And with a flick of its tail it was gone.

Mira went to her mother's stone up the hill from her cottage, and there, climbing over the worn surface, were the most beautiful yellow roses she had ever seen. The roses draped over the words her father had carved like a mother cradling her child.

Mira was very happy. She picked some roses and

trotted back to the house with little Sasha bouncing behind. When she saw her father and Auntie, she told them her story.

Her father took the roses with tears in his eyes and embraced his darling daughter. "You have done well, child, for nothing pleased your mother more than yellow roses. Perhaps she will smell their fragrance and so long to be home that the sea will give her back to us."

But Auntie sat in front of the house knitting and brooding over the great mansion that stood now opposite their small house, across the bay of the Inland Sea.

And when night came, she crept to poor Mira's room again and woke the girl out of a sound sleep. "You did well to think of your mother," she growled into the girl's ear, "but what of your father? He lives here in this poor, ugly house and slaves in the fields all day to grow a little grain. Does he not deserve your attention too? Why should he work so hard and long, straining himself to plant and harvest his fields, when he could be the lord of a grand mansion?" Then she left Mira, sure that her words would pain the gentle soul into wishing for a huge house and servants for her dear father.

And indeed, Mira did think of her father all night. She loved him very much. To see him working all day, bending over his hoe in the fields, was a pain and a worry to her.

So in the morning she woke up before the others and ran down to the water. There she sang out,

"Magic fish, magic fish,
Listen to me,
Your friend little Mira
Wants something of thee!"

The water boiled and the air thickened, and out from between the waves jumped the fish, looking at her even more curiously than the day before. There was a little smile on its pale fish's lips.

"You are not the first caller of my day, pretty Mira. That fisherman came again. Now his wife wants a castle and will stand for nothing less. Look across the bay!"

Sure as her eyes were true, there across the water where their vinegar barrel had once stood and then the cottage and then the mansion, now there rose a magnificent castle with soldiers on the battlements and a great flag snapping in the tower.

"That is a powerful castle," Mira said, "but I have been thinking of my darling papa, who toils over his hoe each day. Would it be too much to ask, dear fish, that his burden could be lightened with a strong horse and plow?"

"Go to your father's shed," the fish said gently. "It is done." And it lingered a bit as Mira smiled and curtsied, then with a flick of its tail it was gone.

When Papa and Auntie awakened, Mira led them to her father's farm shed, and there stood a fine, strong mare with a gleaming black mane and tail and great, heavy hooves. Leaning against the wall there was a plow, a harrow, and a heavy leather harness with shiny bells on it!

And in the back of the shed was a tidy wagon to carry their farm goods to town.

Mira's father gazed in astonishment. "What is this, my dear?"

And Mira told Papa about the fish and its wonderful gift.

"You are a good and loving daughter," said Auntie, though the words burned in her mouth. "This horse and plow will make your father's work much easier. Yet look across the bay. The fisherman and his wife have a great castle where their vinegar barrel once stood. It is a gift of the fish and could have been ours."

"But we did not need a castle," said Mira, gazing in surprise at her angry aunt. "We needed a horse and plow, so that is what I asked for."

Her lazy aunt said no more but spent the day sitting by the fire in the kitchen, knitting and watching Mira bake the bread and wash the clothes. And always her eye slid over to the window beyond which the great castle of the fisherman and his wife stood.

That night she crept up to Mira's attic and woke the tired girl up. "I have tried to help you think of others, stupid girl, but I can see it is no use. Think of your poor Auntie who came to this terrible, small shack to care for you and your lazy father after my foolish sister went gallivanting off to sea. I want a little peace, Mira. I want to be cared for and pampered. I want a life of luxury and ease, in green velvet, with blue flowers in my bodice. Do you not understand? If you cannot understand what I want,

you are a cruel and stupid girl and I'll have no more to do
with you."

Auntie's words cut poor Mira's heart. She thought she
was a good and loving niece. Did she not catch the fish,
bake the bread, and keep the house as neat as a pin? She
did not understand what more her aunt could want. She
thought and thought until daybreak. She went to the edge
of the Inland Sea and with tears in her eyes called out,

> "Magic fish, magic fish,
> Listen to me,
> Your friend little Mira
> Wants something of thee!"

The water boiled and the air thickened, and out from
between the waves jumped the fish. It gazed at her with
sorrow.

"Ah, Mira, you look so sad! What has made you feel so
mournful? If I had known you were unhappy, I would have
come before you called, yet you would not have been the
first mortal I spoke with. That foolish fisherman's wife wants
to be an empress now and must have a palace. Just look!"

Sure as her eyes were true, there across the bay where
the vinegar barrel had once stood and then the cottage
and then the mansion and then the castle, there now
stood a monstrous palace as big as a town. It had a dozen
towers and many gates and armies of people in fancy dress
walking in the garden. It stretched halfway around the
bay, almost to the edge of her father's fields.

"That is a noble palace!" Mira said, forgetting her own sorrow for a moment. She sat down on the dock with her feet dangling in the cool water of the sea and looked at the palace for a while. The fish came closer and watched as, finally, Mira could not hide her sadness, and tears dropped into the water near it.

"Please tell me what ails you," the fish said gently, and it brushed a fin softly against her ankle.

"My Auntie came to stay with us after Mama went away," Mira said, "and she is not happy. I cook and clean and catch fish for the table, but she says that she has no peace. She says that she wants to be pampered and live in luxury and ease with a green velvet dress and blue flowers in her bodice. She says she will hate me if I cannot give her these things. But what more can I do for her, kind fish? I try so hard already!" And tears filled her eyes again, dropping now on the fish's head.

"You break my heart, gentle Mira. Will you not ask for something for your auntie? I can give her a mansion or a castle like the fisherman's."

Mira shook her head miserably. "I know better than to ask for such things. If Auntie is not happy with the sun on the water, good food on the table, people who love her, and a small cat at her feet, how will she be happy with a mansion? She will take her anger with her to her new home. She will hate everyone in the great house as she did in the small, for that is the way of the world. And that is why I cry. There is nothing at all I can wish for her that will make her happy if she is not happy now."

The fish smiled gently at Mira. "Will you trust me to grant you a wish you have not made? I think I know a way to give your aunt what she wants."

Mira nodded her head slowly, a smile of hope growing on her own lips.

"Go back to your house, Mira. I think Auntie is happy now."

Mira ran back to the little house and flew into the kitchen. Auntie's nightgown lay in a pile on the floor, and on the table stood a fine violet in a beautiful silver pot. Around the pot was a green velvet ribbon that matched the violet's green velvet leaves. Delicate blue flowers with yellow hearts grew from the center of the plant.

Mira was amazed. Her aunt was all green velvet and blue flowers. She lived in a beautiful home. She would be pampered and cared for by Mira and her father, and she would sit on the kitchen table and be admired. She was the loveliest thing in the house.

Mira shook her head. Her darling fish had done it! It had found a way for Auntie to be happy, for everyone knows that flowers don't get angry and are rarely ill-tempered.

She ran from the kitchen back to the water's edge and called for her fish.

When it came she jumped into the water and threw her arms around its gills. "You are the cleverest, kindest creature in the world. Auntie will be happy now and always with us. We will pamper and love her and enjoy her beauty."

The fish struggled out of her grip. "My own darling Mira, you must get out of the water. I long for your embrace, but it hurts me, and you will drown if you stay too long."

Mira climbed onto the dock, dripping and trembling.

The fish gazed up at her, love and longing filling its flat eyes. "You have been so kind to those you love, Mira. Do you not have any more wishes?"

"I wish I could be a fish and be with you," she said.

The fish rocked its body in the waves. "This is not a good life," it said. "Much as I love the water, it is cold, and there are so many hooks in it."

"Then, I wish you were a human and could live with my father and me," she answered.

"It is done," the fish said joyously, and in the water instead of a fish swam Mira's mama!

She climbed out of the water, laughing and crying, to embrace her darling girl.

"Ah!" Mira cried, and threw her arms around her mother's neck. Now Mama could return her embrace with all her love.

"How can this be?" Mira asked.

"When my boat broke up in the storm and I would have drowned, I was saved by a sea witch who wanted a sister for company. She promised me half her power if I would stay. My choices were few. I could agree or drown. But even then I could think only of you and your father. So I made the sea witch agree to a bargain. I would stay in the sea and share her power, but if a human asked that I become human again, it would be done. If I spoke a word of the bargain, the witch promised that I would die."

"Mother! What a hard bargain you struck!"

"It took me all this time to get away from the sea witch and find my way back to my own bay. And now because your kind heart made the request, you have your mama back to stay!"

"We are so wet! We should go to our little house and dry ourselves by the fire," Mira said.

Just then she looked behind them, across the bay, to glance once more at the fisherman's palace. It was gone! Where all the fine houses had been, there was once more only a small, crusty vinegar barrel.

"Mama! You took away the great palace of the fisherman and his wife," she exclaimed.

"Yes." Mama nodded. "The fisherman's wife wanted to control the sun and the moon. That was too much to ask, so I took it all away. They'll be happier as they are. They had better be. Now that I am human again, the powers the sea witch gave me are gone."

The two walked to the small house, and there they all live to this very day, with Father, Sasha the cat, and a beautiful violet on the kitchen table.

And sometimes the fisherman and his wife come to visit and talk about the time they were emperor and empress.

The farmer, his fisher wife, and their lovely daughter smile and say nothing.

❧

"'The Fisherman and His Wife'" has always been one of my favorite fairy tales," admits *PAT YORK*. "I loved the notion of getting anything I asked for, and I really loved the fish! But I always wondered why the fish never said no, why anyone would want to be an empress—I had a lot of questions! So I decided to answer a few of them by writing this story. I never did figure out everything, but I had a good time trying."

❧

PAT YORK teaches academic enrichment classes to children in first through fifth grades at Cleveland Hill Elementary School in Cheektowaga, New York. Her poem "A Faerie's Tale" was nominated for the Rhysling Award, and her story "You Wandered Off Like a Foolish Child To Break Your Heart and Mine" was nominated for the Nebula Award. She is currently working on a novel about small shopkeepers on the moon.

THE CHILDREN OF TILFORD FORTUNE

BY CHRISTOPHER ROWE

Ω

It's a good world. There are good places in it like Cane County,
where the air is clearer than glass and the streams sing.
There are good fathers in the world, like Tilford Fortune.

Mr. Fortune was a farmer in Cane County. His farm
was in rocky hills, though, and rocky hills don't make for
the best farms. But he worked hard. His back was broad
and he knew the weather and he kept his children fed. He
kept their clothes mended and the house clean and warm.
He did all these things alone, because his wife had passed
away.

Strong as he was, though, one day Tilford Fortune fell
sick. He'd long dreaded the day he couldn't provide for his
three children anymore. He'd prayed that they'd be
grown, with families of their own, long before his time

came to die. But Tilford Fortune knew the weather, and he could see that a storm was coming for his family.

He called his three children to him. The oldest was a girl of twelve, tall and straight with hair the color of the sun and fine as corn silk. Her name was Sally.

"It's a good world, Sally," said Tilford Fortune, "but sad things happen everywhere. It's been hard work seeing that you children have hot food. And now I'm not going to be here any longer."

Sally began to cry because she loved her father very much. "I don't know what to do," she said. "I don't know how to plant the garden and bake the bread."

"You'll have to go out into the world, then, Sally," said Mr. Fortune. "I have very little to leave to you children, no money at all. But what I do leave to you, you must make the most of."

Sally nodded, though she couldn't stop her tears.

"Sally, I want you to take the rooster that lives in the yard. If you find a person that's never seen a rooster, then that person will give a great treasure for it. Then you can buy food for you and your brother and sister."

Tilford Fortune's middle child was his only son. He was a sturdy little boy, ten years old, his skin as brown as a walnut from playing all day long in the sun. His name was Toby, and if he didn't always like his sisters, we can forgive him.

"It's a good world, Toby," said Tilford Fortune, "but sad things happen everywhere. I've worked long into the night so that you children can have warm clothes. I won't be here to do that much longer."

Toby began to cry because he loved Tilford too. "I don't know what to do," he said. "I don't know how to sew up holes in the old clothes or make new ones, either."

"You'll have to go out into the world, then, Toby," said Mr. Fortune. "I have very little to leave to you. But what I do leave to you, you must make the most of."

Toby nodded, but still he cried and cried.

"Toby, I want you to take the scythe I use to harvest the wheat. If you find a person that's never seen a scythe, then that person will give you gold for it. Then you can buy clothes for you and your sisters."

The youngest child was a pretty little girl named Molly. She was just four and so not old enough to remember her mother. She was a lonesome child and her eyes, green as the river, were always sad.

"It's a good world, Molly," said Mr. Fortune, "but sad things happen everywhere. I've worked hard so that you children would have a safe, dry place to sleep. But I'll soon be gone."

Molly's green eyes glistened. She loved Tilford Fortune most of all, and she began to cry. "I don't know what to do," she said. "I don't know how to make new cedar shingles for the cabin roof."

"You'll have to go out into the world, then, Molly, with your brother and your sister," said Mr. Fortune. "I have very little to leave to you. But what I do leave to you, you must make the most of."

Molly nodded.

"I want you to take the cat that curls at your feet at

night. If you find a person that needs him very much, then you'll know what to do."

Then Tilford Fortune told his children that he loved them, and told them to remember his last words to each of them.

When he was gone, the children of Tilford Fortune mourned for three weeks. But at the end of three weeks, all the food in the house was gone. The shutters had come loose from the side of their old cabin, and there were holes in the elbows and knees of their worn old clothes.

Sally Fortune went out into the yard then and caught her father's old rooster. "I don't know where in the world I'll find someone who needs a rooster, but I have to go look."

Toby didn't like following after his sister, but he remembered what Tilford Fortune had said. He found the gleaming scythe wrapped in oilcloth in the barn and went to stand behind Sally in the front yard.

Molly sat on the porch for a long time, stroking her tabby cat, which was dozing in her lap. She was afraid to leave her home, but she was afraid to be left alone, too. So she put the tabby in a wicker basket and went to join her brother and sister.

The three children walked down out of the hills, then, and into the world.

As they were leaving Cane County, an old woman called out to them from the porch of her house. "Where are you children going?"

Sally was in front of the little group. "Out into the

world to find our fortune, ma'am. I'm looking for some-body who's never seen a rooster so they'll trade me a great treasure for this one."

The old woman shook her head. "You'll have to get a long way from here before you find anybody that's never seen a rooster!" she said.

And the old woman was right. The children wandered a great distance, and everywhere they went they found roosters.

They took a little boat to a hot country covered with jungles. The trees were filled with wild roosters. They were loud and colorful, with a dozen shades of green and red in their wings, and tails as long as a peacock's, but they were roosters still, and no one in that country would give Sally treasure for her father's gift.

But a man who lived there took pity on them. "Sally, Sally," he said. "Do you know what a rooster is for?"

Sally didn't understand his question, but the man wore a friendly smile so she asked him to please explain.

"No one in my country needs your rooster because roosters are for dividing time. And we know how to divide our time here. In the morning, when those wild roosters in the jungle are crying at the sun, we've already risen from our mats and gone to our labors. Some of us fish for a little while in the sea, and some of us gather fruits in the jungles. Some of us go out with our spears and hunt the fierce bears so that we have meat for our feasts. And after a while, when we have enough, we come back to our village and share what we have. We take long naps in the afternoons. At night we light fires and play music and dance. So do you know who to look for now, Sally?"

Sally took her brother and sister and went to find people who did not know how to divide their time.

After a while the children found a great building that was as polished as a mirror. It was made of metal and glass and was sealed off from the sky. The children found their way inside it to a great room divided into much smaller rooms by strange cardboard walls.

There were dozens of people there, rushing around Sally and her rooster while Toby and Molly huddled together next to a plastic tree. The people were frantic and hurried, typing on keyboards and phones, rifling through papers and printouts, paging with pagers and meeting in meetings. They flowed around Sally and her rooster like a stream flows around a limestone boulder.

Sally whispered to her rooster and set him on the gray carpet. He filled his chest with air and let out a loud COCK-A-DOODLE-DOO!

And the people stopped. They all turned to stare and didn't even notice that their beepers were beeping and their faxes were faxing. A dark-haired woman who might have been beautiful if she hadn't looked so tired and worried leaned forward and said, "Little girl, why have you brought that bird into our office?"

Sally said, "To trade him for a great treasure."

The people all laughed, and some of them started shuffling away, blinking in the bright white electric light.

But the dark-haired woman said, "Why would we need a rooster, little girl?"

Sally said, "To show you how to divide your time."

The lady said, "But we know how to do that. See here? My watch shows me the time in Tokyo and Tripoli. My calendar has my days sliced into hours and my hours sliced into minutes. Our big white board has our meetings written out weeks in advance!" All the people nodded because what the lady said was true. They all had watches and calendars as advanced as the dark-haired woman's.

"I don't know what time it is in Tripoli, it's true," said Sally. "And this rooster has never been to Tokyo. But listen here. At every sunrise, he lets out a cry. If you're sleeping, when you hear him you know it's time to rise up. Then you can go out and do your work for a little while. When you have enough, you can all gather together and share what you've made or found or gathered. You can take naps in the afternoons, and at night you can build bonfires and dance."

The people there hadn't taken naps in the afternoons for a very long time. The beautiful lady—and she *was* beautiful, just very tired—took off her gold watch and gave it to Sally. "I could use a nap," she said.

A pale man dropped his great pile of papers to the floor and took a pager from his pocket. He put it in a pile with his portable phone and his car alarm deactivator. "I haven't been dancing since I got this job," he said.

And all the rest of the people there put *their* watches in a pile at Sally's feet. They took the rooster and sat him on top of the watercooler, and then they knew how to divide their time.

Toby looked at all the gold watches that Sally brought out of the sad building, and they made him feel a little more hopeful. He'd been afraid he'd never find anyone who hadn't seen a scythe, but if Sally had found people who'd never seen a rooster, then he could find people who needed the scythe his father had left him.

He lifted his chin because now it was his turn to do the looking. He led his sisters out across the wide world.

And lost his hope. For no matter where they went, no matter how many people he asked, Toby could find no one who marveled at his scythe.

Finally, they came to a misty island full of mountains and gardens. The houses were made out of paper there, and the people wore long silk jackets. The paths around the houses were kept clear of high grass by people swinging scythes much like Toby's. No one in that country would give him gold for his father's gift.

A lady there saw the children, and Toby looked so sad that she took pity on him. "Toby, Toby," she said. "Do you know what a scythe is for?"

Toby didn't understand the question, but the lady was very kind and explained.

"No one on my island needs your scythe because scythes are for clearing a space in the green earth. And we've all found a peaceful place among the trees and grasses. We plant our gardens where good things were already growing. We place our houses among the trees in clearings that the trees have left for us. Look at the brook there, and watch the old carp rise up to chase the dragonfly. We live in the land like he lives in the water, letting it flow where it will, and following the current of the blooms and birds. So do you know who to look for now, Toby?"

Toby took his sisters to find people who didn't have a peaceful place in the earth.

They heard the subdivision before they saw it. The great roar and clash of motors and spinning blades could be heard for miles around. And when they *did* finally come to the great brick wall around the brand-new neighborhood, they saw towering clouds of smelly blue smoke rising into the sky.

The development had a black iron gate across the street leading into it, but the children were small and slipped between the bars. All around them they saw huge houses on small yards. The houses all looked alike, and all of the yards were swarming with people.

There were men roaring around on giant lawn tractors and women blowing grass and leaves with grass and leaf blowers. They were using hedge trimmers with engines to square all the hedges and buzzing weed whackers to whack all the weeds.

Toby unwrapped the scythe from its oilcloth and walked into the middle of the street. The sunlight caught its keen edge, and the sounds of the engines died away until all was quiet. Not even a bird called because there were no trees in the subdivision for birds to rest on.

A sunburnt man set down his electric shears and said,

"Little boy, why have you brought that old hand tool into our gated community?"

Toby said, "To trade it for gold."

The people all laughed, and some of them started to turn back to the dry little lawns they'd been grooming. But the sunburnt man said, "Why would we need a scythe, little boy?"

Toby said, "To clear a place in the green earth."

The man said, "But we know how to do that. See all these machines? I can clear my lawn of unauthorized weeds in five minutes flat with my four speed lawn mower. Our vines never grow where we don't want them to because we spray them with poison spray. Our flowers stay in their tidy white boxes, and this whole subdivision is clear, clear, clear!" All the people nodded. They patted their machines but then hissed and sucked their fingers because the engines were still hot.

"This scythe wouldn't be much for taming vines, that's true," said Toby. "And you'd have to let your flowers grow out of their boxes if this was the tool you used. But see here. When you let the blooms bloom and the trees grow, you'll make a peaceful place on the earth. You can sit quiet in the shade and hear the birds sing. When the vine flows across the path, you can flow around it and have a little peace in the world."

Peace and quiet were hard to find in the subdivision. The sunburnt man thought a minute, then dug a big gold coin out of his pocket and gave it to Toby. "I haven't heard a bird sing for a long time."

A woman pulled off her gardening gloves and found another coin for Toby. She put it on the street next to Tilford Fortune's old scythe. "I'd like a little peace with the earth; I'd like the earth to feel at peace with me."

And all the rest of the people gave Toby coins or gold necklaces. They put the loud, smoking machines away and let the plants and animals come back to live among them.

When the children had walked a little way from the subdivision, little Molly sat down on the ground and started to cry. She hugged the wicker basket she'd carried on all their journeying in her lap.

"Don't cry, Molly," said Sally. "We'll find a man who's never seen a cat. Or at least we'll find out what a cat is for and take it to people who need it."

But Molly cried still.

"Don't worry, Molly," said Toby. "We didn't think we'd find out what roosters or scythes are for, but we did."

Little Molly shook her head. "I *know* what cats are for," she said. "Cats are for holding in your lap when you're sad or lonesome. I'm sad now, so I'm holding this cat here."

The lid of the wicker basket popped open, and the big yellow cat stretched out. He looked up into Molly's green eyes and started kneading her stomach. He purred and purred.

"But why are you sad, Molly?" asked Sally and Toby.

"I'm sad because we have to sell our cat," Molly said. "With all the watches you'll trade for food, and with all the gold you'll buy new clothes. I know we need a new house, but I love our kitty."

Then Sally and Toby were sad too because they loved the cat as much as Molly did. So they sat on the ground, and the cat went around from lap to lap, purring.

Finally, Sally stood up. She said, "We're being silly. There are plenty of watches and coins to buy food and clothes *and* a new house."

Toby said, "But our father told us to take the things he gave us and trade them for treasure."

Molly thought about the last thing her father had told her. "No, Toby. He said to find someone who needs a cat, and that I would know what to do then."

Sally asked her, "Have you found someone who needs a cat?"

Molly nodded. "We do," she said.

Then Toby asked her, "Do you know what to do now?"

Molly nodded again.

Then she stood up and put the tabby back in its basket, and she led her brother and sister home.

They traded the watches and the coins for food and clothes, and their neighbors came and helped them fix the shingles and the shutters on their cabin. In the mornings they woke up and went out and did their work for a little while. In the afternoons they rested among the wildflowers that Tilford Fortune had always let grow right up against the walls. And at night they lit bonfires and danced.

"Like Sally, Toby, and Molly," says *CHRISTOPHER ROWE*, "I live in a rural county in Kentucky. Like them, I once had to leave—and when I did, I had to work in offices and live in neighborhoods like the ones the children of Tilford Fortune visit in this story. I'm glad I found my way home."

CHRISTOPHER ROWE writes a column for a magazine based in his hometown, stories for books and magazines, and is working on his first novel. When he's not writing, he spends as much time tramping about in the woods as possible and working on the farm his family has owned for three generations, which also employs (at last count) 291 cows, thirty-one cats, and one little dog.

THE GIRL IN THE ATTIC

BY LOIS METZGER

@

Sitting on a small wooden bench, Ava could see the blue sky turn orange through the tiny attic window. The air smelled good, like wet leaves, and birds chattered as they always did in the early evening. She could hear her step-mother, too, tearing at weeds in the garden, cursing them for their very existence, despite her best efforts with pesticides and poisons. But Ava liked the weeds—tall and green, they looked good enough to eat.

She went to an all-girls' school, and that morning her stepmother had spoken to the school psychologist.

"She won't talk," her stepmother said to Dr. Fran Munder while Ava waited in the hall. The door was open a crack; she could hear everything.

"I've consulted with her teachers," Dr. Munder said.

"They say Ava talks, maybe not excessively, but when necessary. She's a good student. Maybe she doesn't have close friends, but the other girls don't shun her either—"

"You don't get it," her stepmother said. "She won't talk to *me*. I try—I really try. I think I've done quite well, under the circumstances. Ever since her father died—oh, never mind!"

"No, please." Dr. Munder spoke gently. "Go on."

"Well. He died several months ago. Sudden illness. A little cough—you think it's nothing. Well. It wasn't nothing."

"How frightening. I have a little cough myself."

"We'd only been married a short time. Whirlwind romance, very passionate, you understand?"

Dr. Munder coughed. "I wonder . . . Maybe I'll see the school nurse. This cough. Just in case."

"I didn't have children—never wanted them, frankly— but when Ava came with the package, so to speak, I was pleased. We didn't click right away, but I figured, give it time. Well, I tried—I tried hard. I got her a new wardrobe. Oh, I know she has to wear a uniform to school, but I got her beautiful weekend clothes and barrettes for her hair. She has very long hair—I saw her come out of the shower— it's down below her waist. Did you know that?"

"No," Dr. Munder said. "We ask that our girls wear their hair off their faces, off their necks."

"But she wears her hair like that at home, too—even at night! Does she ever wear anything I got for her? No. She had this old blanket, practically in shreds. Now she has a down quilt. I've created a dream-come-true bed-room for her, with a canopy bed and lace curtains. Does she spend any time there? No. She sits in the *attic*—that musty old place!"

"Perhaps she misses her real mother."

"She was only an infant when her real mother died. Her poor father had to raise her all by himself. That was why he was so happy, so grateful for me. He and his daughter were very close, but when the girl turned thir-teen last year, he felt she needed a woman to talk to. Well. If he only knew!"

Ava was summoned to the room. Dr. Munder had fluffy hair you could see through. Ava sat in a wooden chair next to her stepmother, who adjusted herself in a swivel chair, crossing her long, slender legs at the ankles.

"Ava, is this true, that you won't talk to your step-mother?" Dr. Munder asked.

Ava shrugged.

"You see? You see?" Ava's stepmother was a beautiful woman, even in anger, with high, chiseled cheekbones and large, dark eyes.

Ava, in the attic, watched the sun dip below the tree line. Sparrows and blue jays and even a cardinal flew by, from branch to leafy branch. She liked sparrows because they looked sturdy, and she liked blue jays, too, even their harsh voices. Cardinals, with their shocking redness, might be the most beautiful of all.

But that day a different bird showed up and sat right

on the windowsill. It wasn't much to look at. It was little and round, and had a light brown breast with dark streaks of brown, and darker wings with even darker streaks of brown. It tilted its head at her, stared at her with eyes that were bright and alert.

"Little brown bird," she heard herself say. "Are you hungry?"

The bird looked at the windowsill and flew away.

She ran downstairs to the kitchen, got a slice of bread, and came back to the attic. She tore apart the bread and placed several small pieces on the windowsill.

The little brown bird came back. It ate the pieces of bread and then stared at her.

"More?"

The bird flew away again.

This time she got several slices of bread. Lined up the pieces, and waited. But the bird didn't come back. She put the bread away in a plastic bag.

That night she looked up the bird in one of her father's books—all she had left of him, except for a few photographs. He'd been a bird-watcher and for years belonged to a group that went outside in the early hours with mosquito nets and binoculars. So. It was a house finch—female, because the males had a bright red forehead. So. The bird was a *she*.

The next afternoon Ava sat at the windowsill with the pieces of bread all lined up and ready. It was a beautiful fall day, cool and glowing.

The little brown bird came back.

"Hello! Are you hungry?"

The bird ate every piece. This time she didn't fly away, but sat there looking at Ava.

"More?"

"No," the bird said.

Well.

"Are you really talking?" Ava said, "or am I crazy?"

"I don't have time for this," the bird said, and flew away.

By dinnertime, Ava had convinced herself she had imagined the whole thing—including the tiny bird's surprisingly deep, vibrant voice. As always, she ate in silence, cleared the table, loaded up the dishwasher.

"Honestly, Ava," her stepmother said. "He was my best friend too! You're not the only one who wishes . . . wishes for something she can't have."

Ava went to her room. She slept in a sleeping bag on top of her mattress. She didn't like the new puffy quilt—it was too soft, too warm. She missed her old blue cotton blanket. And that new paisley wallpaper . . . it hurt her eyes to look at it.

The next day she went to the attic, spread out the bread. The bird came, and ate, and stared at her.

"All right, maybe I'm not crazy," Ava said. "Maybe you can talk."

"I can talk. Maybe not excessively, but when necessary."

That sounded familiar.

"You don't understand," the bird said. "Every time, they have to convince themselves they're not crazy. It's so tedious."

"So you've spoken to other people?"

"As I told you. When necessary."

"Why is it necessary now?"

The bird shook her head and flew away again. Such impatience! Ava would have to be careful. Maybe not ask so many questions.

Ava sat quietly while the bird ate the bread.

"All right, then," said the bird. "You may now ask for three wishes."

"I knew it! You're enchanted, and this is your punishment! You're a princess or something, horribly trapped in a tiny bird's body!"

"I am *not*."

Ava had ruffled her feathers, so to speak. "I didn't mean *trapped*."

"Never mind. Let's move on."

Three wishes. But she had only one. "Could you—"

"*No.*"

"But I miss him so much."

The bird said nothing.

Ava thought awhile, but not for too long, given the bird's extreme lack of patience. "I wish I had my old room back, the way it was. I hate what my stepmother's done to it—it's like something in a magazine, all fancy and frilly."

"Have you told her that you don't like your new room?"

Ava shrugged. "Not exactly."

"Never mind. Tomorrow you shall have your wish." With that, the bird flew off.

When Ava got home from school the next day, she couldn't believe it. Her room was her room again! There was a blue cotton blanket, almost identical to the one her stepmother had gotten rid of, and plain curtains fluttering in the window, and even the horrible paisley wallpaper had been papered over—with a lovely design, clouds and blue sky.

At dinner, she didn't say a word.

"I don't know what possessed me," her stepmother said, as if Ava had asked. "I had so many things to do today, and instead I changed your room all around, back to the way it used to be. Do you like it?"

Ava nodded.

Ava couldn't wait to tell the bird all about her room, but of course the bird knew. "Thank you, thank you," she said. "It's perfect!"

"Don't thank me. I wasn't the one who stood on stepladders and put up new wallpaper."

"But—"

"Next wish," the bird said.

She didn't have one ready. Her new room, and how happy and comfortable she felt in it, had occupied all her thoughts. She had to think. . . . "I hate all the clothes my stepmother bought—slinky pants with shiny studs, suede shirts with fringes, hair barrettes that weigh about ten pounds. I wish I had my old stuff back."

"Have you told her you don't like these new things?"

Ava shrugged. "Not exactly."

"Never mind. Tomorrow you shall have your wish."

Ava, home from school, rushed to her closet. Amazing! These were clothes she would have bought for herself—they were her taste *exactly*. Flannel shirts, sweat-shirts, T-shirts, pants with deep pockets.

"It happened again," her stepmother said at dinner. "I had so much to do, but I didn't do any of it. Instead I donated all your clothes to charity and bought you new clothes, like what you used to wear. Do you like them?"

Ava nodded.

"I suppose . . . Well. My mother was always buying my clothes, arranging my room. She said she knew better than I did what a young lady needed. It never occurred to me to question her, so when it came to you . . . Well. I just assumed. But, after all, they're your clothes, and it's your room, isn't it?"

She nodded again.

In the attic Ava couldn't wait to tell the bird how pleased she was. "Thank you, thank you!" she gushed.

"Don't thank me. I wasn't the one who stood on long lines to buy you all those new things."

"But—"

"Last wish," the bird said.

Again Ava didn't have one ready. She had to think. "I wish . . . I wish I had someone to talk to!"

"Tomorrow you shall have your wish."

Ava couldn't sleep that night. What would the bird

come up with? Maybe a new student would show up at school. She would sit next to Ava, of course, and they would hit it off right away. Or maybe one of the girls already at school would decide, out of the blue, to become her best friend. Or maybe the elderly couple in the house next door would move out, and a new family would move in with a girl exactly Ava's age. . . .

None of those things happened.

After school Ava went to the attic with several pieces of bread, but the bird never showed up. She felt cheated. *Three* wishes, the bird had promised! Three, not two!

Ava sulked at dinner.

"What's wrong?" her stepmother asked. "You look upset."

Ava said nothing.

That night she lay on her bed. Even in the darkness, something shiny caught her eye. There was something on top of her bureau, something that hadn't been there before. She got up. It was . . . a hairbrush. With a large silver handle. She ran her fingers over the bristles—not too stiff, not too soft. Exactly right.

She went downstairs and stood right in front of her stepmother, who was on the living room couch, reading.

"Did you get this for me?"

"Oh! Oh! You scared me half to death!" Her stepmother took several deep breaths. "Oh. That's better. Honestly, Ava, it was so quiet, and you haven't said a word in so long—" She looked at what Ava had in her hand. "Well. That hairbrush. It belonged to my mother. I thought . . . I don't know what I thought. I just saw it, and the next thing you know I put it in your room."

"It's wonderful," Ava said.

Her stepmother watched as Ava pulled an elastic band out of her hair. Ava had thick, gleaming, golden hair that covered her like a blanket. "Oh, Ava. You've let your hair down."

"Could you brush it?"

Her stepmother stood behind her and brushed—not too rough, not too light. Exactly right. And as she brushed, Ava talked and talked—the words spilled out of her. Her stepmother didn't say much. But Ava could tell she was listening with all her heart.

❧

LOIS METZGER admits, "I've always been fascinated by 'Rapunzel.' A wicked witch holds a young girl prisoner at the top of a tower. To get to the girl, the witch calls out, 'Rapunzel, Rapunzel, let down your hair!' The lonely, unhappy girl lets her long hair spill out a tiny window and down the length of the tower, and the witch climbs up. In the story for this book, a lonely, unhappy girl is also hidden away—inside herself. But, unlike Rapunzel, when this girl finally lets her hair down, so to speak, she frees herself."

❧

LOIS METZGER has written many short stories and several novels for young adults, including the award-winning *Missing Girls*. She lives in New York City with her husband, the writer Tony Hiss, and their son, Jacob.

THE HARP THAT SANG

BY GREGORY FROST

૭

It was Karla's idea to play on the riverbanks, and Beatrice, who would have preferred to stay indoors that gloomy day, suspected nothing. They played at being pirates. Humoring her younger sister, Beatrice asked what treasure they would seek, and raven haired Karla produced a rag bundle into which she'd put a few trinkets of her own. "You have to put something in too," she urged. Beatrice asked her what, and Karla pointed to the golden bracelet on her wrist. Beatrice clamped her hand upon it, reluctant to part with it. Her father had given it to her for her fourteenth birthday. But Karla said, "It's only for the game, Bea. It's only for a while. It isn't as if we're *throwing* it in the water."

Finally the bracelet went into the bundle.

They set out alone because the river wasn't terribly far from home, and because they were pirates and didn't need to share their schemes with adults. There had been a lot of rain, and the river was high and fast, dark and swirling.

Karla urged Beatrice to follow her, persuaded her to walk along the sharpest bank, above the angry river, to hide the treasure bundle. Then at the last moment Karla seemed to change her mind. She turned back. For a moment they stood almost nose to nose, and Beatrice saw her fate in her sister's eyes. Then Karla pushed her off the bank.

Beatrice cried out, and her fingers pinched at the air for something to catch her, but there was nothing, no root or dangling limb where Karla had turned. Beatrice plunged into the angry river.

Her head broke the surface and she spluttered, calling, "Sister, sister, help!" She choked and waved her hands. But the water turned her every which way. It spun her, tumbled her, hauled her against rocks, to which she tried to cling while the torrent tugged her loose.

High above her, Karla watched, so still that she might have been stone, so still that her sister never saw her. She watched as currents dragged Beatrice under, and dark blonde hair fanned out upon the surface. She watched until even the hair was pulled from sight. Then she knelt and opened the bundle. She took out the bracelet. This was her prize. It was the most beautiful thing in the world, and she had it now. She slid it onto her skinny wrist and tied up the bundle again.

By the time she reached the manor, she was hoarse from screaming. Along the way she threw herself into brambles and bushes. The contents of her bundle lay spilled along the path behind her.

Long before she'd crossed the yard, her parents heard the screams and rushed out to meet her. Servants, too—for her father was a great lord, and many people lived and worked on the estate.

Karla babbled her terrible story of her sister's misstep upon the banks that had tumbled her into the river. Most of the household raced to the river. Over the next few days they combed it, dredged it, took their boats miles downstream until the falls there stopped them. Her father didn't sleep in all those days. He stayed out with the boats, calling Beatrice's name until his voice failed him.

No one found her.

Her mother mourned for months, and Karla closed herself up in her room as if sharing the grief, but actually she was admiring the bracelet. Her father, though he mourned too, watched her so oddly then that she knew he must suspect. Outside of her room, she stopped wearing the bracelet. She worked very hard to make sure she gave his suspicions nowhere to take root. A stone—a cenotaph—was erected in Beatrice's name, and every day Karla took some trinket or flower or scrap of paper and placed it on the stone, creating her own personal memorial.

In time her father's suspicion ebbed. In time the loss of her sister translated into extra attention lavished upon her. Eventually she placed the golden bracelet upon the memorial stone. She didn't care for it anymore. She wanted something else. The marriage that had been arranged for Beatrice was renegotiated, and Beatrice's husband-to-be was pledged to her. Karla acquired everything of her sister's, and no one was the wiser.

Antonio had no idea where he was going, just that he had a sense he would find what he needed before he was finished. He'd lost sight of the rest of the gypsy camp. There was no path through the woods here, but his feet seemed to know the way. The gusting wind nearly blew his cap off twice.

Before he saw it, he heard the roar of the river ahead, and he emerged from the woods onto a low bank that led down to a mudflat bend. Protruding from the mud were two curved bones—two ribs from a rib cage.

Cautiously Antonio made his way down to the mud. There were a few other bones scattered across it. Old bones, from the look of them. Antonio took off his boots and walked barefoot into the muck.

Then it was as if the noise of the river faded away. The bones seemed to sing. Awestruck, he listened. The wind gusted and the bones sang again, a high but mournful note. The bones were small—too small to be a man's rib cage. A fawn's maybe. He crouched beside the ribs, and sunlight glinted on strands of gold so fine that he had to peer closer to see them. They were wrapped around and between the ribs like a spider's web. Here was the source of the odd droning—fine, long strands of golden hair drawn tight like the strings of a harp between the bones, and thrumming in the wind.

So, he thought, this was what I was after.

He dislodged the bones from the muck, then wrapped the silken hair around them. He didn't imagine that the hair and bones belonged together—had ever been part of the same creature—but he was a gypsy, and his world was full of connections and coincidences.

It was a year later that Antonio was invited to perform for a wedding banquet. He had long since finished his remarkable harp made from the beautiful bones, polished and carved with triskeles and small figures. The golden angel hair—and he had come to think of it as strands from an angel's head—he had wrapped tightly around the pegged strings to make them glint; he couldn't say just why. It wasn't the sort of thing one did with a harp, but some instinct had guided him, and the music those strings made was sweeter than that of any other instrument he'd ever built, sweeter than any his companions or anyone else had ever heard. That was how word reached the household of the lord who was throwing a banquet for the wedding of his daughter, and how Antonio, a distrusted gypsy, was offered a handsome fee to make sweet music before and after the ceremony.

He drove his wagon to the estate, accompanied by other musicians from his camp who would play krumhorn and bodhran beside him. It was the gypsy way: Good fortune was shared.

The banquet hall was spectacularly prepared, with flags and streamers all lavender, pink, and white. Rose petals were sprinkled across the floor, and sunlight cascaded in through the leaded glass windows. The musicians sat at the rear of the hall, in a boxed area to the left of the aisle where the bride would come walking. The crowd milled about, and everybody was finely dressed. They chatted and laughed, warming to the celebration. Yet when Antonio began to play, those nearest him stopped whatever they were doing and listened. Even the servants forgot themselves momentarily, in thrall to his music. His harp made it seem as if heaven itself had entered the hall.

Then he began a gentle lullaby. His companions exchanged glances, and Antonio himself seemed bemused by the tune his fingers were forging, as though they played without his command. He glimpsed a woman rising at the other end of the hall, turning, her face alarmed. The lord of the manor hurried to her and from her to Antonio, waving his hands. "Please, not that song," he insisted. Antonio made himself stop, though his fingers seemed almost to want to continue. He had to curl them into fists. "That was a song our long-dead daughter used to sing," the lord went on, "and while you've no way of knowing, it grieves my wife to hear it now. Especially on this occasion."

Antonio nodded. "Forgive me, sir, for in truth, it's not even a song I know." He set down the harp.

"Not a song you know?" asked the lord. "But then, how did you perform it?"

"I can't say, my lord. It was as if the tune were coming from the harp to me instead of the other way about." Folding his hands, he asked the others to play awhile without him, then sat most humbly in the hope that his lordship wouldn't require a more sensible explanation since he had none to offer.

Fortunately for Antonio, the time had come for the lord to retrieve his daughter. He departed from the chamber, and upon that cue people began to line up on either side of the aisle. More flower petals were sprinkled down the middle of it, and a white sash was tied across it at the far end. On the opposite side of the sash, the groom awaited, looking bold and merry, smiling to his friends and well-wishers.

The doors beside the musicians opened. The lord entered the room in a solemn promenade. Beside him his daughter, Karla, clasped his arm. She glanced at Antonio, and the bright excitement on her face clouded, though he could not imagine why. He had never set eyes on her before that moment. She reached up and pulled the white veil over her face.

Even as she hid her unease, the harp at his side began to vibrate, and the plangent music of its gilded strings formed into words that called out, "Oh, sister!"

Karla gasped and took a step away, pushing against her father. She stared into Antonio's eyes, and while his remained an expression of complete innocence, hers were one of horror-fueled guilt. She found her father's gaze sharp-edged with suspicion. Only the veil safeguarded her.

He took her arm again. "Come," he said, and led her forward.

On her first step, the harp's strings sang again: "Oh, sister, how could you treat me so!"

Crying out, Karla tore free of her father's guiding arm. She backed away, but the doors had been closed after her. She pressed against them as if she might melt between the panels.

At the far end of the hall the woman who'd become animated by Antonio's earlier performance now started up the aisle. "Beatrice," she called. "Beatrice?"

The harp sang, "Mama!" and the woman stopped, her hand pressed to her mouth. The young groom followed with uncertain steps behind her.

The lord and the gypsy both stared in wonder at the harp. Their eyes met, and each shared in a realization of what was transpiring here.

Her father returned to Karla. "We must continue down the aisle or give up the marriage," he said. "You know you don't want to do that." She, half mad, could not think how to deny him without confessing everything. His hand closed about her arm, and like a force of nature he walked her forward again. She stiffened as they came abreast of Antonio, but her father drew her on.

"Oh, sister," cried the harp, "envious sister, who drowned me for my bracelet and my place."

Karla wailed, "No, no!" but her father would not let her go this time.

"Sister!" cried the harp.

Karla collapsed at her father's feet. He dropped her arm and looked down upon her.

The harp ceased to speak, but invisible fingers played the lullaby that Antonio had been forbidden to perform. Like a small child, Karla clutched her father and begged, "Forgive me, please!" He stood, unmoved. She lowered her face and drew her arms over her head, as if the gown and veil might swallow her up.

The harp strings fell silent. "Forgive me, sister." Karla sobbed into her skirts, but the harp didn't reply.

His wife came forward as if to comfort the girl, but the lord ordered, "Leave her be." He stared darkly upon her. "I don't know what we'll do now, but love her we dare not. On the day she committed it, I suspected her crime. I saw her sister's bracelet upon her wrist, but I didn't want to acknowledge it. I feared to lose both my children, while this cold and witchy creature set about playacting the mourning sister to misdirect the doubt I had. She's as human as a watch spring. There's nothing she could say to me now that I could ever trust not to be the mechanism's cunning to gull us more." To the groom he remarked, "You're fortunate it was today this harp found its way here." He glanced darkly at Antonio, then took his wife by the arm and left the hall. She seemed ready to collapse as Karla had, but he would not let her, not yet.

The guests were left to wonder, to gossip and surmise. The family of the dazed groom surrounded him and drew him away, and quickly the others followed. They swirled around Karla like water around a rock, never saying a word to her. Soon the hall was empty. When Karla raised her head again, even the musicians had departed and the candles had been snuffed. But the lullaby played through the hall.

Karla got to her feet. The harp was gone. How did she still hear it? She covered her ears and fled the room, but the lullaby followed her into the hall. She ran from the house. The song pursued her there, too. Wedding guests saw her race across the yard and out a side gate.

In the woods the song clung to her. She pounded at her head to drive it out. The voice of the harp called, "Sister, sister, how could you kill me?"

She shrieked finally to drown it out but heard Beatrice even above her own screaming—as if Beatrice floated right beside her, lips to her ear. "Sister, sister."

She beat at her head, tore at the veil, at her hair. Her dormant conscience awoke in that voice. She ran blindly as if she could escape herself.

Without realizing, she ran straight off the bank above the river.

The current snatched her. She surfaced, choking, gasping. Her arms flailed for purchase. She struck a rock but was dragged along before she could grab on to it. Thus her sister had gone, and in terror she looked back at the bank, and maybe for a moment there was a figure standing there—she was spun about too fast to be sure. Her white dress billowed on the surface as if to buoy her, but claws of hidden currents grabbed at her legs and dragged her down. In the dark, swirling waters she heard her sister's voice, and she opened her mouth to cry, "Beatrice!"

After that there was only the uninhabited veil upon the surface, floating along like foam.

The lord caught up with Antonio on the road. The gypsy drove the wagon without speaking to his two accompanists. Despite the failure of the wedding, they'd been paid the promised sum for their playing, if grudgingly.

The two had bombarded Antonio with questions: Did the bones of the harp belong to a dead girl? Had he known all along? He told them nothing. The harp that had seemed extraordinary before now seemed to bear a curse.

Then the lord, riding alone, caught up with them, and the two vanished into the wagon and left Antonio to face what they were sure could be only trouble.

"The harp," inquired the lord when he'd dismounted. "Might I see it again?" Antonio turned, and one of his friends handed it to him. He offered it to the man below him.

With trembling fingers, the lord took the harp. He held it by its arms as if wanting at the same time to embrace it and fling it away. Forlornly he said, "She's gone."

"Not gone," replied Antonio. "She's been with you all this time. She was waiting for this day." He didn't know if what he said was true, but he felt it was something this man needed to hear more than truth.

"Would you—would sell this harp?" asked the lord.

"If you desired it, I would, my lord. It has more of your daughter in it than it does of my talent."

The lord nodded. He offered Antonio a large purse. "I don't know how to play it," he said. "Perhaps you could teach me?"

Before Antonio could answer, the lord plucked a string, idly, and the harp sang—not as before with the voice of his lost Beatrice. Now it sang in two distinct tones forming a perfect harmonic interval. Yet he had touched only one string.

Antonio dropped the reins and climbed from the wagon. The harp had never made such a sound under *his* fingers. He peered closely at his handiwork. Then he pointed at it in wonder.

The strings of the purchased harp were bound, each one, in alternating filaments of gold and raven black.

—*For Kayla and Dolly*

ॐ

GREGORY FROST says, "I love Pentangle. They are one of the great folk music groups, and one of my favorite songs of theirs is a piece called 'Cruel Sister' from an album of the same name. I had been thinking of writing a story from that song for a couple of years, ever since two other writers—Ellen Kushner and Delia Sherman—had invited me to contribute a story to an anthology they wanted to do, in which all the stories would be based on folk ballads. Alas, they didn't get to do it, but they had planted the idea for 'Cruel Sister,' and, thus, by the time Terri and Ellen asked for a story for this anthology, I had already written one in my head. The song ends with the revelations made by the harp, so it was left to me to find a fitting ending for it. I hope I have."

ॐ

GREGORY FROST is the author of six books and more stories than you can shake a stick at (if that's your idea of a good time). He has contributed to other fairy tale anthologies edited by Ellen Datlow and Terri Windling such as *Snow White, Blood Red* and *Black Swan, White Raven.* His latest novel, *Fitcher's Brides,* is a dark, disturbing fantasy that also comes from a fairy tale—in this case, from the story "Bluebeard." He has been a singer in a garage band, an illustrator, an actor in two dubious horror films, and a researcher for a television series. He promises someday to grow up.

A LIFE IN MINIATURE
BY BRUCE COVILLE

Once a poor couple worked at a place called TTT, which stood for "Tomorrow's Technologies Today." They swept the labs, cleaned the windows, and generally picked up after the scientists, some of whom were astonishingly messy. The couple lived in a small cottage at the edge of the TTT industrial park and would have been content with their lot were it not for one thing: They did not and could not have a child.

One dark and stormy night there came a knocking at their door. As they rarely had guests, this so frightened the wife that she threw her apron over her face. But the husband scurried to the door. There he found a tall man with fierce eyes, who was much bedraggled with rain and mud.

"My car has broken down," said the man. "May I take shelter here?"

Though he looked like a vagrant, the husband asked him in, partly because he had a kind heart, and partly because he knew security at TTT was such that no outsider could pass its gates.

What he did not know was that their visitor was Dr. Merrill Lyon, head of research at TTT.

After ushering their guest to the table, the husband dialed up some fresh coffee and hot bread, which the table swiftly delivered.

When Dr. Lyon warmed himself a bit, both inside and out, he noticed the wife peering at him from behind her apron.

"Come come, good woman," he said. "You've nothing to fear from me!"

After a bit more coaxing the wife lowered her apron and edged her way to the table. Yet still she seemed sad, and now that Dr. Lyon saw it, he noticed that the husband, too, had eyes weary with sorrow.

"Why such long faces? Is TTT not treating you well?"

"Oh, no!" cried the husband quickly. "We love our jobs!"

This was not entirely true but was probably the wisest thing to say under the circumstances since he could not be sure that their guest had not been sent to spy on them. "It's just that . . ."

When his voice trailed off, his wife jumped in with a vigor that belied her previous timidity. "It's just that we want a little baby boy, sir, and can't seem to have one. Oh, I want a child so much I wouldn't mind if he were no bigger than a mouse."

And that was how the whole thing started.

In his office the next day Dr. Lyon could not stop thinking about the wife's words, which almost seemed an invitation to test a bit of technology he had been tinkering with. Two days later he invited the couple to his lab, where they signed several release forms freeing TTT from all responsibility, then underwent numerous tests and injections.

Not many months after, the wife gave birth to a perfect baby boy. Well, perfect in all ways save one: He was barely the size of his father's thumb! Despite her comment to Dr. Lyon the mother was not entirely happy with this. On the other hand, the tiny infant was so dear that her whole heart went out to him the first instant she saw him.

Word of the miraculous child quickly made the rounds at TTT. Before long many scientists had come to visit the baby, who Dr. Lyon dubbed "Tom Thumb." (Though Tom's parents were not entirely happy with this name, they preferred it to Dr. Lyon's first suggestion: "The Spacesaver 3000, Mark I.")

Eventually even the daughter of the man who owned TTT came to visit. The girl, Titania by name and but four years old herself, was immediately smitten with the baby. "Oh, the dear thing!" she cried. "Please, can I hold him?"

Tom's mother, being no fool, passed the child to

Titania, who cradled him in the palm of her hand and wept bitterly when it was time for her to leave.

The next day came a knock at the cottage door. Before either man or wife had a chance to answer, in swept the little princess (for that was what the people at TTT called Titania), bearing an armload of gifts for Tom.

From that moment on the baby wanted for nothing in the line of clothing, as it was Titania's delight to dress him as if he were a doll. So it was that the child of the humble cottagers wore silks and satins and shoes made of the finest Italian leather—though it must be said that their cost was all in the workmanship, since an entire wardrobe for the lad could be made from a mere handful of scraps. Titania came to visit often and adored the tiny baby, though it did distress her that she often found him scrabbling around on the floor with the mice, who seemed to look on him as a special friend. Tom even trained one to carry him about on its back, as if it were a tiny horse. He named it "Charger," and the two made quite a sight.

Though he grew no taller, Tom seemed to mature rapidly, and when he was but a year old it was decided that he should join the children of the other TTT employees at their day care.

This did not turn out to be an entirely good idea, for he was constantly in danger of being stepped on by the other children. Moreover, Tom himself was the soul of mischief and loved nothing more than to slip into some child's pita bread then stick his head out from behind a cherry tomato and shout "Boo!" just before the poor

thing took a bite. These antics led to more than one case
of hysteria, several parental complaints, and two lawsuits.
Finally the vice president in charge of employee relations
decreed Tom would have to be schooled elsewhere.

When Dr. Lyon learned of the problem, he invited
the wee lad to come live in the lab. Tom's parents were
reluctant to let their boy go, but the doctor made so many
promises about the fine education he would receive and
the splendid people he would meet that finally, with
heavy hearts, they agreed. Tom agreed too, though he
insisted that Charger be allowed to come along with him.

Dr. Lyon had a dollhouse custom made for Tom to live
in. Though he mentioned it to no one, he also had the
dollhouse fitted with cameras and microphones so he
could monitor Tom's life.

Tom loved being in the lab, for all the scientists who
came through would stop to talk to him and compliment
him on what a fine lad he was becoming. In fact, by the
time he was four Tom had the wits and skills of a ten-year-
old. Dr. Lyon made many notes questioning whether this
was a function of his reduced size.

Tom was enormously curious, and he and Charger
were always prowling the lab to see what Dr. Lyon was up
to. Finally the scientist ordered Tom to stay on the table-
tops, saying he was afraid someone would step on the tiny
boy if he was running loose on the floor. This so frustrated
Tom, who now could not get from one table to another
without being carried, that one of the TTT engineers created a system of towers and bridges for him. Soon every

lab table had a five foot tower at each end, each tower being connected by a narrow bridge to the one at the next table, with the bridges sufficiently high that the scientists could walk below them with no problem. The kindly engineer added a system of pulleys so all Tom had to do was climb into a little cup and then hoist himself to the top of the towers.

Now he could travel freely about the lab and was much happier. Most of the scientists soon became used to the sight of the thumb-sized boy scampering about overhead. Dr. Lyon, however, seemed to be somewhat nervous about having Tom move around so easily. And after a while Tom noticed that every night the doctor carefully locked his center desk drawer. The boy wondered what was in the drawer that Dr. Lyon hid it so carefully, but as the man always took the key with him, he was not able to find out.

The lab was a place of great fascination for Tom. He loved the bubbling test tubes and the crackling power sources and the strange-smelling concoctions so much that even though Dr. Lyon repeatedly begged him to be careful around them, he could not resist getting too close—which was how he happened to tumble into a small pot of something extremely disgusting one afternoon.

The goo, as it turned out, wasn't an experiment at all, but something one of the lab assistants had been cooking for lunch that had been left on the burner too long and gone bad.

Tom thrashed and struggled to get out, but the gluey stuff held him fast. Even when the lab assistant picked up the pot and scraped it into the garbage, Tom wasn't able to make himself heard above the deafening music that the assistant was playing while Dr. Lyon was out of the office.

When the lid of the garbage can closed over Tom, he was sure his end had come. The darkness was so complete it was as if he had been swallowed, the papers in the can stuck to him when he tried to move, and every time he struggled too vigorously, he sank deeper into the trash. Twice someone opened the can to throw something in, but by that time Tom had sunk so far that the papers above him muffled his tiny cries.

He wept bitterly.

Finally the lid was lifted again—and stayed open. For a brief moment Tom thought he would be saved. But swift hands tied the top of the plastic bag lining the can, sealing Tom in. He felt the bag being taken from the can and cried out more desperately than ever. Alas, his voice was muffled by the jumble of trash. The bag was flung somewhere, moved, flung again, and Tom was certain he would soon run out of air or be crushed or something equally terrible. But he was not the sort to despair. With his tiny fingers he began to claw at the plastic that held him in. It was maddening work, for the plastic slipped and slid, but he finally managed to tear open a small hole. Thrusting his hand through, he waved it about, hoping someone would see him.

Someone did—an old seagull who was scanning the

trash heap for something interesting. Landing on the bag, the gull quickly pecked it open and snatched Tom up. Off it flew, Tom dangling from its beak.

The boy struggled and squirmed until he realized that if he *did* manage to get the bird to let go of him, he would be dashed to his death on the rocks below. What a choice: be eaten by a bird, or plummet to a stony death!

But when the gull flew out over some water, Tom quickly swung his legs up, wrapped them around the gull's neck, and began to squeeze. The startled bird opened its mouth to squawk. Tom immediately released his legs and fell to the water some thirty feet below. He struck hard and was stunned for a moment. He began to sink. But before he had a chance to worry about drowning, an enormous pike struck, swallowing him in one gulp—which was actually lucky for Tom, as it saved him from being slashed to bits by the pike's needle-sharp teeth.

Down the gullet Tom slid until he was in the fish's stomach, which burned him like fire.

This time he was sure he had come to his final moments. But as he was waiting for his doom, he felt the great fish jerk and convulse. It was flung around then smacked down, moving so violently that Tom had no idea what was happening at all—until he saw a smear of light. He began to shout and scream and thrash about himself.

"Well, well, what have we here?" cried a rough voice. "Something the fishie et is still alive. Let's have a look, shall we, missy? Always interesting to see what these beasties swallow down."

Tom shrank back as a flash of silver cut open the stomach wall. He covered his eyes to shield them from the bright light that flooded in. Then he felt himself once more plucked up.

"It's Tom!" screamed a familiar voice. "It's Tom! Oh, do put him down. Please, please be careful!"

A moment later Tom was standing on a table, and little Titania was gently pouring water over him to wash away the many revolting things that had covered him that day. "Poor Tom," she kept saying, and sometimes she would start to cry. "Poor, poor Tom."

"Not so poor," he said. "I'm still alive. But how did I get here?"

"That's what I'd like to know," said a deep voice.

"Who are you?" asked Tom, gazing up at the tall bearded man.

"I'm Titania's father, Arthur Kring. We were out for an afternoon of fishing on Lake TTT, and when we caught a fish we caught you as well. Thank goodness the captain here planned to grill the thing now. But how in heaven's name did you get inside that monster?"

After Tom told them of his adventures, Titania said, "Daddy, we can't let Tom stay in that horrible lab anymore."

Her father agreed (he agreed with almost everything his daughter said), and so Tom was brought to live at the executive quarters of TTT.

He sent for Charger to come live with him, but the mouse had disappeared and had not been seen since the afternoon Tom fell into the pot.

Though Tom mourned for his old friend, all in all his new home was very pleasant. He wanted for nothing at all since Titania doted on his every wish. But in time he began to have a hankering to see his parents and asked over and over if he might visit them. Finally Titania agreed and said that she herself would take him. So one morning the two set out for the little cottage where Tom had spent his earliest days. To Tom's surprise, he found his father in a state of gloom, and his mother in even greater despair.

"What is wrong, what is wrong?" he asked.

"We've been let go!" wailed his mother, throwing her apron over her face. "After all these years, we've been let go! They're going to replace us with those mechanical men Dr. Lyon invented. Oh, whatever will we do? Whatever will we do?"

"I shall talk to my father," said Titania decisively.

But now the little princess discovered the boundaries of her power, for Mr. Kring told her this was a matter of business, and in those things she must not interfere.

Titania was so vexed she stamped her foot, but it did her no good.

"I'm sorry, Tom," she said sadly. "I cannot help you."

"Perhaps you still can," said Tom. "There is a desk drawer in Dr. Lyon's office that I would like to examine."

"Why?" asked Titania, wiping away her tears.

"I'm not sure. But he was always so careful to keep it locked that it makes me wonder what is in it. Can you help me check?"

"I'll be glad to."

They decided that Titania would visit the lab with Tom hidden in her pocket. While there she would get Dr. Lyon to show her something on the far side of the lab. She would slip Tom out of her pocket, and he would make his way into the desk drawer to see what it contained.

"Why, Titania, what a pleasant surprise!" cried Dr. Lyon when the little princess entered the lab the next day. "We've missed you around here." He scowled slightly at her then added in mock seriousness, "I'm not sure we can forgive you for taking our little friend away from us."

"He's much safer where he is now, Dr. Lyon," said Titania. At the moment this was quite true since he was clutched in her hand, which was in her pocket.

With her other hand she pointed to the far side of the lab. "What's *that*?" she asked, feigning great interest.

Dr. Lyon, well aware that it was important to keep the boss's daughter happy, agreed to explain it to her. As he turned to lead the way, she deposited Tom onto the desk. Quickly he slipped into the center drawer.

In his hand he carried a tiny flashlight that Titania had had made for him. Shining it around him, Tom saw that the drawer was like a long, low chamber, one in which he could stand with his head just barely below the ceiling. To his right he saw an eraser big enough for him to sit on. Behind him were pencils as thick as his legs. Not far in front of him lay a file folder that would have made a nice tennis court for someone his size.

Tom made his way to the top of the folder.

"Spacesaver 3000, Mark I," read the label.

The words had a familiar ring, though Tom could not say why.

He lifted the edge, crawled under it, and began to read. Soon his tiny heart was pounding with rage and excitement.

Suddenly he heard footsteps. Titania and Dr. Lyon were coming back. "Wait, wait," he heard Titania say. "I want you to explain *that* to me."

"In just a moment, my dear," said the doctor.

Stepping behind the desk, he slammed the drawer shut.

Tom was trapped inside! His excitement turned to fear. Had Dr. Lyon known he was in here? Was he trying to catch him? Even if he wasn't, Tom didn't want to be found inside the drawer—especially not after reading what was in that folder.

Clenching his tiny flashlight in his trembling hands, he made his way to the back of the drawer.

It was sealed tight. He should have expected that; there was no way that Dr. Lyon would have a cheaply made desk. He was trapped.

Hours passed. Tom wondered if he would ever get out. Then he remembered that it was Friday. What if Dr. Lyon left for the weekend? Tom began to wonder if he would die from lack of food or water before the drawer was opened again.

Then, to make things worse, his flashlight went out, leaving him in utter blackness.

It was impossible to know how much time had gone by before he heard a scratching at the back of the drawer. New fear clutched Tom's heart. Was something trying to get in here with him? *Scratch. Scratch, scratch.* something was gnawing at the wood. The sound went on and on until Tom thought he would go mad with terror.

Then it stopped, and he heard a new sound, at first terrifying and then, when he recognized it, soothing. It was the sound of a mouse—and not just any mouse. It was his old friend, Charger.

A moment later Tom felt Charger's furry body rub against him. When he grasped his former steed by the tail, it led him to the back of the drawer where it had gnawed a hole just big enough for a mouse, or a boy the size of a thumb, to escape.

"Wait," murmured Tom. "Wait!"

He returned to the folder and with great effort rolled a piece of paper until it was no thicker than a pencil. He carried it to the hole and pushed it through ahead of him. Then he followed Charger through the hole.

The climb to the floor was treacherous, and Tom nearly fell more than once. When at last he was down, he embraced Charger. With the paper underneath his arm, he went back to the dollhouse where he had once lived, which was still tucked into a corner of the lab, and called Titania.

A few minutes later she arrived, guards in tow.

When Tom showed her the paper he had found in Dr. Lyon's drawer, her eyes narrowed in anger.

"Wait until I show this to Father!" she said.

Her father was angry too, not only at Dr. Lyon, but at the jury that awarded Tom half ownership of TTT in compensation for the company's unethical act of combining mouse genes with his own in order to make him come out so small. Dr. Lyons's plea that he was only trying to help humanity overcome its crowded condition fell on deaf ears.

It took several years, but the technicians at TTT finally managed to find a way to make Tom grow to a full two feet in height. At Titania's request they also found a way to shrink her to almost the same size.

Soon after, the pair were wed in a pavilion in front of the very lake where Tom had been swallowed by the pike. His parents sat in the front row, weeping and smiling, and cheered when the happy couple kissed.

As for Tom and Titania Thumb, they ran TTT wisely and well, doing much good in the world and turning a tidy profit as they did.

It was a short life, but a happy one.

"When I was eight or nine," says BRUCE COVILLE, "my cousin gave me a huge volume of fairy tales as a birthday gift. I doubt there was any book in my childhood that I turned to more often, or pored over more thoroughly, than that one. The mysterious quality of the tales it held was endlessly appealing to me, and thinking of it even now, I can feel myself drifting halfway into that other world it spoke of.

"I decided to work with Tom Thumb for this collection partly because I have always been fascinated by great variations in size. The very first book I published was called *The Foolish Giant,* and I have often written about characters who shrink—or were tiny to begin with.

"I suspect such tales appeal to kids because we all start out trapped in a world of giants. What is life for a character like Tom Thumb but an exaggerated version of what all of us experience as kids, when we find ourselves trapped in a world designed for people more than twice our size?"

BRUCE COVILLE was born and raised in upstate New York, where he still makes his home. He has published more than eighty books, including the best-sellers *My Teacher Is an Alien* and *Into the Land of the Unicorns.* Before becoming a full-time writer, he worked as a toy maker, a grave digger, a cookware salesman, an elementary school teacher, and a magazine editor. He is married to illustrator Katherine Coville.

LUPE

BY KATHE KOJA

Q

*Do you ever go into the woods? Not the park, always so dusty-*dirty, torn paper wrappers and splintery seesaws, four old trees leaned up like broken boards against the fence. No, I mean the *woods*, the place where the town's noise fades away as if there is no town at all; where the trees stand like an army, where the bears and wild pigs live, and Old Blanca the witch, the place all the grandmammas say *Stay away from!*

In the woods everything is different. The light slants different, like underwater; the grass is sharp and pointy with morning frost. And the smells—a hundred scents, a thousand every second: dead-leaf spice and bitterroot, mold and rot and berry, I couldn't guess or name them all but they don't need names, they just are: like the trees, the needle frost, the slanting light: and me.

In town I have a name—Lupe, for Guadelupe—and a family: Mamma and Papa and Fernando—'Nando, my younger brother. When I want to be mean to him I call him Feonando, because *feo* means "ugly" or "awful." When he wants to be mean to me, he waits till I go to sleep, then puts sweetgum in my hair; it sticks like glue, and the sugar-smell draws the ants. Sometimes I hate 'Nando a lot.

For a while we had another brother, a baby brother: Teodoro. He was tiny and chubby and oh, so soft; it made me happy just to carry him around. I used to put my face in the curve of his neck and breathe in his warm baby smell, then breathe out again in little puffs to tickle him and make him laugh. Mamma said I was like his second mother, Mamma said . . . But then the fever came, like a hot wind blowing over Teodoro, blowing like a desert till he stopped laughing and stopped eating, till finally nothing was left. Mamma let me help her wash him, and dress him in his little white nightgown, and Papa buried him in a dark brown box.

All that night I could hear the wolves out in the forest crying for the moon: It was a sound like the wind, or the moon herself, crying to be so cold and lonely in the sky, like Teodoro crying, all alone in his little brown box. . . . Finally I couldn't help it, I sat up in bed and cried too, so loud that 'Nando woke up and yelled for me to stop. I hit him and he hit me and then Mamma came in, screaming, and hit us both.

Everything changed, after Teodoro died. Mamma was

quiet, not the good quiet that means you're thinking, but the bad quiet that means you can't think at all. She walked around our house like a ghost, hardly eating, never seeming to sleep. Papa just worked, worked, hunched at his bench making figures of mammas and babies, lots of mammas and babies, but all of them sad looking, so sad no one wanted to buy. 'Nando spent all his time at the park, acting foolish, getting into fights. And I went into the woods.

It should have been scary—the long crooked arms of the trees, the rustling leaves whispering behind your back—but I wasn't scared. Maybe I should have been. Maybe I was too sad about Teodoro. Maybe I liked it there. It was quiet in the slant of the sun, and if you sat still, really still for a long time, the animals would come out, the squirrels and the birds and the chipmunks, and rush and eat and play right by you as if you belonged there, as if you were part of the woods too.

But you had to be careful, very careful, not to get too comfortable or feel too safe. Because the big animals, the bears and wild pigs, the wolves were in the woods too, and they knew you didn't belong, some human girl sitting there with bare feet, hair the color of tree bark, it didn't matter to them: they *knew*. They would trample you, or drive you trembling up a tree; the wolves, especially, would eat you up.

That very day I'd seen a wild pig, old boar tusking for acorns, his smell as big as he was: like a hundred old cabbages boiling at once, like something dug up from a year underground. I saw him and he saw me and I ran home as hard as I could, hair flying, breathing through my mouth. When I tumbled inside, 'Nando pinched his nose: "¡*Ay di mí!* Where you been all day, Lupe, out by the pits?"

Papa stuck his head out from the workroom; his face was powdered with sawdust, a pale brown mask. "The pits! It's nasty there, Lupe. Why in the world—"

"I wasn't by the pits," I said, and pinched 'Nando, a hard twisty nip on his leg. He let out a yelp, danced out of reach and "The woods," he called. "That's where Lupe goes. Carlos and Aimi told me, they said she goes there every day."

Papa came all the way out now, frowning lines in the sawdust mask. In his hand was another mamma-and-baby, just born from the ragged wood. "The woods, Lupe? What do you do there?"

I sit and watch the trees, Papa, and the squirrels dancing like falling leaves. I listen to the sounds that are so small you can hardly hear them. I look for wolf tracks. I drink water from the stream I found. I think of Teodoro. "Nothing," I said.

"Nothing," hollow, like an echo from right behind me, so close I jumped—but it was Mamma, her hair hanging down like black seaweed, her eyes red. "Nothing she does all day, lazy girl. Why don't you help your mamma? Poor Mamma, there's no one for her now."

Papa clutched the mamma-and-baby. 'Nando edged closer to the door. None of us spoke. Mamma squeezed my arm; her hand was damp and hot, as if she had a fever, like Teodoro. "I'll help you," I said. My voice sounded strange, as if I were far away. I wished I were far away, back in the woods, so far inside no one could find me. "What do you want me to do?"

"Go to the woods for me," Mamma said. "Go and see Old Blanca."

Papa's lips went tight; he set the wooden people down. "No, Maria," he said, hands on Mamma's forearms, his face close to hers as if he would kiss her, as if they were alone in the room. "That's no errand for a child. Old Blanca is—"

"A *bruja*!" 'Nando shouted. "She eats children, she's a witch!"

Mamma wrenched away from him, her eyes redder now, an awful red; they made me think of the wild boar, fierce and tusking, blind to everything but hunger. "Who else can help me? Who else will give me back what I have lost?"

"Maria, no! Maria—"

"I'll go," I said; I had to say it twice to make them hear. "I know the way, Mamma, I'll go to Old Blanca for you."

'Nando's eyes were round and bright; Papa's lips parted, but he said nothing. Mamma scrambled to fill a basket, the split-oak basket she used for the market, piling it with tidbits and scraps of shiny cloth, some wheat cakes, a spill of fat purple grapes, the half-made mamma-and-baby, and "You take this," she said to me. "Take it and give it to Old Blanca. She'll know what to do."

"Take this too." Papa held out one of his carving tools,

a wicked little scraping knife with a yellow handle. "Be careful, *querida*," he said into my ear; he had tears in his eyes. "And hurry right back."

The basket was heavy on my arm, as if it were filled with rocks, or bones. I tucked the knife into my skirt pocket and reached for my cloak, but it still had the smell of the boar, rank and fresh, so I took Mamma's instead, long and soft and red. It brushed the ground as I strode toward the woods, the afternoon shadows pointing like fingers back the way I had come, the sun warning me to turn back, but how could I do that? Mamma needed me. And I wasn't afraid, not really. Not of the woods.

I kept a wary eye for that old boar; I was wary anyway, I'd never come here this late before. The trees arched dark above me, like the inside of a church at night. Birds flew, branch to branch, heading for their nests; the squirrels scolded. I stepped rock by rock through the stream, careful to keep Mamma's cloak dry. As the sun dropped lower still, its rays brushed gold through the trees, gleaming gold, like the eyes of wolves.

Old Blanca. *She eats children,* 'Nando had said, which wasn't true, how could it be true? But she did strange things there alone in the woods: dug for bones, brewed roots for poison, built altars of antlers to the harvest moon. People said she could see in the dark; people said she could fly. People said she could change into an animal—an owl, a mule deer, a wolf—any animal, whenever she wanted.

I knew where to find Old Blanca, we all did, knew

enough to stay away. Past the stream there was a clearing where the leaves had been brushed carefully away, the mulch and dirt beat into a ring as if someone had been dancing there, or walking in a circle. And past that, so tumbled down and covered with vines that it seemed like a pile of brush, was the *bruja*'s hut.

With one arm I tugged at the tangled brush, searching for the door; the basket handle dug into my arm as I knocked, one, two, firm with my fist and "Excuse me!" I called—and scared myself, my voice sounded so loud in the quiet. "Excuse me, Grandmother Blanca, I have something for you!"

No answer, only the faraway bird sounds, the brooding quiet of the hut. Something rustled behind me, a stealthy sound. I turned fast, the scraping knife snatched from my pocket—but no one was there.

Heart pounding, I knocked again, more firmly this time. Maybe she was sleeping inside; maybe she had turned herself into a spider with tiny little ears. "*Abuela* Blanca! Please, my mamma needs you!"

Still there was no answer. Perhaps she was not home after all. My shoulders slumped; I thumped the basket down. Now what? Leave it there for the mice to nibble, the raccoons to gnaw to bits? Go home and tell Mamma that I had failed? *Who else can help me? Who else will give me back what I have lost?*

A third time I pounded at the door, hard now, with all my strength. "Let me in! Let me in, *Abuela* Blanca!"

—and just like that, like magic, the door opened,

swinging on its hinges as easily as a breeze. My heart galloped like a racing horse. I took a step, two steps, I was
inside.

It was a strange place, but pleasant, as if the woods
had come indoors: jumbled, dark, and fragrant, with
hanging roots and tumbled apples, big jars of clear stream
water, a squat black stove like a little campfire—but no
one was there, no one but a skinny white cat curled, half-
dozing, by the stove.

"*Abuela* Blanca?" I asked, feeling frightened and foolish and excited all at once: Maybe it was her, maybe she
truly could change her shape! But the cat just opened pale
eyes at me, and blinked, and yawned—then leaped up,
bow-backed and hissing, not at me but at something
behind me—

—as the room faded away like a candle snuffed, and I
whirled on my heel so fast I dropped the basket, grapes
and cakes and wooden people spilling on the floor, the
knife again bright in my hand—

—to see a gray wolf, timber wolf, *lobo* with hard yellow
eyes. Big, oh he was big, he seemed almost as tall as I was,
his great gray haunches and paws, he stared at me and I
stared at him, the cat beside me, her puffed-up tail brushing my legs—

—as the wolf lunged forward, so fast I couldn't move,
his red jaws open and I think I screamed, a wild wailing
little scream and the cat screamed too, a pink shriek as the
wolf snatched up in those red jaws the wooden people,
mamma-and-baby and *crunch! crunch!* he bit them in two,

their bodies falling one way, their sad little heads another, and for some reason this took away all my fear, took it and turned it into rage, the way Old Blanca turned roots into poison, turned herself into birds and beasts and "Stop it!" I cried, and struck at the wolf, drove the knife with all my might—

—but he was gone, disappeared, as if he had never been at all: I stood there trembling so I almost dropped the knife. The room came back to life around me, the crackle of the stove, the cat sniffing my sandals, the smell of the herbs so strong I felt dizzy and had to sit down, right there on the floor beside the cat. "*Abuela* Blanca," I said out loud, although I knew she could not hear. "I'm going now. I'm going to tell my mamma—"

"Tell her what?"

I think I screamed again, a tiny scream; I know I fell over, right on my back like a turtle, staring up from the floor at a tall gray woman in a dirty white dress standing over me, arms crossed; she wasn't smiling.

"What are you going to tell her? That Old Blanca was busy? I *am* busy." She had a voice like two sticks rubbed together, raspy and dry. "Too busy for you, *niña*. Take your clutter and go."

"I brought—I brought you . . ." the basket, where was the basket? But now the grapes were squashed, the wheat cakes scattered, the wooden people ruined—

"Are you looking for this?

Like magic, her hand was under my nose, long hairy fingers holding the mamma-and-baby but somehow—more magic? real magic?—they were whole again, heads and bodies, the mamma with her arms around the baby . . . and they were smiling, both of them, happy carved smiles as "Go home," Old Blanca said. Was she smiling, too? "Go home and tell your mamma to wait for the moon."

Wait for the moon? What could that mean? I got to my feet, took the wooden people, pulled my skirts in a curtsy and "*Gracias,*" I said. "I will tell her." I curtsied again, turned for the door but "You," said Old Blanca, *Abuela* Blanca. "You like the woods, don't you, Lupe?"

Golden eyes like the wolf's, gray hair like the wolf too. "I do," I said; how did she know my name? The cat wound around my legs, sniffed my sandals again. "I come here every day."

"Come back and visit me," she said. There was no mistaking her smile now. She ran one hand across my face lightly, like a breeze, like a brushing leaf, like the tickle of fur; gray fur. "I'll show you some things you'll like to see. . . . But hurry home now," in the first, hard, dry-stick voice. "Your papa is very worried."

"*Gracias,*" I said again, and I did hurry, fast and sure though the woods were pitch-dark, I could barely see my hand before my face—but that didn't seem to matter, I knew where I was going, I never lost my way or stumbled once.

On the path to my house I saw all the lamps were burning. 'Nando was waiting at the door and "Where were you!" he shouted, as if I'd been away a year. "What took so long, what did she say? Is she really a witch?"

I felt in my pocket for the smiling wooden people. "Where's Mamma?" but here came Papa to swoop me up, hug me so hard my breath whistled out, and "Thanks be," he said. "Your mamma is sleeping. . . . What happened out there, Lupe?"

How could I tell him? What should I say? So instead I showed him the smiling mamma-and-baby. He looked at it for a long time, his face still and solemn in the lamplight. Then "It's late," he said. "Time for bed. 'Nando, you too."

⠀⠀⠀⠀⠀⠀⠀⠀⠀🦋

Wait for the moon. I never did find out what that meant, but Mamma slept all that night and long into the morning, and when she woke up she was the old Mamma again, talking, eating, no more tears. Her red cloak was dirty-brown at the hem, and black on the back where I'd fallen, but she didn't scold me, or even seem to care. She just added it to her basket of washing and went down to the well.

The wooden people were set up on the table, a little bunch of flowers tucked beside them. Papa started carving lots of smiling mammas-and-babies; people liked them, and bought them, as many as he could carve.

And then one morning Mamma came crying to breakfast, and we all got worried, but she was smiling through her tears and "What do you think?" she said, one hand reaching for Papa's. "We're going to have another baby soon!"

Papa's eyes filled up too, and he kissed Mamma's

hand; 'Nando started hollering about another brother but "The baby's a girl," I said. "Call her Blanca." Everyone looked at me, and I felt my cheeks get pink. Where had the words come from? I didn't know, they just popped out. But I knew I was right.

When I asked *Abuela* Blanca about it later, she smiled and nodded, but didn't explain, just gave me the pestle and mortar and set me to grinding: wild thyme and pepper-grass, bright yellow lupine, while she sat on the stool beside me and braided her long gray hair.

"'Lupe,'" says *KATHE KOJA*, "is my second retelling of the Red Riding Hood story—the first was in a book of fairy tales for adults—and I find her even more compelling this time around. There's something very brave and cool and mysterious about that girl walking into the dark woods all alone. I wonder if I could do it? Maybe that's why I wrote this story: to take another walk, to test myself again in that dark wood."

KATHE KOJA is the author of *Straydog* and *Buddha Boy,* as well as several novels for adults. She lives in the Detroit area with her husband, artist Rick Lieder, and her son, Aaron.

Awake

BY TANITH LEE

That first night she woke up, which was the night after it had just *happened,* Roisa had been surprised. She'd been upset. She knew something had previously gone terribly wrong—exactly like when you have a bad dream, and you wake and can't remember what it was, only that it was awful, and the *feeling* is still there.

Now, of course, she was used to waking like this. She looked forward to it every night near morning, when she lay down to sleep again.

She sat up, threw back the light embroidered cover, and slipped from the bed. She slept clothed always, in the rose silk dress she had been wearing the evening *It* happened. Yet the silk was always fresh, as if just laundered and pressed smooth by hot stones. She herself was also always fresh, as if just bathed and scented, and her hair washed in the essences of flowers. She had long ago ceased to puzzle over that, though before That Night keeping herself so perfect had been a time-consuming daily task.

Roisa was sixteen. It had been her sixteenth birthday, the day it happened. Now she was still sixteen, but she had done and learned such a lot. She knew that the cleanness, and everything like that, was simply because of Great Magic.

By the bed was a little (magically) new-baked loaf, apples and strawberries (magically) just picked, and a china pot of mint tea, (magically) brewed and poured.

Roisa made her nightly breakfast.

Then she left the attic room.

Outside, the narrow stairway was as it always was, dirty and cobwebbed, thick in dusts. But when the skirt of the silk dress brushed through the muck, nothing stuck to it.

She was used to that also.

As she was to the people standing about lower down, absolutely stone-still, as if playing statues in some game. There were the ladies-in-waiting first, the three who must have meant to follow her up to the attics that evening. Unlike on Roisa, webs and dust *had* gathered on them, spoiling their gorgeous party clothes and jewelry and carefully arranged hair. It was a shame. Roisa still felt sorry for them, if in a rather remote way.

The first time, it had really shocked her. She had shouted at them, pulled at them, tried to make them move. Then, worse than these, the other things—for example, the cat that had become a furry *toy* cat on the lowest landing, the bird that stood on the still with its wings fanned out, never lowering them, never using them to fly off. And the young guardsman she had always liked, standing motionless, already dusty in his splendid uniform, his blue eyes wide open, not seeing her at all.

Worst of everything, however, had been to find her parents—her funny, pretty mother, her important, grand father—sitting there like two waxworks in the carven chairs from which they'd been watching the dancing in the Hall. The dancing from which Roisa had escaped, actually, to meet secretly with the guardsman—but somehow she had missed him—and then—then instead she had, also somehow, gone up into the attics of the palace . . .

Roisa had cried when she woke that first night. She had felt no longer sixteen, but about six. She had put her head into the lap of her mother's dress, clutching her mother's body, which felt like a cold rock. Sobbing.

That was when *They* came.

They—the ones who told her. The ones with the magic.

When she got down to the palace Hall tonight, Roisa did pause, only for a minute or so, to dust her mother.

She always did that. It seemed essential. Because of Roisa's attention to her mother, the Queen still looked glamorous—her hair and necklaces still shone.

The King, Roisa didn't try to dust. She would never

have dared because in the past he had seldom touched her, and then only with the firmest of hands, the coolest of kisses.

Beyond the Hall lay the royal gardens, into which, her dusting done, Roisa ran.

Oh—it was full moon tonight.

Once, wonderful scents had drifted here from lilies and from arbors overgrown by jasmine. A gentle breeze blew this evening, and not one of the now-scentless flowers, not one of the tall, graceful trees stirred. Not a single leaf moved, nor even the wind chimes hung in the branches.

By the fountain—whose jetting water had stopped in a long, faintly luminous arch, like rippled glass—the two white doves sat, as they had done now for years. The doves didn't move. Nothing did. Not even the moon, which lived in the sky—at least, it never did when she saw it. Only the night wind, the breeze, only that ever moved.

Roisa glanced about her, by this time no longer worried over the time-frozen gardens. Not even the fish in the pool, still as golden coins, concerned her anymore. There was nothing she could do about any of this.

Just then something seemed to ride straight out of the moon.

They had come back. As they always did.

With the brilliant flutter of sea spray, thirteen white horses landed on the lawn. On the back of every one sat a slim, clever-faced lady with flowing hair, each of a different color—and these tints ranged between apricot and copper, between jet and mahogany, from flame to pewter to violet. Everything sparkled—horses, ladies—with gems, beads, *fireflies*—Then the thirteenth horse came trotting forward, and the thirteenth rider swung from her gilded saddle, light as air. Even though by now she knew this person so well—better, probably, than she'd known her own mother—Roisa never quite stopped being surprised by her.

She was a Fey, of course. One of the Faery Faer, the Elder Ones.

"Awake, I see," said the Thirteenth Fey, whose name was Carabeau (which meant something like *My-friend-who-is-good-looking-and-has-her-own-household*). "Up with the owl, my Roisa. Come on, let's be off."

So Roisa mounted the horse behind Carabeau, as she always did.

After which the thirteenth horse and all the other twelve horses lifted up again into the sky. They weren't winged, these faery steeds—it was just that they could, when they or their riders wanted, run as easily through the air as over the earth.

In seconds the great palace and its grounds became small, far off and far down. It was possible to see, all round them, the high wall of black thorns that kept out all the world. And beyond the thorn-wall, the deserted town, the deserted weedy fields, and ruined cottages from which everyone had, over the years, dejectedly gone away. For the palace was under a curse that would last a century, and everybody knew it.

❧

Roisa laughed as the horses dived up and up. The moon was like a huge white melon, hung on a vine of milky clouds. The shadows of the horses ran below them over moonlit forests, over looking-glass lakes and gleaming, snake-winding rivers, over sleeping villages and marble cities that had also intended to stay wide awake.

"Look, do you see, Roisa?" asked Carabeau, and she pointed with her long, ringed finger at an open courtyard in one of the cities. There was torchlight there and music and dancing—but all stopped utterly still. Exactly like the scene in the palace they had left behind.

"Do you see the banners?" asked Carabeau. "The lights and the colored windows. Look at the girls' rich dresses and the fine clothes of the men. Look at that little dog dancing."

And the little dog *was* dancing, up on its hind legs, cute as anything. Only right now it didn't *move*.

Roisa sighed.

"What, my dear?" asked the Faery.

"I wish—" said Roisa.

"Yes? You know you can say to me or ask me anything, my love."

"Yes, I know. I'm only—sorry I can't ever see—what it's *really* like—I miss it, Carabeau. Only a little bit. But I do."

"Your old life, do you mean? Before you fell asleep and then woke up with us."

"Yes."

"Before the Spinning Wheel and the Spindle with its pointed tip."

"Yes. Oh—it's marvelous to fly about like this, to see everything, and all the foreign lands—the towers and spires so high up, the splendid rooms, the mountains and seas—I remember that forest with tigers, and the procession with colored smokes and elephants—and the great gray whale in the ocean, and the lighthouse that was built before I was even born—"

"And the libraries of books," said Carabeau softly, "the treasure-houses of diamonds, the cathedrals, and the huts."

"Yes," said Roisa.

She hadn't known before she began that she would say any of this. She hadn't known she *felt* any of it. (Nor did she think if Carabeau might be testing her in order that she be sure of this very thing.)

"Is it because," said Carabeau, "when you visit these sights with us, time has always stopped?"

"Yes—no—"

"Because, Roisa, one day that may change. How would that be for you, if the people moved and the clocks ticked?"

"Of course—of *course* I wish everything was like that—so I could see it properly *alive*. But . . . it isn't only that. I want—to live *inside* it—not outside all the time."

"Even if you are outside with us, who love you so well? Even with me?"

"Oh," said Roisa.

Not long after that the horses dipped down. They galloped between scentless streamers of low cloud that should have carried with them the smells of spices or fog or rain. They brushed the unmoving tops of trees with their glittering hoofs and skimmed over a wild night-valley.

This time they landed in the courtyard of a vast old temple. Though some of the building had come down from enormous age, still lines of carved pillars upheld a roof whose tiles, blue as eyes, remained.

In the past they had often come down into the places of human life and walked the horses, or walked on foot, among markets and along busy highways, mingling with the people and the beasts who, "playing statues" like everyone in the palace and everywhere, stayed motionless as granite.

That very first night—so long ago it seemed now—Carabeau and the other twelve Feys had explained to her how, while Roisa and her palace slept their magical sleep, the rest of the world went on about its usual affairs. And how, when she woke up each night, it was inside a timeless zone the Faery Faer could make and carry with them. And then, though she and they might spend all the hours of darkness traveling to the world's four corners and back, no time at all would pass in mortal lands.

"It isn't," Carabeau had said, "that we stop their time—only that we move aside from the time they keep. For them less than the splinter of a single second goes by—for us it is a night."

"But the *wind* moves—" Roisa had cried.

"That wind that blows is not a wind of the world, nor subject to the laws of the earth. That wind is magical, and its own master. But the moon doesn't move, and the sea doesn't. The clouds don't move at all."

Astonished, Roisa had never really understood, which she saw now. She'd only accepted it all.

Of course she had. Thirteen Faeries had told it to her.

Only one thing. That first night she had asked if the other people in the palace—her parents, the guardsman—if they could wake up too, as she had done. Because, as she knew, now the curse had fallen they, like her, were meant to sleep for a hundred years.

"They won't wake," said Carabeau. "Not until the proper hour. Or else there would be no point to any of this."

Tonight they dismounted from the horses in the ancient temple courtyard. It was full of the (magically raised) perfume of myrtle bushes, which had once grown there. Faery lamps of silvery amber and cat's-eye green hung from spider silks or floated in the air. An orchestra of toads and night crickets made strange, rhythmic music. Invisible servants came to wait on the Thirteen Feys and Roisa, bringing a delicate feast of beautiful, unguessable foods and drinks.

They picnicked while the temple bats, caught in that second's splintering, hung above like an ebony garland thrown at the moon.

Roisa once more sighed. She'd tried hard not to.

Carabeau looked into her eyes. But the eyes of a Fey, even if you look directly into them, *can't* be seen into.

"Do you recall, Roisa, what happened that evening when you were sixteen? Then tell it again."

So Roisa told Carabeau and the others what they all knew so well. They listened gravely, their chins on their hands or their hands lightly folded on the glimmering goblets. As if they had never heard any of it before.

But this story was famous in many places.

At Roisa's birth twelve of the Faery kind had come to bless the child with gifts. These gifts were just the sort of thing a princess would be expected to have and to display. So they made her Lovely, Charming, Graceful, Intelligent, Artistic, Well Mannered, Dutiful, Affectionate, Patient, Brave, Calm, and Modest.

But all the while they were giving her these suitable gifts, the Twelve Feys were restless, especially the two that had to give the baby the blessings of good manners and dutifulness, and the other Faery who had to make her modest.

Every so often, one or several of them would steal closer and stare in at the cradle. The court believed they were just admiring the baby. Of course she was exceptional—she was the king's daughter.

Eventually the Feys left the room, leaving it loud with congratulatory rejoicing. By magical means they'd called to their own queen, the Thirteenth Fey, whose name was Carabeau.

Now this was unusual. And in the town, which then thrived at the palace's foot, people looked up astounded to see the Queen Fey ride over the sky in her emerald carriage drawn by lynxes.

When she entered the King's Hall, courtiers and

nobles stood speechless at the honor. But Carabeau looked at them with her serious, wise face, and silence fell. Then she spoke.

"The princess shall be all that's been promised you. You'll be proud of her, and she will fulfill all your wishes. But first she shall have time for herself."

At that a hiss had gone up like steam from a hot stone over which has been flung some cold water.

The king frowned. His royal lips parted.

Carabeau lifted her hand, and the king closed his mouth.

"The Spinning Wheel of Time shall stop," said Carabeau, "because this child, by then sixteen years old, shall grasp the Spindle that holds the thread time is always weaving. Then she shall gain a hundred years of freedom before she becomes only your daughter, and wife to the prince you approve for her."

The king shouted. It wasn't sensible, but he did.

The rest—was history.

When Roisa finished recounting this, which was all she knew, and all the Feys had told her, Carabeau nodded.

"You remember too that night, and how you went to meet the guardsman—you, always so dutiful, but not then—and somehow you missed him, as we intended, and climbed into the attics, and found me there. And when I offered you the chance of a hundred years of journeys, of adventures—of freedom—you gripped time's Spindle, and the Time Wheel stopped."

"I don't remember that—I never have," said Roisa

doubtfully. "Only—going upstairs, and perhaps finding you. But when I first woke afterward, I was frightened."

"But now you are not. Understand, my love, for you this wasn't a curse or doom. It was my gift, the thirteenth blessing. And anyway, at last the hundred years are at an end. This night is your final one among us. Let me tell you what has been arranged for you when you return to the world. Tomorrow a powerful and handsome prince, even more handsome than the guardsman, will hack a way in through the thorns. He'll climb up through the gardens, the palace, mount the attic stair, wondering at it all. He'll find you asleep, as always you sleep by day. He'll wake you up. You'll fall in love at once, and so will he. Then everyone else will wake. The birds will fly about, the cats will purr, the earth's own wind will make the leaves rustle, the sun and the moon will cross the sky. You will live happily till the end of your days, you and your prince, admired and loved by all. The life that, perhaps, now you long for."

The Thirteenth Fey paused. She waited, looking at Roisa.

Roisa realized that something was expected of her. She didn't know what it was—should she thank the Faeries excessively for all the pleasures and travels, the feasts eaten and sights seen? Or for their care of her, their kindness?

Roisa didn't know that the Thirteenth Faery was actually waiting to see if Roisa would say to her, *But I don't really want that!* For Roisa to burst out that No, no, now the choice was truly hers, really she wanted to stay among the Faery kind. Providing only that they would lift the spell from those left in the palace (as she knew they could), then she would far rather become one of their own—if that were possible (and it was). Even if it lost her a princess's crown and all the rough romance of the human world.

But Roisa, of course, *didn't* want that, did she.

She wanted precisely what she had been supposed to have, before the magic of the Spinning Wheel and the hundred years' waking sleep.

And so, when Carabeau murmured quietly, "Are you glad your century of freedom is over?" Roisa sprang up. She raised her head and her arms to the sky. She crowed, (not modestly or calmly) with delight, imagining the fun, happiness, glory that was coming.

And then, startling herself, she found she was crying. Just like on that first night. Just like then.

And when she looked down again at the Feys, they seemed pale as ghosts, thin as shadows, and pearls spangled their cheeks, for the Faery People can't cry real tears.

Then they kissed her. The last kisses of magic. The next kiss she would know would be a mortal one.

"Shall I remember—any of *this*? she asked as, under the static moon, they rode the sky to her palace.

"Everything."

"Won't anyone . . . be jealous?" asked Roisa.

The Thirteenth Faery said, "You must pretend it was all a dream you had while you slept." And in a voice Roisa never heard, Carabeau added, "And soon, to you, that is all it will be."

TANITH LEE says, "The story of the Sleeping Beauty, along with many fairy tales, has always haunted me. I'd considered if, sleeping, she ever dreamed. It took my husband and partner, John Kaiine, to suggest to me that, more than dreaming, she might actually, unknown to any, be regularly waking up. The idea that the thirteenth Fairy might not be as bad as she'd been painted followed swiftly. To me the result here is rather sad—for the fairies and Roisa. Then again, of course she wants her own life back! What, I wonder, would you or I have chosen?"

TANITH LEE, who lives on the coast of England, has written a number of novels for children and young adults, including *The Dragon Hoard, Princess Hynchatti & Some Other Surprises, Prince on a White Horse, Islands in the Sky, Black Unicorn, Gold Unicorn, Red Unicorn,* and *Law of the Wolf Tower,* first of the Wolf Law trilogy.

INVENTING ALADDIN

BY NEIL GAIMAN

Q

In bed with him that night, like every night,
her sister at their feet, she ends her tale,
then waits. Her sister quickly takes her cue
and says, "I cannot sleep. Another, please?"
Scheharazade takes one small nervous breath,
and she begins, "In faraway Peking
there lived a lazy youth with his mama.
His name? Aladdin. His papa was dead. . . ."
She tells them how a dark magician came,
said he's Aladdin's uncle, with a plan.
He took the boy out to a lonely place,
Gave him a ring he said would keep him safe,
down to a cavern filled with precious stones,

"Bring me the lamp!" and when Aladdin does,
in darkness he's abandoned and entombed. . . .

There, now.
 Aladdin locked beneath the earth,
she stops, her husband hooked for one more night.

Next day
She cooks
She feeds her kids
She dreams . . .
Knowing Aladdin's trapped,
and that her tale
has brought her just one day.
What happens now?
She wishes that she knew.

It's only when that evening comes around
and husband says, just as he always says,
"Tomorrow morning, I shall have your head,"
when Dunyazade, her sister, asks, "But please,
what of Aladdin?" Only then, she knows. . . .

And in a cavern hung about with jewels
Aladdin rubs his lamp. The Genie comes.
The story tumbles on. Aladdin gets
the princess and a palace made of pearls.
Watch now, the dark magician's coming back:

"New lamps for old," he's singing in the street.
Just when Aladdin has lost everything,
she stops.

    He'll let her live another night.

Her sister and her husband fall asleep.
She lies awake and stares up in the dark,
playing the variations in her mind:
the ways to give Aladdin back his world,
his palace, his princess, his everything.
And then she sleeps. The tale will need an end,
but now it melts to dreams inside her head.

She wakes
She feeds the kids
She combs her hair
She goes down to the market
Buys some oil . . .
The oil seller pours it out for her,
decanting it
from an enormous jar.
She thinks,
What if you hid a man in there?
She buys some sesame as well that day.

Her sister says, "He hasn't killed you yet."
"Not yet." Unspoken waits the phrase "He will."

In bed she tells them of the magic ring
Aladdin rubs. Slave of the Ring appears . . .
Magician dead, Aladdin saved, she stops.
But once the story's done, the teller's dead,
her only hope's to start another tale.
Scheharazade inspects her store of words;
half-built, half-baked ideas and dreams combine
with jars just big enough to hide a man,
and she thinks, *Open Sesame,* and smiles.
"Now, Ali Baba was a righteous man,
but he was poor . . ." she starts, and she's away,
and so her life is safe for one more night,
until she bores him, or invention fails.

She does not know where any tale waits
before it's told. (No more do I.)
But forty thieves sounds good, so forty
thieves it is. She prays she's bought another
                    clutch of days.

We save our lives in such unlikely ways.

❧

NEIL GAIMAN says, "In *The Arabian Nights,* Scheharazade is married to a king who is going to kill her in the morning. She has her sister join her in the bedroom and ask her for a story—and Scheharazade tells stories of such magic and suspense that the king does not kill her, because then he would never know what happened next. She keeps her stories going for a thousand and one nights, and even manages secretly to give birth to several children before she is finally done and the king changes his mind.

"I have a number of stories to tell this week. No one's going to cut off my head if inspiration fails. At least, I hope they're not. I wish I knew where the inspiration comes from, but I don't, and perhaps it's wisest not to inspect too closely.

"There are two stories from *The Arabian Nights* in the poem: 'Aladdin and His Magic Lamp' and 'Ali Baba and the Forty Thieves.'"

❧

NEIL GAIMAN is the author of the *Sandman* comic book series and the adult novels *Neverwhere, Stardust,* and *American Gods.* His first novel for readers of all ages, *Coraline*, was published in 2002. He has found that so far most of the kids who have read it have enjoyed it as an adventure, while the adults who read it have the kind of nightmares from which they wake up screaming, which proves that there is some kind of justice in the world.

My Swan Sister

BY KATHERINE VAZ

My sister, Rachel, was born wrong. There was a mistake in every cell in her body. She lived for a while in an incubator at St. Vincent's Hospital in New York City and looked so tiny in her glass nest. "She's our little swan," said my mother. Rachel was wild and beautiful and seemed ready to fly away. She stared upward, each of her eyes just one drop of pale blue. "Hello," I whispered. "Don't you want to stay with me?" I was eleven and had been waiting for a sister for a long time. She was rose pink. Her head was like a soap bubble, the kind that has panes the color of a rainbow on it. My father put a toy elephant on the top of the glass, to lasso her with its trunk if she tried to float off before we said good-bye. She was going to leave us very soon.

One night while holding Rachel I saw my uncle Jack tapping on the outside of the window of the intensive care unit. He and my mother had not spoken in years. He walks fast, talks fast, reaches high; my mother is slow. She's a young spirit with no sense of time. Sometimes instead of going to work, she decides to go to Central Park and sketch the trees, and my job is to call the pet store where she's a cashier to say she has the flu. Thin as one of her drawing pencils, she forgets to untangle her short black hair. Humming, staring into space, she escapes in her mind to places I can't always reach, and when my father comes home from working at his fruit stand, he helps me make tomato soup filled with carrot pieces cut into daisies. Mother taught me how to twirl around until I'm too dizzy to stand; she made us both necklaces from chains of paper clips.

Uncle Jack is an old spirit who decided he didn't have the patience for us. But there he was in the hospital with his arms around Mother. Rachel had worked a miracle in summoning him back to us. And suddenly our mother was calm and strong, so the little swan must have performed wonders inside of her as well. Uncle Jack was the one to cry. Mother said only, "She's my joy for as many hours or days as I have her."

"You have me now too," he said.

When Rachel was allowed to come home, I invented a plan. I would show her New York. It was the city of my birth, and my mother's birth, and my father's. If Rachel saw how astonishing it was and how much I loved it, she would decide she could not possibly leave us. We lived in our own small nest on West Eighteenth Street, high enough to see the river turn into melted silver when the sun went down. I held Rachel up to our window and said, "It's so exciting here your heart won't ever stop beating!" The clouds were like white wings drifting along above the wide world, bird-high.

The doctor said it was a fine idea to help Rachel enjoy every single minute. We were given permission to take her out. She had a tube attached from her nose to an oxygen machine that was green and thin and had wheels and a handle so that we could push it around. Mother offered to steer the machine and I could carry Rachel. One bright morning, the light dripping gold, we bundled her in a blanket covered with sailboats and took the elevator down fifteen flights. The first man to fall in love with my sister, other than my father and Uncle Jack, was Rafael, the doorman. "Who is this angel?" he shouted when we crossed the lobby.

He took my sister from me and said, "She's a sweetheart."

"Oh, yes," said Mother, happy as a breeze. "Jessica and I are going to show her the city."

"Will you marry me?" Rafael asked Rachel.

Her face was too weak to smile, but she politely shined some light off her eyes.

We made a strange parade, Mother wheeling the machine and my sister in my arms and the tube connecting her to the canister of air, as we strolled in slow motion down West Eighteenth and stopped at Tillmore Bakery Supplies, with its ballerinas for cakes, candles with sparkles, and sugar roses. She would have no birthdays, but we wanted her to see a giant store that held out the promise of every celebration that anyone could imagine. In the narrow aisles, shoppers stepped aside as I showed Rachel the bins of confetti, party hats (I put one on), and the books on how to make wedding cakes that looked like white temples. I showed her cookie cutters shaped like half-moons and turkeys. Rachel slept. "Please try and pay attention," I said. It was almost like our first sisterly quarrel. Mother giggled and took the party hat off my head and pretended it was a megaphone that she held to her mouth to boom out, "Earth to Rachel!"

My sister perked up and grabbed my finger with her right hand as we went back onto the street. Summer was already tipping toward fall. The leaves were turning their usual fire colors, and they scuttled through the streets until people, or taxis and cars, crushed out all that fire under their feet or tires. Maybe it was Rachel's second miracle (or third, fourth, one hundredth) that when people saw us walking at half-speed with the oxygen machine and my sister attached to it, instead of being in a hurry (like my uncle Jack), they also slowed down and said, "Oh, heavens," or "Oh, my," the way people sound the first time they see a tide pool—how pretty, how easily crushed.

We walked under some scaffolding around a bank. "Look, Jessica! Look, Rachel!" said Mother. A construction worker had taken off his metal hat and was bowing at us.

We turned down Sixth Avenue so that Mother could show Rachel the pet store, Animal Kingdom, where she worked. Chihuahuas jumped at the glass in the window display when I lowered her into view. My sister's legs had no strength, but I felt a tremor in her, telling me that she would kick with pleasure if she could. She had raw, thin skin so much like the flesh of these puppies that they forgave her for being a bird. The pet store smelled of grain, leather, newspaper, and the milky scent of baby animals. My mother introduced Rachel to her boss, Doris, who had red hair that she brushed upward into a flame. She was the person I lied to whenever I called to get my mother out of work, and I often feared that Doris would explode into a torch that would burn its way to the truth.

Instead, Doris gave us a toy cloth mouse with a small bell attached to its collar. I shook it in front of Rachel and her head tilted.

"You taking care of yourself, sweetie?" Doris asked my mother. Doris has a voice like a volcano erupting.

"Rachel is taking care of all of us," said Mother.

We visited Mr. Wing, who runs the stationery store where I buy pens and notebooks for school and fold-out maps of the subway. I call him my "Quarter Friend" because one day I was fumbling with my money, and customers were impatient behind me, but I could not bear to use my special quarters with the mementos of the states on them. Mr. Wing laughed and said, "I'm also a collector."

He likes Georgia with its huge peach, which leaves me no choice but to roll my eyes and say, "But Mr. Wing, how *common!*" He never fails to act like this is the richest joke he's ever heard. He keeps a shrine with joss sticks and oranges on a shelf with a red paper poster of the Double Happiness symbol. "Ask for happiness and also a long life, Jessica. A long life without happiness is useless, and a happy life that isn't long is not good either," he once explained to me.

Today he gave Rachel a red envelope with a dollar in it and said, "For good luck."

Oh, the wonders we took in, my baby sister and Mother and me! We saw fish with open mouths, like trophies, in the window at Balducci's, and the bricks and spires of the old courthouse that makes me think of a palace in Moscow. It's now a library. Rachel whined and fussed; was she sad because she could not read books? Mother said, "I'll take you to the big public library with its stone lions, and Jessica and Father and I will read to you at home." I would take her to art museums and show her Monet, who paints the world as if it's melting. And to gardens with birds-of-paradise, lilies, and other children.

We backtracked to West Fourteenth Street for a surprise visit to Antonio's, my father's store, where he sells fruit, vegetables, bread, and candy. Sometimes in the alley behind, the pale green and yellow wrappings from the apples and pears get loose and fly about. They look like the moltings of canaries. When I handle the fruits there, I imagine them full of bird-singing. I put them to my ear and listen. Today I held one to Rachel's ear; she'd been born knowing the language of the skies.

Father was cutting open a burlap sack of lemons when we walked in, and he stopped and smiled. The world froze. "My girls," he said.

He helped Mother steer the oxygen machine around a stand with a pyramid of red apples. They gleamed. They had white kisses on them from being polished and stacked in the light.

Father said, "Rachel isn't too tired, is she? Are you, dear?"

He wiped his hands on his apron. He is skin and bones, and his hairline is already receding. Even his mustache is thin. He handed me a caramel and suddenly, unwrapping it, I was struck as if I had been sleepwalking through my many foolish days and now I was jolted awake—because all of us were here, my sister fluttering against my chest, my Mother exhausted but at peace. There was sweetness in my mouth. We were surrounded by fruit that could be split open to hear better the birdsongs inside them. My father is quiet (Uncle Jack once said he had no ambition), but on the day of Rachel's great adventure, I put my head to my father's chest and discovered that there was singing, loud birdsong, inside my father, too.

The weather turned colder after that, and we agreed to keep Rachel inside. But I longed for the day to take her out again, and I began to knit a jacket for her. Mother bought me thick yarn, blue and white. I wanted to work small waves of blue into a white background. I sat by

Rachel in her crib and my needles clicked out a little music that made my heart sing. They made a *tap, tap* that lulled her to sleep—but many nights she fussed, and many mornings she awakened short of breath. "That's part of a swan's story, Jessica," said my mother when she saw me worrying. "Swans disappear at night and perform bold deeds and must race back by daylight, panting." Mother taught me a cable stitch, and I kept unraveling my work until it came out just right. I did a front panel, the blue yarn peaking along, and started one of the sleeves—not easy! "You'll be wearing it by Halloween," I told Rachel.

I imagined the night as a swarm of crows biting at her feathers. They must have nipped her without mercy because often at first light she was red and crying. I finished the collar. It was rough, not as smooth as it should have been, but I knew I had to hurry.

We ventured into the city one more time: Uncle Jack called to say that he was getting an award for the best sales of stocks and bonds for his company that year. Invitations engraved in gold arrived, including one for Rachel. And one for me: I ran my fingers along my name, indented on the page: *Jessica*. We took a taxicab because we thought Rachel's life would not be complete without a genuine ride in one. The driver kept saying, "Poor child, poor child," until Mother said, "What are you going on about? Sir? She's off to Wall Street. She's in heaven." Mother was in her black velvet dress, and I wore my cranberry velvet one with a matching sash. Rachel was in green togs that made her skin less yellow.

Uncle Jack was wearing a black suit in a theater-like room. When he saw us, he stopped talking to some people and came to hug us. He took Rachel in his arms and said, "It wouldn't be the same without you here."

We could not stay long because Rachel began to cry again, but Uncle Jack ordered a limousine to take us home. I said, "Rachel! Maybe people will think we're rock stars." I'd brought along my knitting in a brown paper bag because I knew that time was running short. I still needed to fix the hem, and one more sleeve was left to knit.

That night I sat up even though my eyelids kept dropping. I stitched the hem in place. Just as I was starting on the right sleeve, Rachel returned early from her night flight, wailing, and I had to comfort her. Father got up; it was almost his usual time. There's a courtyard below us, and I showed Rachel that pieces of the moon had gotten caught in some of the bramble bushes. Father nursed a cup of coffee and stood with us. The sky flipped stars into his cup, tiny ones, a size that could fit over Rachel's eyes. He said, "It's my favorite time. The night is finishing and the day is starting, and they're both together for a moment, right now. It's like there's no one else awake."

"Almost no one," I said.

"Right," he said. "There's us." It was four in the morning. Rachel screeched worse than ever, and he took her from me to see if he could quiet her. Her screams brought Mother to us. We tried to pat Rachel, sing to her. She hollered, she raised the roof. She hit high notes and then low ones and started in again all over.

"She's in pain," said Mother.

An ambulance took Rachel and Mother to the hospital, and Father and I rode in a police car, but I was frantically knitting. I needed to finish the jacket. Hospital clothing is so horrible and unpretty, and Rachel liked to look nice.

When Father and I got to St. Vincent's, Mother met us in the emergency hallway. She was serene, so I thought Rachel would be fine. I had ten rows started of the last sleeve. I'd been getting the thread wet with sweating. The soles of shoes in the corridors made a squishing sound, and some nurses were laughing and I almost yelled at them to shut up. I was still hearing Rachel's screaming inside me.

"They tried to revive her," said Mother. "But they couldn't."

Her insides were too small and too wrong for her to live.

Father and Mother did not want me to see her, but I said I needed to. I had that jacket to give her.

She was lying alone on a table in a room without much light. A white plastic tube like a pretend cigar was still in her mouth, and Father took it out. He was weeping, but Mother was quiet. I stared into Rachel's blue eyes. They were half-open, looking at me—didn't that mean she was alive? Mother closed them with her finger. That's when I began to cry and bellow. I was going to be sick. I'd failed her. I hadn't taken her to the museum, or the library. I hadn't even finished her autumn jacket.

"Never mind," said Mother. She took the jacket from my hand and threw the ugly white hospital blanket off my sister and dressed her in the white-and-blue knitting. I shrieked enough to shatter walls and take the color out of paint. A sleeve was missing! I hadn't been fast or good enough!

"Let me tell you the last part of Rachel's Story," said Mother. "It goes like this: Everyone knows that swans only sing once, the most stunning song of their lives, but unfortunately, it's right before they die. Remember how she screamed tonight? Well, it's only because we're people and she's a swan that we couldn't tell at first that it was the most beautiful song in the world. And the mistake, the terrible mistake, that most people make when a swan dies is that they wrap it completely up tight. They cover its wings! And so, in the grave, a swan turns into a skeleton of a person, nothing more.

"But Rachel has a wing free. That was very thoughtful of you. Now she gets to fly wherever she wants. You'll have to look carefully; she's blue and white, so she's in the ocean and the sky. She wants to stay with you, and do you know why? Because it was brave of you not to turn away from her. You gave her a full life.

"She went to a place of many parties and a hundred candles. A man asked to marry her! Friends greeted her wherever she went. Like a wise old woman, she soothed me and then won over your uncle Jack. Can you believe he loves us again? That was Rachel's doing. Most people in a long life don't do as much good as she did in thirty days. She made the crowds stop and gape at her: What fame!

She dressed up for fancy financial-street events. The city was at her feet; she was already soaring above it. How can she give that up?"

Uncle Jack came to the funeral at the cemetery, and I thanked him for walking in step with me, gripping my hand, because I kept shutting my eyes not to see the graves.

"She won't be able to breathe in the earth," I said.

He pointed at the sky. "She's everywhere now," he said.

Nowadays the subway rumbles and I think, "Listen, there's life underground." I see a white cloud and it's Rachel's swan-like wing, waving to me. Her blue and white jacket fills the air, but it's her bare wing that I want to touch when my feet feel like stone. I'll have to rethink the idea of Double Happiness: One can have a complete, amazing existence in just a few days, and it's joy as big as creation. Rachel is a generous sister because often, as I walk along, she dips down to let me catch hold of her feathers. I lift my sad face and gaze around. The buildings here, they want more and more of the sky, past the simple blue of it. They wear that blue on their collars and keep on stretching. I want the sky of New York, too, and beyond it. I sprout wings on my back, wings on my ankles. My swan sister, Rachel, whispers, "Hold on tight," and what a shock. What a surprise. I'm the one flying.

KATHERINE VAZ says, "The stories of Hans Christian Andersen have always enchanted me, especially 'The Wild Swans.' Elisa, the heroine, must knit shirts made of nettles to change eleven swans back into her brothers, but she runs out of time and cannot finish one of the sleeves. Her beloved younger brother is restored—except that one of his arms remains a wing. What's so beautiful in that notion is that we might do our best to save or repair our loved ones, but the result isn't always as we want or expect. And somehow that falling-short, that affectionate error, that mistake, that wing, strikes us as even more radiant and powerful because it is a visible mark of how much love we had.

"Rachel was a real little girl who did not live long, but—pretty as a swan, light as a feather—she managed to remind my family that even when time runs short, even when we cannot speak, we can still work wonders."

KATHERINE VAZ is the author of two novels and a collection, *Fado & Other Stories,* which won the 1997 Drue Heinz Literature Prize. She has published stories for children in *A Wolf at the Door* and for young adults in *The Green Man: Tales from the Mythic Forest.*

ELLEN DATLOW has edited and coedited many anthologies, including *Snow White, Blood Red* and *The Year's Best Fantasy and Horror* annual volumes (both with Terri Windling). She has won seven World Fantasy Awards, the Bram Stoker Award for *The Year's Best Fantasy and Horror #13* (with coeditor Terri Windling) and *The Year's Best Fantasy and Horror #17* (with coeditors Gavin J. Grant and Kelly Link), the Locus Award for Best Editor in 2005, and the Hugo Award for Best Editor in 2002 and 2005.

TERRI WINDLING has edited over thirty anthologies, many of them in partnership with Ellen Datlow, including (for young readers) *The Green Man*, *The Faery Reel*, and the Borderland series. She also edits *The Journal of Mythic Arts*, an online publication devoted to myths and fairy tales (www.endicott-studio.com). She has written adult novels, nonfiction on myth, and several children's books, including *A Midsummer Night's Faery Tale*, *The Winter Child*, and *The Faeries of Spring Cottage*. She has won seven World Fantasy Awards, the Bram Stoker Award, and the 1997 Mythopoeic Award for Novel of the Year.

MARS HAS A MILLION DIFFERENT WAYS TO KILL YOU. . . .

The year is 2085. Mars Experimental Station One, a colony built to test humans' ability to live in an alien and hostile environment, has been in existence for ten years. This functioning city of two thousand people includes only twenty teenagers, each hand selected from the billions on Earth as part of the controversial Asimov Project.

The Asimov teens each have reasons to doubt themselves and distrust each other. But one thing is certain: Mars offers them something Earth never could. When the existence of Marsport is threatened, the group must overcome their fears and join forces, for their survival depends on nothing less.

FOLLOW THE ADVENTURES OF THESE TEENS IN THE MARS YEAR ONE TRILOGY:

#1 MAROONED!

#2 MISSING!

#3 MARSQUAKE!

ALADDIN PAPERBACKS
SIMON & SCHUSTER CHILDREN'S DIVISION

Aladdin Paperbacks is the place to come for top-notch fantasy/science-fiction! How many of these have *you* read?

The Tripods, by John Christopher

❑ Boxed Set • 0-689-00852-X

❑ The Tripods #1 *When the Tripods Came* • 0-02-042575-9

❑ The Tripods #2 *The White Mountains* • 0-02-042711-5

❑ The Tripods #3 *The City of Gold and Lead* • 0-02-042701-8

❑ The Tripods #4 *The Pool of Fire* • 0-02-042721-2

The Dark is Rising Sequence, by Susan Cooper

❑ Boxed Set • 0-02-042565-1

❑ *Over Sea, Under Stone* • 0-02-042785-9 (rack) • 0-689-84035-7 (digest)

❑ *The Dark Is Rising* • 0-689-71087-9 (rack) • 0-689-82983-3 (digest)

❑ *Greenwitch* • 0-689-71088-7 (rack) • 0-689-84034-9 (digest)

❑ *The Grey King* • 0-689-71089-5 (rack) • 0-689-82984-1 (digest)

❑ *Silver on the Tree* • 0-689-71152-2 (rack) • 0-689-84033-0 (digest)

The Dragon Chronicles, by Susan Fletcher

❑ *Dragon's Milk* • 0-689-71623-0

❑ *The Flight of the Dragon Kyn* • 0-689-81515-8

❑ *Sign of the Dove* • 0-689-82449-1

❑ *Virtual War*, by Gloria Skurzynski • 0-689-82425-4

❑ *Invitation to the Game*, by Monica Hughes • 0-671-86692-3

Aladdin Paperbacks
Simon & Schuster Children's Publishing
www.SimonSaysKids.com

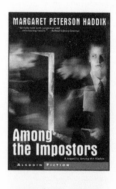
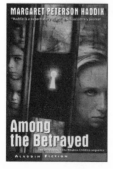